# Buried
# Secrets

I0587010

S.D. Tooley

Full Moon Publishing

## *From the Author*

**This book is a work of fiction. Names, characters, places and incidents are the product of the author's imagination. Although some actual historical events and locales have been fictionalized, they are solely used to fit into the creative narrative and in no way meant to slight any people, places, or organizations.**

Library of Congress Catalog Number: 2017939398

ISBN 978-0-9976707-1-4

Published June 2017

Printed in the United States of America


Full Moon Publishing LLC
433 Mystic Point Drive
Bluffton, SC 29909
www.fullmoonpub.com


Logo Design by Lesley Staples

# PRAISE FOR THE SAM CASEY SERIES

"Entertaining reading in what looks to be a solid series."— *Booklist*

"Author S. D. Tooley delivers the exciting Sam Casey series with suavity and grace in a writing style which will rivet the reader to the roller-coaster plotting."                    — *EuroReviews*

Tooley entices through nuanced characterizations, intricate plotting, and detail-laden prose."                 — *ForeWord Reviews*

"An exciting mix of police procedure, spiritual 'intuition,' creeping suspense, and page-turning narrative."         — *Library Journal*

"…an action-packed mystery that will garner much attention from fans who enjoy a police procedural with a twist."
                                             — *Midwest Book Review*

"For those readers with an interest in the religion of Native Americans and specifically the Sioux, they will find tantalizing hints of these practices within the pages."         — Leslie Doran, *Mystery News*

"Sam Casey is amazing—a beautifully described and magically interesting character…the plot, characters and pacing are all excellent."                    — 4 Star Review, *Romantic Times*

# 1

Sunlight stabbed through tattered drapes, shocking his eyelids into a frenzied dance. He tried to turn his head away from the rude attack, but it hurt too much. Tongue, dry and parched as a sheet of sandpaper, tried to coax moisture from his mouth. Hungover? Where had he been? What day was it? Couldn't remember that either. With a groan he slid his legs to the side of the bed and levered his body into a sitting position. A stale odor mingled with another odor that was familiar. Where had he smelled it before? He wasn't sure if he had eaten, but something in his stomach was bubbling to the surface. How far was it to the bathroom? He closed his eyes and waited for the nausea to pass. His eyelids fluttered as drapes billowed from above a rattling air conditioner. Popcorn ceiling and yellow walls didn't spell high-end hotel to him. Who painted popcorn ceilings anymore? A picture of fruit hung haphazardly above a marred dresser. Even in his condition he had to resist the temptation to straighten it. One thing he knew for certain…this wasn't his house.

Alarm bells clanged in his head. He hadn't had more than two drinks any given day since college. Well, maybe a few more at his retirement party. Was he having a stroke? Heart attack? His groggy mind assessed that he wasn't in any pain, except for his stomach and head. Drugs? He didn't take them, except for the rare aspirin or Tylenol when his knees acted up from too much cycling. The bells clanged louder, not so much that someone might have drugged him, but because he couldn't remember last night, who he was with, much less what he might have done. All of yesterday was a total blank. Someone had slipped him a drug of some type. He pressed the heels of his hands to his eyes, then rubbed his nose as though that alone could clear the odor from the air.

He looked down at his legs, still clad in slacks. Then he looked at his shirt, one sleeve stained in dark red. His left arm appeared to float from his body, flashing blood like a road-side billboard.

His drug-addled body moved with surprising speed as he leaped from the bed and spun around. The woman lying next to him was nude, auburn hair sprayed across the pillow, eyes open in surprise, a knife buried in her blood-smeared chest. He had seen and smelled enough bodies to know she had been dead for sometime. Only one problem—he had no idea who she was.

# 2

"Isn't he a little young to be playing golf?" Abby Two Eagles refilled her glass from the pitcher on the serving cart. She was seated on a chaise lounge, the glass in the cup holder.

"Jake thinks if he starts early enough, Dillon could be the next Tiger Woods." Sam said it with a smile even though she agreed with her mother. Her fifteen-month-old son was a mini-version of her husband, from the square jaw line, light brown hair and taupe-colored eyes, to the broad shoulders and muscular build.

Sam grabbed another orange scone as she propped her legs onto a nearby chair. The July heat forced her to pull her long, unruly hair into a high ponytail. The mornings were tolerable; but by afternoon, temperatures were expected to reach into the nineties. The Midwest summer humidity hung in the air like a sticky gauze. She didn't know how her mother continued to wear the traditional long skirt and blouse. At least she had kicked off her moccasins and hiked up her skirt to reveal olive-toned skin that had little need for the sun's tanning rays. Sam, on the other hand, easily burned so she preferred to sit under the shade of the table umbrella.

Alex Red Cloud emerged from the garage dragging a hose and carrying an oscillating sprinkler. Trailing behind him was Poco, his Irish Setter. Dillon dropped the golf club and ran toward the swim trunk clad Indian. Alex was a family friend who lived in the gate house located in the back of the one hundred acre property. He hadn't been too fond of Jake chewing up the sculptured Bermuda grass with his golf club. Instead, Alex had positioned six large landscaping stones and covered them with fake turf so Jake would have a driving range. Sam and Abby had even caught Alex hitting a few balls when he thought he was alone.

Jake maneuvered between numerous perennials landscaped by the house in order to hook up the hose. Alex centered the sprinkler on the lawn between two flower beds. Once Jake turned on the water, he and Alex took a seat on lawn chairs a safe distance away and watched Poco and Dillon run through the water.

It had been agreed not to buy a swimming pool. Sam and Abby were afraid just one turn of their heads away from Dillon in a pool of water could be disastrous. Alex was afraid of what a pool, even though a small blowup one, would do to his precious lawn. So they had agreed that a sprinkler was the safest choice.

"What are we doing today, Mom?"

"Absolutely nothing." Abby turned her face toward the sun, soaking in the warmth.

"Wonderful." Sam sighed and closed her eyes. "Sounds like a plan." Sam's relaxing moment was interrupted by chirping from Jake's cell phone. She picked it up and checked the screen. It was a number she didn't recognize. "Another irritating telemarketer." Sam pressed the green icon, prepared to read the caller the do-not-call registry riot act. "Hello."

"This is Jonathan Doe. I need to speak to my lawyer."

Sam knew that voice, but why was he using the name John Doe? Having heard the phone ring, Jake hustled up the two steps and crossed the patio. She cast a puzzled look at Jake. Why was his former boss using a fake name, and why was he referring to Jake as his lawyer? No one could ever accuse Sam of not being quick on her feet. Their family attorney was Jason Coleridge. He was old school. Semi-retired, he did everything by hand, shunning anything electronic. Without a website presence or any type of social media, anyone would be hard-pressed to verify Jason's identity. She pressed the speaker button and placed the phone on the table.

"You do know you are calling Attorney Coleridge at his residence. He values his family time." Sam heard a sigh on the other end.

Jake looked puzzled, but played along. He tossed his sunglasses on the table and took a seat. "This is Jason Coleridge."

"Sorry to bother you on your day off, Jason, but I need your help. I woke up this morning next to a dead woman with no idea where I was or who she is."

Sam almost dropped her glass of iced tea. Had she heard correctly? She glanced at Abby who looked just as shocked.

"Have them do a drug test."

"That's the first thing I insisted."

Jake knew Carl Underer had a law degree. He could easily represent himself. Then again, can't do too much investigating from inside a jail cell. Last time Jake had talked to his ex-boss was when Carl had sold Sam's family home he had been renting on the Island of Martinique.

"Do you need bail money?"

"No bail on a murder charge, unfortunately."

"Where are you, John?"

"Heyward Bluff, South Carolina."

"Where?" Jake wanted to ask him what the hell he was doing in South Carolina. "Never heard of it."

"It's north of Savannah, Georgia, and about twelve miles west of Hilton Head Island."

Jake looked at Sam and she shrugged. He still had a couple

weeks off for medical leave. "Do you need me to come down there?"

"That would be great. And, Jason, could you bring your assistant? I think I'm really going to need her help."

# 3

Jake rubbed the red marks on his arm as they drove out of the Savannah airport.

"Sorry about that, Jake. It's been a long time since I've flown. Why do you think Mom and I have never used the house on Martinique?"

"I think some of your nails are still embedded."

Sam unfolded the map until she found their location. "We need to take I-95 and head north. It looks like the police station is about thirty minutes away." Carl hadn't had too much time to explain how he ended up in South Carolina, how long he had been there, or why he didn't stay in Martinique after selling the house. Her thoughts were interrupted by the roar of the car engine as Jake passed a semi and merged onto the interstate. "You know, the Volkswagon convertible looked really cute. We didn't need this gas guzzler."

Jake turned his mirrored sunglasses her way. "Always wanted to drive a Charger. Besides, that was our agreement. I agreed we would drive home if you let me rent the car I wanted."

"Guys and their muscle cars. I will never understand it," she said with a sigh. "What's the plan?"

"Police station first. We need to talk to Carl."

Sam folded the map to the area where they were headed. "Let me guess. You are going to play it straight, cop-to-cop, and hope they share all their information." She lowered the visor to block out some of the sun's glare. A *Welcome to South Carolina* sign was flanked by tall palm trees on the side of the interstate. With a good tailwind, it had only taken two hours to fly to Savannah. Jake thought of waiting until the next day to fly out, but the worried tone in Carl's voice was one Jake had never heard in all the years he had worked for Carl.

"Something like that. You have a better plan? Although I'm almost afraid to ask," he added under his breath.

"Carl used a fake name for a reason, and he let on that he is expecting his attorney." Sam pulled a business card from her purse. "You are Jason Coleridge. Leave your wallet, gun, and cell phone in the car. I am your assistant."

Jake looked down at his Bermuda shorts and pale yellow shirt. "I don't exactly look like an attorney."

"You have a client accused of murder. You came right from the airport. Besides, down here I bet even the judge wears shorts under his robe." Sam's phone beeped. "That should be Tim."

"Tim?" Jake didn't like the sound of that. Tim Miesner had been one of Sam's sources for years. He was a young hacker who had proved useful on a number of cases. His talents had caught the eye of the FBI so he spent his summers during high school interning for the feds.

"Don't get your by-the-book briefs in a knot. Tim is getting us whatever reports he can find from the crime scene so we don't walk into this case blind."

Jake's sigh sounded more like a groan. Sam's way of doing detective work blurred the legal lines. He had to admit, they were walking into unfamiliar territory. From what they had researched, Heyward Bluff was a small town. Images of the small towns Lee Child's character, Jack Reacher, stumbled into came to mind. But then, what were the ramifications of falsifying their identities? Would they be doing Carl more harm than good?

"Here, Exit Eight," Sam said. "We can always check into the hotel first if you feel you need to change clothes."

"No need. I didn't pack anything resembling a suit." They no sooner exited the expressway then the familiar arches appeared. "Great. I need a cup of coffee."

"It's eight hundred degrees out and you are drinking hot coffee."

Jake already knew Sam would prefer an iced tea. He took the drive thru, received their order, and quickly got back onto the road. "Are you going to keep Tim's report a secret?"

"I thought I would wait until we parked." Sam stored the extra napkins in the glove compartment, then settled back to admire their surroundings. The tall trees and green underbrush they had encountered on the interstate were replaced with trees draped in a gauzy moss. Palm trees and lush flowering plants landscaped the businesses along Route 278. "Wonder what those trees are with all that creepy stuff hanging from it."

"Live oak, and that's Spanish moss. It will attach itself to most trees."

"What about the trees with those scarlet-colored flowers?"

"Crepe myrtle. If you had read the travel magazine on the airplane instead of mangling my arm and sleeping, you would be an expert on South Carolina."

"I wasn't sleeping. I was praying we wouldn't go down in a ball of flames."

Jake reached over and squeezed her hand. Sam noticed he was smiling more these days, not that she had expected him to drop his bad cop demeanor. He gained back the thirty pounds he had lost during his ordeal, and was back to exuding all two-hundred-ten pounds of danger.

They passed a manicured fairway beyond a wrought iron fence. A flag on the green fluttered softly while two golf carts zipped along a cart path. "Now that's where Carl should be living." They passed a sign that said, *Sun City Hilton Head.* "It's an over fifty-five community," Jake said. "Leaves us out."

A large group of birds were gathered around an object on the side of the road. They resembled turkeys and appeared to lope rather than walk. "Are those vultures?"

"Nature's garbage disposal. They can smell a carcass from a mile away and strip a deer clean in less than three hours."

"Thanks. You just killed my appetite."

They continued east across a marsh where white sticks poked from between tall weeds.

"Before you ask, those are egrets. The birds wait to catch the fish as the tide recedes. According to the article, high tides occur twice a day and can reach close to eight feet."

"See. I didn't have to read the travel magazine. I can get the *cliff notes* from you."

After several minutes, a robotic voice on the console's GPS instructed them to turn right at the next light. Sam pulled out a map she had printed off the computer showing the location of their hotel, the location of the police station and one substation, as well as a map showing the various restaurants in the area. "Turn right again after this gas station. The police station is that building at the end where the flags are."

Jake saw cameras on the outside of the police station so he pulled into a parking space two buildings away and turned off the engine. While he emptied his pockets of his wallet, phone, and removed his gun and holster, Sam brought up Tim's email. "What was he able to find?"

"Preliminary coroner's report, some photos, and initial findings from the CID officer."

"This small of a town has a Criminal Investigation Division?"

"Comes from the county. Doesn't mean it's fully staffed. Might just be a fancy title." Sam opened the first attachment showing photos of the deceased from different angles. There was bruising around her neck in addition to the knife wound in her chest. Her arms were at her sides, no defense wounds visible or bruising on any other part of her body. Another photo showed the deceased's clothes piled on the floor. They studied each photo with a cop's eye. "Looks like she was killed somewhere else and placed in the bed. No blood spatter anywhere. Doubt the killer had time to clean up."

"Not much blood on the sheets either. The Sunset Motel. Sounds like a snazzy place."

"Beautiful woman. At least Carl has good taste," Sam said. Next she opened the responding officer's report.

Jake leaned close to read along with her. "She hasn't been I.D.'d yet. Approximate age thirty to thirty-five. Carl is the one who called it in. No witnesses. Motel manager on night duty didn't hear anything nor did the guests in the other rooms. No cameras outside of the building. No other homes or businesses in the vicinity. And the room had not been rented out so someone broke in."

"Not much to go on." Sam closed out the email then tossed her phone in her purse. "Here."

Jake took the business card from Sam and studied it. "What if they call Jason's phone?"

"I already called him and told him not to answer any calls from an unknown area code."

Jake shoved the card in his shirt pocket. "Where's the gym bag?"

"In the back seat." They had packed a change of clothes and toiletries for Carl. Whether the police would let him keep it or not, they weren't sure. "You know this would be so much easier if Carl would just tell them his name."

"I'm sure he has his reasons. Are you ready?"

# 4

Jake approached the window where a woman was just finishing up a phone call. She was wearing what looked like a staff uniform and a *don't piss me off* smile. "Can I help you?"

Jake slid the business card into the tray under the security window. "I'm here to see my client, John Doe."

Her steely glare moved from his face to the card. One eyebrow twitched with either skepticism or amusement. "Long way from home, aren't you?" Her gaze drifted to the welted scars circling Jake's neck.

"Needed a vacation anyway."

She gave a cursory examination of Sam's feathered earrings, especially the third one which touched her left shoulder. The clerk shoved away from the desk and turned to a uniformed officer standing in the doorway.

"Is there a problem, Kate?"

Kate handed the business card to a thin-faced officer whose name badge identified him as Mike Montrey, Shift Sergeant. "This here is John Doe's attorney, Mike. Came all the way from some place in Illinois."

"It's near Chicago," Jake said.

"Ahhhh." Kate said it with what sounded like disdain. "Guess our lawyers down here aren't good enough." Her gaze again found its way to the scars. It looked as though someone had wrapped barbed wire around his neck and dragged him behind a truck.

"Why don't you let the chief know he has visitors, Kate." Mike waved a hand at them as he pressed a buzzer. "Right through that doorway, folks, and stop at the first desk."

The door opened to a room of neatly arranged desks and chairs with offices lining the back wall, not unlike most police stations Jake had entered. The building still had that new paint smell; and by the looks of the wood, chrome fixtures, and planked flooring, it appeared this small town had a lot of money to spend. A hallway near the back led somewhere, and stairs and an elevator on the right led to the upper floor. Another hallway to the left Jake assumed lead to a breakroom since one officer was approaching carrying a cup of something steaming. Jake doubted there was a basement so expected the holding cells to be down one of the hallways.

Sam placed the gym bag on the table by the door while Jake emptied his pockets of change and car keys. The sergeant tore his eyes from Jake's neck and studied the pile of change and car keys. "That's it? No phone? No wallet?" He swung his gaze to Sam. "No purse?"

"We pack light." Jake scrutinized his surroundings, assessed the number of staff while snatching bits and pieces of phone conversations drifting from the cubicles. He had given up buttoning his shirts all the way to conceal the scars. It never completely hid them; and he didn't much care for turtlenecks, even in the coldest of weather. Two staff members stared at the visitors before returning to their work, while a young woman at a desk nearby studied them with mild interest.

"What's in here?" Mike nodded toward the gym bag Sam had placed on the desk.

"A change of clothes and toiletries for our client," Sam said.

Mike barked out a laugh as he unzipped the bag and pulled everything out. "You must think our murder suspect is going somewhere." He inspected each item as though he were a TSA agent. Then his gaze dropped to the leather pouch hanging around Sam's neck. "What's that?"

"A medicine bundle." She noticed his fingers motion in a gimme gesture. "Which I'm not removing."

"Guess you're staying out here, then."

"Sam," Jake said.

Sam sighed, slipped the leather pouch from around her neck, and placed it on the table. "It's sacred so if you don't mind, I would appreciate it if you…" She watched in horror as Mike loosened the drawstring. Just as he was about to dump the contents, the young woman a few desks away stood quickly.

"Don't, Sergeant. It's bad mojo." The woman had dark, piercing eyes and wore her jet black hair in what was known as a TWA, a teeny weeny Afro. When she smiled, dimples cratered her cheeks.

Mike sighed. "Our resident Voodoo expert. Okay, Milla. What happens if I empty out the contents?"

The young woman approached, picked up the medicine bundle and closed her eyes. She was dressed in a white blouse and dark skirt. The empty holster on her hip indicated she was definitely not a file clerk. Her eyes snapped open so fast, Mike took a step back. Sam slowly smiled.

"Midwest? The Dakotas?" Milla asked. "Very powerful." She handed the medicine bundle back to Sam.

"Yes, on all three counts," Sam said, studying the young woman curiously.

"When I said very powerful, I didn't mean the medicine bundle."

"I knew what you meant." Sam slipped it over her neck and

tucked it inside of her sleeveless top. Mike's eyes slanted from Milla to Sam.

"Mike," a voice from a far doorway yelled out. The man waved his hand. "Show them in."

"Follow me." Mike led them to a stocky man with a receding hairline standing in the doorway. "This is Chief Ray McComb. Chief, Attorney Coleridge and...who are you?"

"Misses Coleridge," Sam said as she leveled her ice blues on the man who had wanted to strip her of her medicine bundle.

Mike closed the door behind them and the chief motioned to the two wooden chairs in front of his desk. "I understand you are representing John Doe. I certainly hope you can tell me his real name."

"I'm sure you took his prints when you booked him."

McComb shot his guests a strange look as he took a seat behind a desk cluttered with reports and yellow sticky notes. The walls were filled with framed awards and photos. Family pictures were lined up on a side credenza. "And I bet you are completely shocked to know that results came back as classified."

Jake said nothing.

"You do know he was the only person found with the victim." The chief averted his eyes from Jake's neck and feigned an attempt to look at the notes in front of him.

"I understand he was the one to call it in. Does that sound like a guilty party to you?"

"True. However, he was also quick to demand his lawyer so my detective couldn't question him." He studied Sam with subtle curiosity. "And what is it you bring to the table?"

Sam gave a slow smile. *Oh, if only you knew.* "I've never been to South Carolina so I thought we'd make a vacation of it."

"Of course." McComb smiled just as slyly and swung his attention back to Jake. "Has John Doe told you anything useful during your phone call?"

"Did the tox screen come back? He believes he was drugged."

"That will take about thirty days."

Jake engaged in a staring contest with the police chief, then averted his eyes to the framed certificates: Commendation, Field Training, Special Merit, and several Firearm Competition awards. "Any emergency room could have those results in minutes. We all know they can't wait thirty days when a patient comes in dying from an overdose. I bet you've got those results already."

It was the chief's turn to say nothing.

"What about the detectives on the case? Can we talk to them?" Sam said.

"Detective Lawson is still out gathering evidence." McComb checked his watch.

"All we need," Jake said, "is a quick ten minutes with my client. If he says we can share information with you, then we will tell you all we know." Jake was unaware the door had opened behind them.

"Over my dead body."

They turned to see a man leaning against the doorjamb. Dark hair matted his forehead and sweat stains ringed the shirt collar. It was obvious from the muscles pressed against the short sleeves that the detective spent copious hours in the gym. It was his eyes, though, that were uncomfortably familiar. Sam could sense Jake tensing.

"I have a Jane Doe found dead lying next to your John Doe. If anyone is going to get answers, it's me."

Jake slowly stood and turned toward the detective. "You do

understand what it means when a suspect asks for his attorney, don't you?" Although Jake's death stare was enough to intimidate even the roughest of suspects, it didn't appear to phase the detective. Lawson instead seemed more curious about Jake's neck.

"She was actually dead before she was placed in the bed," Sam said, hoping to deflate any threat of a dispute that might be brewing. "Her neck was broken first before someone stabbed her for good measure."

"What the...?" The detective turned to his police chief. "How did they get...?" But he stopped when the chief raised his hands.

"This is Jason Coleridge and his wife from..." McComb referred to the business card..."Chasen Heights, Illinois. He is John Doe's attorney. Detective Lawson is working the case. Let's give the suspect ten minutes with his attorney." McComb stood and led Sam and Jake down a long corridor, through a heavy steel door and over to a desk. A cop who looked close to retirement turned a clipboard toward Jake.

"Henry will take you from here," McComb said. "When you are through, I'd appreciate having a few more minutes of your time."

McComb watched them leave, then walked over to Milla's desk just as Mike set the gym bag on a chair next to the desk. Lawson, fists still jammed onto his hips, opened his mouth to speak. "Wait in my office. I want an update on the investigation." He watched Lawson leave in a huff.

"Did you see the attorney's neck?" Milla asked.

Mike rubbed a hand across his own neck. "What the hell's his story?"

The chief held out a business card to Milla, careful to only touch the edges. "Most attorneys I know rarely get their hands dirty, let alone put themselves in danger. If he's an attorney, I'm an Olympic swimmer. Run the prints on Attorney Coleridge's card. Let's see what we come up with."

# 5

Carl shuffled into the conference room looking in desperate need of sleep and a shave. It was a far cry from his typical well-groomed, starched appearance. There was a slight tremor in his hand as he pulled out a chair. The tan jumpsuit looked hot and heavy, and the odor drifting from him smelled pungent. When the door closed behind him, Carl sank into the chair across from them.

"You look like shit. Have you eaten?"

"Hi to you, too, Jake. I don't have much of an appetite, as you can imagine."

Sam checked the walls for cameras and listening devices, then eyed Jake's mentor from across the table. "She was half your age, Carl. What were you thinking?" Although she wouldn't have been surprised to find a thirty-something on Carl's arm. He had always kept in shape, was tall and handsome in a Peter Graves sort of way. However, right now he was looking like a haggard sailor in from being out to sea for a month.

"We have ten minutes and that's all you have to say?"

"Oh, I have plenty more." But Sam bit back her retort when Jake squeezed her thigh. He was definitely paying her back for mangling his arm on the airplane.

"Tell us what you remember," Jake said.

"Not much. Some of it is coming back. I remember being on a boat."

"Fishing boat?"

Carl shook his head. "Tourist boat of some sort. A ferry I think, to an island. Or was I only on the pier? Damn, can't remember."

"Is that where you met her?"

He washed his hands over his face. "Don't know where I met her or how I got to that motel. Was my car there?"

"Not according to the police report, and there's no record of anyone reserving that room," Jake said. "Obviously, your wallet wasn't in the room since they don't know your name."

"Shit. Either the killer has the car and my wallet or I left my car somewhere." He scrubbed his hands over his gray-tinged face again, as if trying to erase the last twenty-four hours. "I'd kill for an aspirin."

"There wasn't any activity on your credit cards so I doubt the killer has your wallet," Jake pointed out.

"How did you get my credit card numbers?" Carl sighed. "Never mind. I don't need to know."

"What are you doing in South Carolina, Carl? Did you buy a house? Are you just passing through?" Sam didn't know Carl as well as Jake did, and her husband didn't appear too worried about Carl's situation.

"Got island fever down there, Sam, not that I don't appreciate your hospitality. A little too French for me. And there's only so much pineapple and bananas a person can eat. Spent a bit of time in Florida and then someone told me about the golf courses in South Carolina. I'm renting a house near the bridge to Hilton Head Island. Gave a fictitious company name and paid upfront for a three-year lease with an option to buy."

"And that is because...?" Sam prompted.

Carl shrugged. "You know me. Can never be too careful." When he sensed Jake's bullshit meter banging like a mariachi band, he added, "There are always a few enemies through the years that might carry a grudge. The Bureau keeps close tabs on them. Until then, I'm keeping a low profile."

Jake asked, "Think one of them may have set you up?"

"No. This is amateur hour. Enemies in the Bureau's radar are pros. They would have fed this woman to the alligators and put a bullet between my eyes, not tried some college date rape drug." His gaze rested on the raised scars. "How are you doing, really?"

"Better. Quantico helped."

"I know. I got daily updates," he added with a wink.

"Going back to work in a couple weeks."

"That's good. Now, what about the drug test?"

"When the chief told me I have to wait thirty days, I reminded him that he could have it in minutes if he tried hard enough."

"Good. Thirty days my ass," he added under his breath.

"We did see the police and crime scene reports," Sam offered. "No witnesses, no one heard screaming. Too many prints in the room to isolate just the killer's. If he was smart, he probably used gloves. We think the victim was already dead when she was placed in the bed. No defensive wounds so we're sure she knew her killer. I left my phone in the car or I'd show you the emails." She suppressed a smile, but it wasn't easy. "In case you are interested, she did not have sex before or after she died." Carl wasn't amused at Sam's added comment.

"They shared that information with you?"

Sam shrugged, a slight smile on her face.

"Of course." Carl knew Tim Miesner did side jobs for Sam. And although he frowned on Tim's side hacking jobs, Carl welcomed them now that his life and reputation were on the line. "What did you find out?"

They relayed what they had read in the emails and described the pictures from the crime scene. Tim was still waiting for the official autopsy report.

"Broken neck? Shit. Bet my prints are on that knife, too. Just hope to hell they didn't abduct me from my home."

"With any luck," Jake said, "the killer may have neglected to place your hands around her neck. Those skin samples won't match the DNA on the knife."

"They seem pretty smart to me, so far." Carl shrugged into his FBI demeanor. "I want you two to go to the cottage, check it out, stay there instead of a hotel. Do a trace on my car if it isn't at the cottage. I have a spare set of house keys in a coffee can of nails on the work bench."

Jake didn't have to write notes. Carl had taught all agents to keep notes in their heads.

"Sam, I need you to check out the motel room, see if you can pick up anything. Naturally, they may still have rent-a-cops watching the place so you may have to get creative. There won't be crime scene tape. It's tourist season and the last thing this town wants is to advertise crime. I wish you could get a look at the body, but it's all the way over in Beaufort. Don't waste your time going there, not when I'm due in court on Tuesday."

"Thought it was Monday," Sam said.

"Monday's a holiday of some sort. Lucky me."

The door opened and the portly retiree stuck his head in. "Time's up. Say your goodbyes."

Carl stood and shook each of their hands. "Thanks for coming on such short notice."

Sam reached out and palmed two Tylenol into his hand. "We left a change of clothes and toiletries with the desk sergeant."

The guard found that amusing. "Good luck with that."

# 6

The police chief had one cheek perched on the corner of his desk when Sam and Jake returned. His fingers gripped two pages of a report. "Well? Is your client going to cooperate?"

The wooden chairs were just as uncomfortable as the first time. "Not yet. He wants to know the results of his drug test first."

McComb flipped the pages over and handed them to Jake. "He was right. Someone used a date rape drug on him. Or he could have used it on himself."

"Really? You think he's at the partying age?" Sam leaned closer to Jake to read the report. "That was a pretty high dose."

"You wouldn't believe what kind of trouble seniors get themselves into down here. Just wish I had stock in those erectile dysfunction drugs."

"He had that in him?" Sam couldn't imagine Carl popping little blue pills. "He's a little too straight-laced to try that."

"No. Just saying what's possible."

"This my copy?" Jake asked.

"Yes. Now your turn. Did your client say anything more?"

"Memories are coming back in bits and pieces, but nothing to even give us a hint what happened last night. He wants to give it another day for the drug to get out of his system."

"Is it worth my detective's energy to take a go at him?"

"Would be a waste of his time."

McComb tilted his head as if trying to coax more information from the air. "And his name?"

Jake shrugged. "Not ready yet."

Sam checked the outer office. Milla was pounding away at her computer, but Sam didn't see Detective Lawson anywhere. "You only have one detective working the case?"

"Detective Millicent Boles was assigned to work with Phil at first. He's a bit of a stickler, says he won't work with *that* woman. His words, not mine."

"Boles? Like in Valerie Fennel Aiken Boles?"

"Yep."

"Who's that?" Jake asked.

"*Midnight in the Garden of Good and Evil.* The voodoo priestess?" When that didn't ring any bells with Jake, Sam turned back to the chief. "Is she related?"

"No. Her grandmother likes to claim they are very distant relatives. Milla's family humors the old woman who had owned a voodoo shop in New Orleans called Madam Udo's House of Voodoo. Get it? You do voodoo? Catchy," McComb added with a laugh. "Had voodoo altars, sold charms, amulets, would even make voodoo dolls, perform spells. You name it. Maybe it's true, maybe not. I personally think the old woman might have taught Milla a few tricks of the trade. Once people start thinking of that reclusive Savannah voodoo priestess, you can see them keeping their distance from Milla." He gave a nod toward the leather medicine bundle hanging from Sam's neck. "Has one of those, too, although she calls it an asphidity bag. Great detective, though. Seems to have a good instinct for the job. Unfortunately, Phil tries to hide his superstitions. My gut says he's afraid she's gonna put the root on him."

"The what?" Jake would have dismissed any reference to an occult of any kind. But after marrying Sam and witnessing firsthand Native American mysticism and lore, he wasn't as quick to reject different belief systems.

McComb suppressed a smile, whether from amusement or skepticism. "Jinx, bad mojo, or moco in Gullah terms. Spells, hoodoo, voodoo, take your pick. You ain't in Kansas anymore. Or in your case, Illinois."

If he expected to see shock on their faces, he would be disappointed. Jake had witnessed Alex talking to various animals in the back acres, and he could only guess what happens in the sweat lodge back by the teepee Alex had erected. He still wasn't comfortable talking about what Abby and Sam were capable of with their talents.

"Let me walk you out." McComb led the way to the outer office. Sam stopped briefly in front of Milla's desk, and the chief watched her slip one of Milla's cards into her pocket.

# 7

Sam was studying the area map on Jake's laptop where a blue light blinked on the screen. "According to the map, Carl's car isn't too far from his house. Keep driving east to the last light before the bridge."

They drove past more golf communities, some looked private with guard houses and gates. Most of the shops and strip malls they passed were tucked behind walls of shrubs and trees. You obviously had to know where you were going. No wonder they allowed U-turns along the road.

"Look at how blue that sky is."

"The sky is blue at home, too, Sam."

"This is a different shade of blue, though. Not a cloud in the sky. It's so, I don't know, so…"

"Tropical?"

Sam looked up from the screen. "Are you making fun of me?"

"I have to remember, you aren't exactly a world traveler."

"Thanks…I think." Sam pointed at the light ahead. "Turn right."

Jake turned, his attention split between the road and the computer screen. "How far down?"

"Only a couple blocks." A sign for the Palmetto Bar and Grill pointed to the left at the end of a long building anchored by a locksmith shop.

He steered the car into a paved lot. The restaurant at the end of the building was fenced in with outdoor seating to the side. At the end of the lot was a black Cadillac SUV. "Is that his car?"

"Yes."

Jake parked the Charger next to the Cadillac. They exited their vehicle and walked up to the SUV. Jake checked the door. "Locked."

"There's a sports coat on the back seat. Looks like a briefcase underneath." Sam tried the back door. It was also locked. "Now what?"

Jake pulled out his phone and dialed Carl's number. Within seconds they heard a phone ring inside the SUV. "Now we know where his phone is. All we need are keys." He noticed the door to the restaurant was propped open by a stool. "How's your dumb blonde act?"

"Never better." Sam released the band from her ponytail and raked her fingers through the tight curls. She unfastened the top button of her blouse and followed Jake into a dimly lit bar. A wall of stale beer and strong cleaner odors greeted them the moment they crossed the threshold. The tiled floor looked freshly mopped, chairs flipped on top of the tables. Posters of college teams hung on the walls.

"Sorry folks. We're not open til four." The man hefted a chair from one of the tables. Although balding, his grey hair was pulled back in a ponytail and his arms looked as though he had dried off with the cartoon section of the newspaper.

One step up past the jukebox led to an open room with several pool tables. Jake imagined this place could get pretty rowdy on weekends. "My wife thinks she lost her car keys last night and we were hoping she left them here."

Sam twirled a lock of hair with her finger. "Shoulda never had that last tequila."

Butch's gaze scoured her body as if her car keys were tucked in her cleavage. "You musta been part of the bus group." He walked behind the bar and hefted a container onto the counter. Using a pen, he lifted a pair of red thong underwear. "Tequila makes your clothes fall off?"

Sam unexpectedly blushed and tossed a guilty look at Jake. "Oh, we don't need to talk about that, do we?"

"Red isn't her color." Jake glared at the bartender, wondering what kind of bar Carl had walked into.

"Wouldn't believe what I find on the floor and in the bathrooms after closing. Ben Cassidy is the name. People call me Butch. I own the place." He tossed cell phones and three sets of keys onto the counter.

"What kind of bus group was this?" Jake studied the keys as he waited for a reply, having no idea which keys belonged to Carl. One set had a collection of tags for a number of stores, such as Kroger, Walgreens, and a few he had never heard of. Another had a Harley logo. Neither would be something Carl would own.

"Every Friday customers park their cars here and take a bus to Hilton Head. Some go to the nature preserve, some to the ferry which takes them to Daufuskie Island, and some who just want to shop on the island but don't want the hassle of parking during tourist season. The bus returns in the evening. I usually have dinner and happy hour specials. Did the pretty little lady take the boat trip?"

"I don't think so." Sam chewed on a nail as she avoided Jake's eyes. "The girls talked me into going out, baby. You know how the girls like to party."

Jake suppressed a smile. "Looks like you lost the latest little trinket you hang from your key ring." He picked up the one key ring that didn't have bling attached. "These look familiar?"

Sam winced. "Not sure?" She made it sound more like a question as she bit her bottom lip. "My head's a bit fuzzy today."

Jake grumbled, walked over to the door and pressed the open button on the key. The lights on the SUV flashed. "You are lucky, hon." He walked back to the bar and glared at Sam. "Next time your sorority sisters are in town, tell them you're busy." He pulled a twenty from his wallet and placed it on the bar. "Sorry to bother you, Butch." He grabbed Sam's hand and pulled her along.

"Bye, Butchie." She blew him a kiss as they exited the door. They hurried to the SUV before Butch grew suspicious. "Wow. Never thought it would be so easy to steal a car."

Jake opened the back door and checked the pockets of the sports coat. "Wallet's here." He fanned through the bills. "Close to four hundred dollars so he wasn't drugged for his money." He opened the briefcase. "Laptop is here, too."

Sam climbed into the passenger side and placed her hand on the gearshift, ran it along the steering wheel, then rested it on the center console, waiting for the familiar tingling sensation, the chill that ran up her spine. Sometimes, if the death were violent, she would actually see it taking place. Usually, the sensation was immediate. Not today.

Jake slammed the door shut then opened the driver's side door. "Why don't you drive the Charger and follow me to Carl's house."

"We are breaking a ton of rules not letting Forensics go over this car with a fine tooth comb."

"You, sweetheart, are better than Forensics. Did you pick up anything?"

Sam shook her head. "Nothing sinister so the killer didn't set foot in here nor did the victim die in the car."

# 8

The asphalt drive led to a two-story cobblestone structure with a wrap-around deck worthy of a plantation home. A three-car carport was on their right, but Jake took the turn-around in front of the house instead, motioning for Sam to park the rental in the carport. Sam popped the trunk, climbed out, and started emptying the trunk. She grabbed the carry-on and laptop. Jake grabbed the suitcase.

Planting beds on either side of the front stairs were in need of a seasoned landscaper. Weeds were growing between rocks and perennials in full bloom were hidden behind tall fescue. The property was separated from the empty lots on both sides by three-foot high retaining walls which were being overrun by a vine of some type.

"Carl called this a cottage?" Sam studied the white trim and railings, the red metal roof, and the enclosed sunroom on the right side of the house. "This is more like a waterfront villa."

"Carl said to take the stairs on the left. It leads to the walkout and the workbench where we'll find the house keys."

What looked like a moderate-sized villa from the front morphed into a waterfront home with a deck on each floor overlooking a massive body of water. "What are those things on the sides of the windows?" Tracks attached to the frames held metal structures the size of a retracted projection screen. "Are those hurricane shutters?"

"That would be my guess. And I would bet they are remote control."

The back of the house extended past the walkout, supported by numerous concrete pillars. A kayak leaned against one wall near a work bench. Next to a set of stairs leading to a back door were patio chairs stacked neatly against another wall near a pegboard of rakes, shovels, long handle brooms, and other gardening tools lined up with precision.

Jake found the coffee can and poured the contents onto the work bench. He grabbed the keys, then scooped the nails back into the container. Stairs led to the back entrance. He set the suitcase and cooler down while he worked the key into the lock.

The door opened into a vestibule. They stood silent for several seconds as though listening for movements. The vestibule appeared to be a mudroom since it had a faucet and drain for washing sand from one's feet, and shelves which held stacks of towels. Sam made the first move and entered a spacious kitchen. Floors in a grayish blue tone resembled driftwood.

"Look at this kitchen." A granite counter dissected the kitchen. It contained a cooking area and sink. A double-range cooking area was inset into a bricked wall on their left. Grey cabinets were numerous and lined two of the walls. A curved counter separated the kitchen from the great room. Four stools were situated on the opposite side. "This is gorgeous," Sam said in a hush.

Jake set the suitcase on the floor and followed Sam into the great room where a formal dining table rested under a rustic chandelier. Thick crown molding hugged the recessed ceiling while large area rugs covered the driftwood flooring.

Sam set the carry-on on the floor and walked through a room of rattan furniture upholstered in a nautical theme of ships and birds. "Definitely manly. I would have gone with palm trees and beach scenes." She opened the French doors and stepped out onto a covered screened deck dotted with various rugs.

Jake grabbed the laptop from Sam, placed it on the table, and turned it on. While it fired up, he gazed over the water at the kayakers paddling in the distance. "Nice view. I think that's the Harbor River, if I remember correctly."

"The way the house is angled, I bet Carl has a great view of both sunrises and sunsets." Sam nudged her husband. "Shall we check out the rest of the house?"

"Save it for later, Sam."

She recognized that tone. Jake was not in the mood for a house tour.

He inspected a cabinet against the wall and discovered it was a refrigerator. After grabbing two sodas, he joined Sam at the table. Although it was hot and muggy, the breeze off the river and from the overhead fans provided some relief.

"We haven't eaten all day." Jake handed her his cell phone. "Check that list you printed out and find us a restaurant. I don't like to break-and-enter on an empty stomach."

"Then you check my emails. Maybe Tim has the autopsy results. Besides, you're better at deciphering autopsy lingo."

"Do you want steak or seafood, although I would assume restaurants would have a variety."

"You did notice the traffic on the bridge," Jake said with a nod to the bumper-to-bumper line of cars on the bridge in the distance. "Tourist season means traffic jams and long waits for a table. And if there's an accident on that bridge, we may be stuck on the island for a long time."

"Okay then. We will stick to Heyward Bluff, although the Old Town section is probably crawling with tourists, too." Sam continued her search while Jake read. The list she had printed out showed a map with the location of various restaurants. However, she had to refer to each restaurant's website for the menu and hours of operation. There was a wide variety of offerings from burgers to high end steak joints. One even boasted a fifty-four dollar steak. Unfortunately, she hadn't packed any clothes worthy of a restaurant with valet parking.

"Nothing fancy, Sam. A burger is okay with me."

"Everyone has burgers, except for this tofu vegan place. Yuk."

"Victim didn't have any drugs in her system. Not too much alcohol either. Hadn't eaten dinner. Blunt force trauma to the back of the head. The knife wound was post mortem. Had a tattoo of a snake on her back and a rose on the right upper arm."

Sam leaned over to see the snake which was positioned head down. "Tramp stamp. Not quite her back, sweetheart."

"Force of the trauma broke her neck. Probably knocked against something rather than hit from behind."

"In other words, we didn't learn anything different from the initial examination."

"It's just strange that she didn't have drugs in her system. Maybe she's the one who drugged Carl. But for what reason?" Jake checked his watch. "I want to get into that hotel before dark. Don't want to have to turn on lights and garner attention from anyone."

"Okay. There's a Captain Woody's in Old Town. We can get a burger there and then the motel is just a short ride down the street by one of those outlet centers."

# 9

How anyone could find a motel tucked behind an outlet center and hidden in a cluster of trees was a puzzle. The concealment did work in their favor, though. There was only one car in the parking lot and an alley behind the building. The building's stucco was painted in flamingo pink. Fake evergreens in pots stood sentry at the office door. With all the high-end hotels around, it was a wonder the small motel had any business at all, although it was evident money and effort was spent to make the exterior presentable. A quick glance at the end unit showed empty parking spaces. Not even a police vehicle.

Jake parked the SUV in the alley behind the building. He exited first and walked up to a window in the last unit. A noisy air conditioner made it difficult to hear if anyone was in the room. They would have to take their chances. The screen easily lifted out of its track. With a gentle tug, the storm window slid up. Sam exited the vehicle and joined Jake. The window was two feet from the ground gaining them easy access. Once inside, Jake pulled the screen into the room and closed the window. He crossed the room to the windows facing the parking lot and parted the drapes.

"No police stationed anywhere. Not even an unmarked car."

"I'll leave the drapes on the back windows open so we can get some light in here." Sam sniffed the air which was pungent with strong odors. "They didn't waste time sanitizing the place."

"Police took the mattress and bedding so it appears the motel staff already replaced it."

The queen-size bed was covered in a bedspread with pink

flamingo designs. Walls were painted in a pale yellow, the popcorn ceiling a stark white. A nightstand was on one side of the bed while a dresser held a television set.

Jake turned the light on in the bathroom. The tub and sink had also been cleaned. He turned off the light to find Sam sitting on the bed, her hand slowly sliding across the bedspread.

"Feel like I need to wear a hazmat suit. Should have brought my blue light."

"Not quite the Astoria, but probably much cheaper than the resorts on the island." He moved back to the windows by the door and parted the drape. "I'll keep watch. Don't take too long."

Sam rose from the bed and moved to the center of the room. She closed her eyes as though listening for voices or cries from the victim. If the murder weapon were still in the room, all Sam had to do was touch it. After several minutes, she opened her eyes with a sigh. "Nothing. It's all been sterilized, too many people disturbing the aura. Not one blood stain missed by the cleaning people." She bent down and studied the surface of the dresser. "They even cleaned up all the fingerprint residue."

"She had to know her killer. No struggle, according to the police report. My guess is they drove her someplace first, either in her car or the killer's. There weren't any abandoned cars at the Palmetto Bar and Grill, other than Carl's."

"All I know for sure is she wasn't killed here. I just don't understand why they would kidnap Carl. He certainly wouldn't have gone willingly."

"At gunpoint maybe." Satisfied an officer wouldn't make a surprise visit to the motel room, Jake moved away from the window. He stared at nothing in particular. It wasn't unusual for him to work things out silently, get inside the head of the killer. It was something Carl had trained him to do which was what made him an exceptional cop.

"It is possible Carl was the mark and the victim is part of some theft ring that preys on tourists."

"And because Carl didn't have his wallet on him, he had nothing to offer."

"So her partners get pissed and she gets killed."

"Not intentionally," Jake said. "Why get rid of the one person who can lure the quarry? They need her. They could have killed Carl." Jake thought about that, then shook his head. "No. I've checked the town's crime reports. Unless they are hiding it, there aren't any records of tourists being set up in this fashion. Besides, Carl could smell a scam a mile away."

Sam cocked her head as though listening to voices only she could hear, but either the voices were too inaudible or made no sense. "What about a jealous husband? Did she wear a wedding ring?"

"M.E.'s report mentioned a number of very expensive rings. Guess any of them could have been a wedding ring. What are you thinking?"

"Maybe he didn't mean to kill her. Domestic fights sometimes get out of hand, are meant to scare or intimidate, but sometimes the boyfriend or husband goes too far. Maybe the boyfriend thought she was cheating on him."

"Possible. I still say Carl would have never put himself in that position. What we need to do first is identify her."

# 10

The next morning Sam awakened to the smell of bacon. They had taken the bedroom on the main floor near the kitchen. After a quick shower, hair dripping wet and lathered with a conditioner to tame the frizz, Sam joined Jake on the back deck where scrambled eggs, bacon, and biscuits greeted her. "You are the best." She kissed him on the cheek while he poured her a glass of orange juice.

"Anything for the love of my life and the pain in my ass."

"Ooooh. I don't know if I should feel insulted." It was only eight in the morning and the humidity was already stifling. The overhead fans were set on high, but the view was too perfect to hide indoors. Sam noticed a sports coat on an adjoining chair. "Are we getting dressed up for a reason?"

"It's Carl's. I took it out of the back seat of his Caddy." He handed Sam a napkin. "This was in the inside pocket."

Sam turned it over. "Palmetto Bar and Grill. We already know he was there."

"Check the other side."

Scribbled in a fluid handwriting she recognized as Carl's was written *Mossy Belden*. "Sounds like an exotic plant. Did you check the phone book?"

"Not sure where Carl keeps it." He pushed his plate aside adding, "By the way, Abby wants to Skype this morning. Might be any minute."

"Good. I miss Dillon."

"She said he's been walking around the house searching for us."

"It's the first time I've been away from him."

Fifteen minutes later, their breakfast finished, a sing-song tune blared from the laptop. Jake pressed several keys and the monitor came to life. Alex and Abby were seated at the kitchen table, Dillon on Abby's lap.

"Look, Dillon. Who is that?" Abby raised Dillon's arm in a wave. A confused look crossed the boy's face.

"Hi, baby. It's Mommy." Sam waved at the screen.

"Hey, Sport. What are you doing?" Jake smiled at his son's antics. Dillon twisted in Abby's lap to see behind the monitor as though expecting them to be on the other side of the table. He looked up at Abby and pointed a finger at the screen.

"Yes, it's Daddy and Mommy. Can you say hi?"

Dillon stuck a finger in his mouth.

"How was the trip?" Alex asked.

"Interesting. We saw Carl, visited the motel where the body was found. So far, no clues other than the name of a woman scribbled on a napkin. Our only hope is that it identifies the victim. Other than that, no progress."

"What about you, Sam?" Abby asked.

"Nothing. The only thing I know for sure is she wasn't killed in the motel room or in Carl's car. They took the body to a town about forty-five minutes away. You should see Carl's house, Mom. The view is fantastic." Sam spent ten minutes describing every room in the house, the décor, wood flooring, and the decks. "And the birds down here, herons, egrets, ibis, woodstorks. So many palm trees."

"Sounds like you plan to go house hunting." Alex winced as Dillon pulled on one of his pigtails.

Sam sighed. "It would be nice to have a place to unwind, even if it was only for a couple weeks. And I think it's driveable."

"About fifteen hours," Jake offered. "Sam didn't enjoy the plane ride so we are driving back."

Dillon squirmed and babbled in Abby's lap. She had to hold his hands so he didn't pound on the keyboard and disconnect Skype. She waved one of his hands. "Say bye-bye, Dillon. Mommy and Daddy need to get back to work."

Dillon babbled a string of da-da-da-da's.

"We'll Skype again soon," Jake said before disconnecting the call.

Sam swiped at her eyes and pushed away from the table. "They look okay, right? Dillon didn't cry."

"Not like you," Jake said, wrapping his arms around her. "Come on. Let's clean up the table and occupy your mind."

They carried the plates, bowls, and cups to the kitchen. While Sam cleaned up the kitchen, Jake located the phone book in an end table in the living room. He set it on the island counter and thumbed through the *B's*. "There's a Mossy Belden right here in town." He grabbed his cell phone and did a search. "She's near Old Town."

"Mossy could be the name of a bartender or realtor Carl met, not necessarily the victim."

"It's worth checking out. If Mossy is home, then we know she isn't the deceased. If she isn't, we'll ask when she was last seen and hopefully find a framed picture of her we can compare to the deceased."

# 11

Jake punched in the address on the dashboard GPS. Immediately a map appeared on the monitor with pulsing dots showing the location of the Cadillac as well as their destination. Carl's Cadillac had every bell and whistle offered.

"Doesn't seem that far away." He turned onto 278 and headed west. Entrances to private communities boasted canopies of trees. Palm trees guarded attractive entry signs, their fronds swaying in the gentle breeze. It took several blocks until the car's air conditioner dropped the inside temps to a breathable degree.

Jake turned at the light and drove past strip malls, a church, and restaurants until they came to a circle drive in the middle of the road where cars jockeyed for position. "This looks like a catastrophe waiting to happen." He maneuvered it without incident, staying in the outside lane so he could continue straight. As soon as the circle spit him back in the same direction, the view morphed from modern structures and industry to older homes, worn sidewalks, and empty lots overgrown with weeds. The map instructed him to turn right at the upcoming stop sign. Cars were parked on both sides of the street. Businesses appeared wall-to-wall, a mixture of restaurants and retail stores. He turned left at the next street which was even more crowded than the previous one with tourists of all makes and sizes clogging the sidewalks and wandering in and out of a variety of shops and restaurants.

"This must be where all the action is." A sign near a gravel drive advertised a weekly farmer's market. It was a quaint small town setting attracting locals and tourists alike. Homes were older and trees leaned with age. "Let's solve this case quickly so we can spend a week shopping and doing touristy things." Sam could swear she heard a faint groan from her husband.

"It should be up ahead on the right." In the distance they could see an expanse of water dotted by a number of boats. He slowed the vehicle down to a crawl.

"It's a church," Sam said. "Are you sure you have the right address?"

Jake parked in a space in front of the brick walkway and turned off the ignition. They sat for several seconds admiring the two-story frame. It appeared constructed of barn wood, the window frames painted in a burnt orange. A sign out front read *Church on the Bluff, Established 1767, Built 1854.* It also listed the days and times of services.

"Looks like there's another service in about an hour," Jake said. "Maybe we can catch an usher or someone who can tell us something about Mossy."

They exited the vehicle and followed the brick path to the front door. The thrumming started the moment Sam started for the church. It was a vibration that reverberated through her body, almost as though the very ground she stood on had a heartbeat. She tried to ignore it as they entered the vestibule where a *Docent on Duty* sign greeted them. They crossed a threshold and were met with the odor of aged polish. Sunlight streaming through arched stained glass cast a warm glow onto the polished wood. The church had already emptied out from the eight o'clock service, except for a few stragglers by the altar.

"Beautiful." A cacophony of whispers erupted drowning out Sam's thoughts. Why was this happening? Why here?

Floorboards creaked as they walked down the aisle, passing

pews, each with its own half door. Visitors stood in clusters listening to a man near the altar. Were those the whispers she heard? Sam turned and spotted a choir loft with a large organ above the entrance. What was it about this church that the spirits were so active? She knew the area had a history even before the first settlers, and it had been a hotbed of action during the Civil War. But those deaths occurred more than a century ago, certainly too long for her to feel any aura. Strangely, the thrumming and whispers ceased, replaced by an overwhelming feeling of peace and comfort.

"Sam?"

She jumped at the sound of Jake's voice, then smiled. "I'm fine. Everything feels fine."

"Can I help you?" A white-haired man limped toward them, assisted by a cane with what looked like a brass lion head for the grasp. "I'm Jerry Nolan, the docent here. Did you have some questions?"

"The church is beautiful," Sam said. "Who built it?"

"E.B. White was the architect. He leaned more toward a gothic revival design with the fanned arches and latticed shutters." Jerry braced a hand on one of the pew's doors and relaxed into speaker mode. "They sent all the way to England for that rose-colored glass you see in them windows. Now, the altar and lectern had to be remodeled after the fire."

"Fire?" Sam said. She pulled out her phone and took several pictures of the windows, pews, and the pipe organ in the loft.

"Oh yeah. Union soldiers practically burned down the entire town of Heyward Bluff on June 4, 1863. Why, the 150th anniversary was a few years ago with nary a peep. Seems they just don't teach that part of history in schools these days. At least we have some Civil War reenactors."

"That's why you became a docent here?" Sam thought Jerry spoke and looked as though he might have been around in 1863 and witnessed it firsthand. If he had a pipe, she wouldn't have been surprised to see him light it and lean back for an hour's worth of reminiscing.

"Yep. Church has a lot of history. It was one of the few buildings spared. Course, all the residents fled. Then we had the hurricane of 1898 which caused more damage, but all was repaired and open for business in 1900."

"What made Heyward Bluff so popular?" Jake checked his watch to let Sam know they had work to do and little time before Carl was hauled into court on Tuesday.

"There was a ferry route between Savannah and Beaufort. Heyward Bluff became a stopover for those traveling between the two towns. We were a resort area back then, much as it is today. When you go on out back, you'll see how it sits on a bluff with a beautiful view of the May River. The church has been listed in the National Register of Historic Places since 1975. It's an Episcopal Church, but all faiths are welcome during Saturday and Sunday services."

Jerry reminded Sam of their family friend, Alex Red Cloud. He also had an excellent grasp of history, although his leaned more toward Native American. "Who is the town named after?"

"Thomas Heyward Jr. Few people know he was one of the signers of the Declaration of Independence and the Articles of Confederation. Served as a judge when he returned."

"You are a wealth of information, Jerry." Jake brought the conversation to their original purpose. "Do you know a Mossy Belden?"

Jerry's eyes lit up. "Mossy? Why, she's in the house right next door. Her son is the pastor here. He runs a summer youth camp near Statesboro, but is home most weekends for the services."

"Is she home now?" Sam asked.

"Should be. She attended the earlier service. I don't usually do my docent duties during service. Being tourist season, it's always busy around here so I make myself available on Sundays. Can't leave my post or I'd show you the way."

"We'll find our way. Thanks for your time." They left quickly before Jerry recited the entire four year history of the Civil War. "The victim was only in her thirties," Jake said. "Certainly not old enough to have a grown son."

"I thought the same thing." As they exited the church, the thrumming started up again. Sam tried to ignore it as she focused on the tourists sitting on the grass overlooking an expanse of water broken up by what looked like sandbars. Piers jutted out from docks where families walked along the gravel shoreline. Others sat on the bluff enjoying a picnic. "Let me get a few pictures." Sam brought out her phone and started snapping pictures of the view, the manicured bluff, the boats in the water. She turned and took pictures of the church and its tall peaks, the large oak tree and lush landscaping. A house nestled close to the church had a back porch with a freshly painted white railing. A woman in a sleeveless dress sat on a swing, head cocked, staring curiously at them. Her steel wool hair was kept short, her skin the color of warm toast. The house appeared made of the same timber as the church.

She tucked her phone back into her purse and followed Jake to the back steps. The whispers started up again. This time instead of a chorus, she heard one voice, just three words that made little sense. It definitely didn't sound like English. Jake tapped her arm. The whisper stopped abruptly. Sam looked up to see the older woman rise slowly to greet them.

"Blessed day, isn't it?"

"Absolutely beautiful," Sam said, although the sweat she felt trickling down her back made her want to tell her exactly what she thought about the temps and humidity in this neck of the woods. "You have a perfect view."

"Yes I do." She turned her head more in the direction of Sam's voice than actually seeing her. "Used to be able to see better, but you know how it is. Guess the Lord wanted to enhance my hearing and other instincts."

"I'm Sam Casey and this is my husband, Jake Mitchell. We were looking for Mossy Belden." They climbed the wooden steps to the porch.

The older woman felt behind her for the swing's armrest and sat down. "Why, you found her. I'm Mossy Belden."

# 12

Sam carried a pitcher of sweet tea and three glasses from the kitchen while Mossy followed close behind with a plate of wafer-type cookies. It was obvious that her ailing eyesight didn't slow Mossy down one bit. Sam filled each of the glasses, then set the pitcher on the coffee table. They pulled two Adirondack chairs close to the swing and sat down. Jake described Carl to her, hoping she might have met him before.

"So you think this friend of yours is supposed to know me?" Mossy wrapped her hands around her sweet tea as she rocked the swing. "I'm sorry, the man you described doesn't sound familiar. I rarely leave the house other than for doctor appointments. Don't know why he would have written down my name. There ain't no other women around with my name to my knowledge."

Sam took a sip of the tea and winced. It tasted like sugar water.

"You ain't in the South unless you've had sweet tea," Mossy said with a chuckle.

"Guess it takes some getting used to." Sam bit into a wafer cookie. "Are these sesame seeds?"

"You ain't in the South unless you've eaten a benne wafer." Mossy chuckled again and shoved the plate toward Jake. "My son would prefer chocolate chip but chocolate don't last long in this heat."

A hummingbird fluttered near the bird feeder attached to the porch railing, then hovered while its long beak poked into the red liquid. Another hummingbird approached, chasing off the first one. Sam watched this little dance for several seconds, then turned back to the older woman. "Is Mossy short for something, like Margaret or Maureen?"

"I was named after my grandmother. Guess the name dies with me, unless my son gets married and has a daughter." Her face saddened as she kneaded her hands. "His fiancée died last Christmas in a car accident. He tries to hide it but I know he's still hurtin' inside." She shook her head and forced a smile. "It doesn't appear I have been of any help. Do you think someone stole my identity?"

"No, not at all." Jake didn't want to show Mossy the picture from the crime scene. That would have been too much for the woman to see, especially if she had known her. "We think the woman our friend met must have known you if she used your name."

"Can you describe her?"

Sam scrolled through the emails on her phone until she found photos of the victim. "She has auburn hair about shoulder length, slim, five foot six, one hundred twenty pounds, green eyes. Very attractive."

"My, that sounds like Angie. She's my home companion. Well, was. I haven't seen her in several weeks. My son hired her to help with chores, do my shopping. I told him I could get along fine on my own, but you know sons."

"Sort of like that Home Help Network program we've seen on the billboards?"

"Yes, although I haven't had the heart to tell Jonah she hasn't been showing up. He said it's a free service for the disabled. I doubt that so I looked up the place, called them and told them she hasn't been around. Funny thing is, they didn't have anyone by that name working for them."

Sam and Jake exchanged looks. "What is Angie's last name?" Sam brought out a notepad and pen.

"Douglas, I believe. Yes, Angela Douglas."

Jake asked, "When will your son be back from the youth camp?"

"Not sure. One of the visiting pastors conducted services this weekend which is why I don't expect Jonah home."

"Do you have a number for him?"

"He has a cell phone. Service ain't good up there, though. When he goes to a nearby town, he can usually get reception and will call me. Would you like me to ask him something?"

Jake would usually have asked for the phone number and called Jonah and left a message. Or, if he had more time, he would drive to the youth camp. Unfortunately, they didn't have that luxury. "What I'd like is for him to come home."

Sam managed to finish off the last of her sweet tea. How soon til the sugar rush hit? "Did Angie have any relatives?"

"She never talked about herself much. When I would ask her personal questions, she would change the subject. I didn't press." Mossy turned her head slightly, as though seeing them from her peripheral vision. "Something happened to Angie, didn't it?"

"We aren't sure. Until we actually locate Angie, we won't know."

"Are you two cops?"

"Not around here. We're trying to help our friend out of a predicament, and somehow Angie figures into it. Angie might be able to clear things up."

Mossy nodded and looked out at the water. It appeared she had been fond of the young woman. She grabbed her glass and clasped it tightly in her hands. "She started working six months ago. Good worker, though a lousy cook, bless her heart. She'd do the laundry, run the vacuum, do my grocery shopping."

Jake tried to avoid the sugary water as long as possible until his thirst got the best of him. The paddle fans overhead provided little reprieve from the heat. "Did she seem worried or afraid of anyone?"

"Nothing she bothered me with. Like I said, rarely talked about herself and I'm not one to pry. If people want to offer information, fine."

Sam refilled her glass and looked over to see if Jake's glass needed filling. He waved her off. He did not have the sweet tooth Sam had, but even the sweet tea was too much for her to handle. "She may not have talked about herself, but I bet you are good at noticing things. Do you think she was from around here?"

"Her accent was more blue grass. There is a difference." Mossy appeared to think about that for a few seconds. "I did ask her once if she had kids, but all she said was once she got rid of her good for nothing husband, she didn't want anything more to do with a man. Then she clammed up."

"Ever notice any bruises on her, maybe a black eye, or a limp?" Sam knew Mossy might not be able to see all the details of abuse, but she might have detected a limp.

"Nothing like that. She was interested in the history of the south and the Civil War, but I believe she was just making small talk. Asked if I ever traced my genealogy. Like I said, all idle chit chat and nothing personal."

Mossy didn't appear that fragile to Sam, and she doubted much got past her keen intellect. "Anything you might remember could give us more information on Angie and help us to find her."

"I think she liked to read because she mentioned going to

those book fairs, you know, the ones they have in Savannah and something held every year on the island. She also liked to go antiquing. I overheard her talking to my son once when they thought I was asleep. My bedroom is right above here."

Sam snapped her gaze to Jake. "Did they have a close relationship?"

Mossy's face suddenly turned serious. "Like I said, my son is still mourning his fiancée."

Sam wanted to say it sounded as though her son and Angie were around the same age and Angie was an attractive woman. But she didn't want to alarm Mossy with an accusation. "Being a man of the cloth and someone who could easily get a person to open up, perhaps Angie mentioned things she was uneasy mentioning to you. Perhaps she had an abusive boyfriend or ex-husband."

Mossy relaxed a bit and set her glass of tea on the table. "Yes, Jonah has a very understanding heart and many people take him into their confidence. He's very good with children, too, and there have been numerous occasions when they have confided in him."

Sam stood and grabbed the glasses and pitcher. "We should get going. I'll take these in for you." She heard the whisper again and caught a fleeting glimpse of a figure darting around the side of the house.

Mossy stood and reached for the plate. "I can take that in."

"You sit and relax." She checked the yard again, but other than the tourists by the shore, Sam didn't see anyone.

"Yes, the heat takes some getting used to." Mossy grabbed the bannister and made her way closer to Jake.

"Did you know where Angie lived?"

"In town, only because it didn't take her long to get here in the mornings. Course, Hardeeville is right down the road, as is Hilton Head. Beaufort and Savannah are more like forty-five minutes, but I never heard her once grumbling about traffic, as most people will if they work in this area and have to drive that distance. I do have her phone number written down in the address book by the end table."

Having heard Mossy's comment, Sam brought the book out to the porch. She found Angie's phone number and read it off to Jake who punched it into his phone. They thanked Mossy for her time and left.

# 13

They sat in the car while Jake called Angie's cell phone number. It rang six times before Jake hung up. Next, he entered her phone number on the console to obtain the owner name and address.

"You were right. Carl's car has all the bells and whistles," Sam said.

"Looks like she's in a community just off of Bluffton Parkway. Heron Lakes. Sounds like it might be a private community." Jake kept one eye on the GPS screen while Sam did an Internet search. The route on the screen took a number of twists and turns.

"There's a restaurant on the property that's open to the public called Heron's Point. Guess we just have to mention it at the gate as our ticket to get inside. You're coming up on that circle thingy again," Sam pointed out.

"It's a round-about, Sam. Actually ingenious. Keeps traffic moving."

"Right. Try maneuvering it after three martinis."

He reached over and pulled a strand of hair from her face. The humidity had forced Sam to pull her hair up into a ponytail. Having a mind of their own, the strands did what they wanted. She had always wished she had Abby's straight black hair rather than her father's natural blonde curls.

She had met Jake on the job when Jake and his partner, Frank Travis, had been assigned to her department. She resented his FBI clinical eye to every case and by-the-book demeanor. He was skeptical of her methods in solving cases and thought it bordered on witchcraft. She had moved up quickly through the ranks through the benefit of being the police chief's goddaughter. Jake discovered it was Sam's talent the chief exploited to dig up dirt on his rivals. She didn't seem to mind digging up dirt as she relished using her gift and focusing a spotlight on those who deserved it while refusing to believe her godfather was no better than his enemies.

She and Jake were oil and water back then, but were married after six months. Jake was now a sergeant in Homicide and Sam was an investigative consultant for CHPD, preferring to spend more time with their son and have the flexibility of picking and choosing her cases.

"Watch the road, big guy."

Jake squeezed her hand one last time. "You know, this private community sounds a little too expensive for someone who works as a home companion."

"Maybe it's her way of volunteering her time."

They passed blocks of empty properties until they came to the sign for Heron Lakes. Jake turned at the entrance and found the guardhouse just a couple blocks from the turn. After telling the guard they were going to the restaurant, they received a visitor card to place on the dashboard and directions to the restaurant. Instead of following the directions, though, they followed the map on the console to the Douglas residence.

They passed houses with turrets and cobblestone arches. Brick drives led to three-car garages, each house sitting on what looked like one acre lots, most with piers extending into man made lakes.

"Turn left here." Sam checked the house numbers on the mailboxes.

"I'm going to drive past the house first. See if there's a car in the driveway."

Angie Douglas' house resembled a mini-tudor with sharp peaks and rounded bay windows. The lawn looked freshly mown and the plants in full bloom. Sam turned to check the backyard as Jake drove to the end of the block. She saw a wrought iron arch covered in a vine of red blooms, and a bird bath surrounded by squatty palms.

"I don't see anyone in the backyard. Quite a few empty lots on this block, too." Sam didn't see any neighbors in the few houses across the street. "People must be shopping or at the beach. I don't see any signs of life."

Jake turned right at the end of the block, then right again onto a worn path at the back of an empty lot. He turned off the ignition and studied the lots between the car and Angie's house. "You take the front, Sam. Ring the doorbell. I'll come in through the back. If no one answers the door, join me in the back."

They went their separate ways, Jake along the back tree line, Sam toward the street. Lawn mowers could be heard from down the block where landscapers scurried like ants around one property. Even in the humid air they were clad in long pants, long-sleeved shirts, and hats. Jake was sweating just looking at them. He slipped behind a huge oak tree as a car zipped by, and wondered how often security drove through the area.

Sam walked with a purpose, aware there might be prying eyes behind curtains across the street. She kept her eyes on the bay window on Angie's house while questions invaded her thoughts. Why would someone of obvious means work as a home companion? It was a job she would be paid for yet she obviously didn't need the money. If she wanted to volunteer her time there were all kinds of food kitchens and thrift shops. Perhaps there were more people than positions. Or did Angie seek out Mossy Belden specifically? If so, for what reason?

Sam marched up the brick drive and approached a double glass door with what looked like pewter insets. Her gaze made a quick sweep of the outside looking for security cameras, but there didn't appear to be any. A floral garland framed the door while a large urn filled with colorful faux flowers and tall grass was tucked in an alcove near the door. She pressed the doorbell and heard a chime echoing. She listened for footsteps, a dog barking, some sign of life. She pressed the doorbell again. If she waited too long, she was afraid it might garner the attention of neighbors.

After several more seconds of silence, she made her way around to the back. She climbed the deck stairs and found Jake peering through the glass in the door. "Anything?"

"No. Looks like this opens to the kitchen." He covered his fingers with the edge of his shirt and slid open the screen door.

"Please tell me you aren't going to break the glass."

Jake pulled latex gloves from his pocket and handed one set to Sam. After slipping into his pair, he tugged on the handle. The door slid open. "No need to. For some reason people think they are safe in a gated community." Jake entered first and Sam followed close behind. They stood for several seconds listening to the sounds of the house—the ticking of a grandfather clock, soft hum from the refrigerator, a hissing from one of the appliances on the counter. By all indications, they were alone.

The kitchen had marble counters and oak flooring. It looked lived in with dishes and cups in the sink, powdered cream next to an elaborate home brewing system. One thing the room was lacking was a woman's touch. Sam didn't see cutesy knickknacks like ladybug canisters, country patterned placemats, or bright-colored curtains. Everything was in brown and gray. Other than the floral garland around the outside of the front door, everything had a masculine touch.

"What do you think?"

"Hard to believe a woman lives here. At least the air conditioning is on." Sam checked the sink. "Food left on the plate looks pretty dry. No water in the sink. Probably a couple days since they were placed here." She opened a cabinet door and pulled out the trash can. "Ripped envelope on top is addressed to Angela and Gordon Douglas the third."

"Now all we need is to find a photo of the happy couple and confirm that the dead woman is Angela."

They stepped gingerly around the island counter, through a broad entryway, and into a war zone.

# 14

What was obviously the living room had been transformed into the center of chaos. Chair and couch cushions had been ripped open. Pictures removed from the walls, their backing pulled from their frames. An empty bookcase sat against one wall, its contents scattered on the floor. "Someone was looking for something." Jake eyed the sweeping staircase and weighed his option to search the entire house. Not their job and he didn't want to disturb any evidence the local police might find.

"If he was looking for a wall safe, it wasn't here. Not one picture was left hanging." Sam also noticed the staircase.

"See any proof that Angie is definitely the deceased?"

Sam stood still, as though absorbing the aura in the room. Not one hair stood on end nor did a familiar chill creep up her spine. If Angie had been killed in the house, Sam should have felt something the moment she walked in. She moved carefully through the debris and bent down. She pulled a pen from her purse and flipped over a framed picture of an attractive woman with an elderly man in a wheelchair. "Definitely looks like Angie. He looks old enough to be her father, though. She may have found herself a sugar daddy." She pulled out her phone and took a picture of the happy couple and several of their surroundings.

Jake stepped over the rubble and picked up a larger picture frame. "Fancy wedding." Since the backing had already been removed, he could see a stamped date on the back of the photo. "Definitely not her father. They have only been married a couple years."

"Explains the lack of a feminine touch in this house. He must have lived here with his previous wife or he was always single and didn't care for the womanly touch. Wonder if he is still alive."

"The envelope you found had both names on it."

"Yes, but it was from a retail store. The account must still have both of their names on it. Course, if he is still alive, where is he?"

Now Sam's gaze lingered over the staircase. "I don't smell anything fermenting."

"Sweetheart, you always have a way with words."

"The picture showed him in a wheelchair." Sam stepped over to a door near the staircase and opened it. "It's an elevator. He could be bedridden and in need of help."

"The trouble you get me into." Jake relented and they stepped into the elevator. After pressing the *UP* arrow, a glass door slid closed and the elevator silently rose, stopping just as quietly. The door emptied them into a hallway with a large atrium at the top of the staircase.

They exited and searched the hallway. There was a doorway at each end and two others near the atrium. They started at the far end of the hallway. Force of habit, Jake pulled his Sig from its holster. Even if Gordon Douglas was bedridden, he could be holding a shotgun. Jake motioned for Sam to stay back. He turned the doorknob, pushed the door open, and quickly surveyed the empty room. The bed was unmade, its comforter littering the floor.

Jake quickly checked the bathroom. "It's clear."

Sam stepped in and opened the door to a walk-in closet. "All women's clothes. Angie obviously had her own room."

"How are your spidey senses?"

"As quiet as a church mouse."

The other doors led to a hallway powder room, two guest bedrooms, and at the opposite end of the hallway a large master suite. Sam opened the door to a huge walk-in closet which held suitcases and a wall safe. Papers were scattered on the floor along with jewelry and some cash. "Come look at this."

Jake entered and stopped when he saw the money and jewelry. "Looks real even from here. What else could have been so important that the killer left the money and jewelry?"

A word seeped into Sam's consciousness. *Montana.*

"What?"

Sam shrugged. "The word Montana just popped into my head. Has to be a reason."

Jake studied his wife's face. His stubborn skepticism tried to rear its ugly head, but the seriousness in Sam's voice helped to tamp it down. "Maybe the husband is from Montana."

"Maybe they kidnapped him and are forcing him to empty his bank accounts." Sam doubted a man in a wheelchair could have killed Angie. Did he hire someone? "Did you find a wheelchair anywhere?"

"Nope." Jake pulled out his phone and tapped in Gordon's full name. There were a number of men with the same name. On a hunch, Jake tapped the entry which was an obituary. "Angie's husband died a year ago from a brain tumor. Was diagnosed three years ago. Survived by his wife, Angela, no children. Preceded in death by his first wife, Meredith, ten years ago." Jake skimmed the rest of the article. "Seems he inherited a shitload of money. His father was in the airplane business. Followed in his father's footsteps, then sold the business twenty-five years ago when he was fifty years ago. He was an avid bird watcher and a Civil War enthusiast."

"Does it give Angie's maiden name? Maybe we can find out more about her background."

Jake ran his finger over the screen. "No. And she obviously isn't in the system because the police haven't come up with an I.D. on her prints. Maybe the Bureau's experts can do better."

"We don't need the Bureau, and I bet there are all kinds of prints in her bedroom." Sam made her way back to Angie's room.

"We don't have any equipment with us, Sam. Hell, we are contaminating the place with every step we take."

"Just a quick peek." She snapped the latex glove at her wrist. "At least we have these." Sam first checked the mirror above the white dresser. Sunlight revealed dust and little else. The surface of the dresser was also tidy with one silk floral arrangement of magnolias occupying one corner. "What is with these cleaning people. They are far too OCD."

"Just as well. I'd like to stay on the good side of the police chief."

Sam ignored her husband as she studied the floral wallpaper and heavy brocade drapes. Artwork on the walls were ink sketchings of nude women. From the hairstyles and body shapes, they depicted the Michelangelo era rather than modern. "Why don't you see if there is a safe behind one of those pictures, although I'm surprised these weren't torn down during the search."

"Maybe security was driving by or they knew there was only one safe in the house and they had already found it." Jake checked behind each picture anyway.

There was an alcove outside of the bathroom with a dressing table. Sam opened the top drawer and smiled. There were several compacts of eyeshadow, blush, and makeup.

"No safe here," Jake called out.

Sam found one compact with a smooth surface, then located a small can of talcum powder. "I think I can get a print off of one of her compacts." She sprinkled the powder onto the top of the compact."

"Don't blow on it," Jake cautioned.

"Why?"

"You'll contaminate it with your DNA."

"Never said I was a crime scene investigator." She picked up the compact and shook off the excess powder. "Perfect." She snapped photos, then checked the results. "I'll have Tim run these through all the databases, just in case Angie Douglas is an alias."

"Great. Now let's get the hell out of here."

# 15

Carl studied the wall behind Detective Phil Lawson. If this punk thinks he can beat him at a silence contest, he was sorely mistaken. The detective's tie was knotted so tightly, Carl didn't know how the guy could swallow. If he didn't stop going to the gym, he'd have to go to the next size shirt just to fit his neck.

Lawson busied himself jotting down notes. Carl knew the routine. If the detective stayed silent long enough, the suspect would start to fill the void with words. Even if a suspect was told everything would be off the record, even though the detective knew the suspect had asked for his attorney. No offer for something to drink or eat. He closed his eyes and listened to the scratching of the pen against paper. Carl could wait him out til Christmas. He heard the door close and opened his eyes to discover he was alone. Another trick. Next, the air conditioning would be turned down. When sweat started clinging to Carl's shirt, the detective would return with a cold can of something and let Carl watch the condensation drip from the can.

This guy appeared to work alone. He should have a good cop to his bad, unless Lawson planned to play both parts like a quick change artist.

Fifteen minutes later, when the sweat started trailing down the sides of Carl's face, Lawson returned with a can of soda, chips of ice dripping from the can. Carl couldn't help it. He laughed out loud. Lawson snapped his dark eyes in his direction. The detective wasn't expecting that. He dropped the pad of paper on the table and took a seat.

Now Carl was ready to play.

"I know all the tricks, son."

Lawson bristled.

"Let's see, you've been here for less than a year, not from around here. I'd say NewYork? Chicago? Nah. You're too tan. Came from some place sunny. Maybe Florida. Big town, touristy town. Miami?" He saw Lawson blink. "Yeah. Lotta years on the force. What are you? Maybe forty, forty-two?" Carl waved a hand through the air. "Doesn't matter. Means you've been on the force for about twenty years. Why'd you leave Miami?" Lawson was working up a head of steam. Carl could sense it. He wasn't enjoying being under a microscope. "Bet you didn't leave on good terms." He waggled a finger at the detective. "That's why you have a perpetual chip on your shoulder, that *I work alone* condition you probably worked into your contract. No need to deny it."

Lawson took a long sip of soda and eyed Carl over the can top. If his eyes were loaded, he would have emptied a clip into Carl about now. If Lawson was waiting for him to bring up details about the case, he had a long wait. Besides, he was having too much fun rattling Lawson's cage. Besides, every suspect has usually been clued in by his defense attorney by now. Why repeat what the detective already knew?

"What kind of trouble could you have gotten into? Shoot an unarmed minority? That's usually pretty good for skipping town, although you didn't run too far. Questionable arrest? Dipping into the till, or..." Carl rubbed a hand across the stubble on his face. "Or dipping something else where it doesn't belong? Yeah. And it had to be someone important, like the mayor's wife, or your partner's wife." Carl cocked his head as he watched Lawson's jaw grind. "No, maybe your partner. Was that it?"

Lawson raked the papers off the table, grabbed the soda, and slammed out of the conference room.

Carl smiled.


McComb walked out of the observation room, having watched the exchange between John Doe and Phil Lawson. "He certainly has your number."

"Damn sonofabitch. Who the hell is this guy?"

"Maybe we can find out. His so-called attorney is waiting in my office."

"Good."

"Not you, Lawson. Attorney Coleridge informed us he I.D.'d the victim and found her house trashed."

"What the hell?"

"I don't have time for territorial disputes. The mayor is on my ass to solve this case, and I'm going to ride yours like a jockey at Tampa Bay Downs. In the meantime, I'm releasing John Doe. Can't hold him when we've got zip to go on."

# 16

"Okay, let me get this straight." Chief McComb was perched on the edge of his desk, arms folded, Sam and Jake in wooden chairs in front of him like two students headed to detention. "You tracked John Doe's car to a sports bar near his house. The car contained his jacket and wallet. In the pocket was a napkin with the name of a woman you assumed to be the deceased. So without informing my detective, you took it upon yourselves to locate Mossy Belden. To do what?"

Sam started to open her mouth but McComb raised his hand, silencing her as he had done three previous times. "I'm sure you weren't going to circumvent my department's investigation by notifying relatives of her death."

"Give us credit. At least we got Angela Douglas' name and address."

"Where you entered said premise without informing my department." McComb raised a hand again and glared at Sam when she started to protest. He swiveled his head to Jake. "You need to keep her on a tight leash, Detective Sergeant Jake Mitchell of the Chasen Heights Police Department."

A smile quivered at the corner of Jake's mouth. "May I commend your department for running the prints I left on the business card."

"Well gee golly. Bet you thought we country bumpkins wouldn't think to verify your identity. Besides compromising our investigation, you also misrepresented yourselves." He swung his glare back to Sam. "Former Detective Sergeant Sam Casey."

"Hey, you would have never let us talk to John Doe if…"

"Quiet." The chief washed his hands over his face and sighed heavily. "Sundays are pot roast and mashed sweet potato day at my home. Sweet corn dripping in butter, homemade apple pie. And here I am." He sighed again, then picked up a report from his desk. "Your John Doe was drugged so he has that much for his defense. After you called from the Douglas house you broke into…"

"Door was open," Sam whispered.

"So you say. Anyway, after your call, I sent my detective to the house. Other than the place being trashed, he hasn't found any sign that she was killed there before being dumped in the motel. He's still waiting for the forensics team to finish going through the house."

"She wasn't killed in the house." Sam expected McComb's eyes to start bleeding.

"And you would know that how?"

"I've been trying to tell you but you keep shutting me up."

McComb turned to Jake. "Please tell me all the newspaper articles I found on the Internet when searching her name is just check lane fodder."

"I have tried to chalk it up to great guessing, but when she was able to locate the remains of fourteen buried bodies just by…" His voice trailed off and he turned to Sam to explain.

"The dead speak to me." She watched a skeptical grin spread across the chief's face. "Not always in words. Sometimes whispers, images, even Nature itself. With the fourteen bodies, the animals pawed at the ground where the bodies were. Grass and foliage bent as though pointing toward the remains. If I touch the deceased or something the killer touched, I can pick up clues, sensations, a prickling of the skin. I didn't feel anything in the Douglas house nor the motel room."

McComb straightened. "Wait. You were in the motel room? Geezo Pete. I should lock both your asses up." He walked around his desk and sank into the leather chair with a groan. "I don't even know what to think about your supposed psychic abilities. Never believed in any of that shit."

"How about we make you a deal," Jake said.

"You are in no position to…"

"I'll tell you who you have in lock up if you release him today."

"Jake, maybe we should run that by John first."

"The test already proved he was drugged. It's obvious her killer was looking for something in her house and that he was there after her murder. They should have surveillance cameras at the guard house. Anyone can get in by claiming to eat at the restaurant."

"Or…" Sam thought about that for a few seconds. "Did your detective find Angie's car in her garage?"

"No, just an old Chevy registered to her husband."

"There weren't any abandoned cars at the bar where we found John Doe's car," Jake said. "Maybe the killer used it to gain access to the property because Angie's car would have had a resident sticker on it."

"Besides, you can only keep him for twenty-four hours without charging him and you don't have any evidence."

McComb glared at Sam. "Don't push your luck. And I'll have you know we are already checking the video from the guardhouse."

"Bad publicity is bad for tourism," Sam said under her breath.

"Are you threatening to go to the press?"

"You don't exactly have the *Chicago Tribune* reporters posted at your door so obviously your small town newspaper doesn't monitor the police scanner."

"Well, you'll be quite surprised that down here in Hicksville we'all have modern computers in our pole-eze cars."

Sam laughed. "That's good." There was Jake's hand again, clamped on her thigh.

"John is the only one who can tell us more about the victim," Jake said. "If we take him back to the bar, maybe try to retrace his steps, he might remember something. It's better than him sitting in a cell while your detective is spinning his wheels."

The chief's phone rang. "McComb." He listened for several minutes, then scribbled something on a notepad. "Good job. Keep me posted." He hung up and turned to his guests. "Forensics is still going through the house. Miss Douglas' car did go through the gate yesterday morning. All that can be seen is a male driver from the chin down and the leg of a male passenger. We checked with their security. Miss Douglas owned a 2015 silver Cadillac sedan. We have a BOLO out now. Still doesn't prove they killed her or how they got her car. But I confess, I don't have enough to hold John Doe. So, I'll bite. Who do I have in lockup?"

"Carl Underer," Jake said. "Former FBI director."

McComb stared at Jake, as though doubting him. After all, if a former FBI director had moved into his town, someone would have said something. But then few people can name the vice president. "I'll be damned. No wonder he was so secretive."

"He prefers a low profile."

The chief opened the door and led them out. "Sergeant Mitchell."

"Jake."

"Okay, Jake. You can go on back and help our guest. He's still a little shaky on his feet." The chief cut a glance toward Sam. "You and your medicine bundle can stay out here." McComb instructed one of the clerks to accompany Jake. Then he steered Sam back to his office doorway. "What's the story on him?"

"What do you mean?"

"His neck. Those are some mean scars."

Sam wondered when McComb would bring up the subject. It wasn't hard to miss the two inch high dark bruising which circled Jake's neck, nor the raised welts from the studs in the dog collar he had been forced to wear. "Jake was held captive in the basement of an old sanitarium. A former cop had a vendetta against us, kept Jake drugged and in the dark for three months. His girlfriend shot me up with labor inducing drugs which killed our twins."

"Holy shit."

"Yeah." Sam had tried hard not to think about the ordeal, but as Abby once said, they each had to face it head-on. It would always be a part of their past. "Sal Marino was his name. He had an ingenious plan. Made it look like Jake died in an explosion. Changed DNA records so that we actually did believe Jake was dead. You can Google Sal's name on the Internet. Our local paper, the *Post Tribune,* has the full story, although they omitted most of the graphic details. Jake's been going through therapy and he still has a couple weeks before he goes back to work. But it's been rough on all of us. The scars will never go away. Neither the external nor internal ones."

McComb touched Sam's arm. "Sorry you both had to go through that. It's bad enough we have criminals to watch out for.

When it's one of our own, it's just unthinkable."

"Which brings me to a related subject. If Jake was a bit abrupt with Detective Lawson, it's because he reminds us a little of Sal Moreno. Not so much physically, but more in his know-it-all, I don't take any bullshit attitude. Sal was cocky, bent rules, falsified reports. Not that I'm saying Detective Larson is like that. I just think one day someone is going to put him in his place."

"Guess what some people consider cocky, I consider self-assured. He is a bit ambitious, which does cause a bit of friction here. But he's good at his job, even though he's a bit demanding. Has ruffled a few feathers here."

"Like Milla's."

"I thought she could learn a lot from Phil, but he had to be an ass about it."

"What happened to taking orders?" Sam had to choke back a laugh since she had side-stepped many an order in her day.

"You have to understand. We're a small department and don't like a revolving door of officers. Try to keep it a tightknit group. Unfortunately, there's always that one person in every department, every office...hell, in every type of business...who makes a boss' life a bit challenging."

Sam recalled how many gray hairs her former boss claimed she gave him.

"Anyway," McComb added, "thankfully, you both won't have to deal with him any more. When are you going back to Illinois?"

"We're going to spend the week sightseeing, make sure Carl is okay."

"Good."

A clean shaven Carl Underer was led down the aisle by a plain-clothed officer. Carl touched his shirt and lasered a stare at

Sam. "Really, Sam? Do I look like a fuckin' tour guide?"

"Hey, at least it's in a boring two-tone of cream and navy. I thought you would like a harbor scene."

"And shorts? With these knobby knees of mine?"

"Have you been outside? I thought the heat back home was stifling. Think I saw Satan at the end of the street."

Carl grabbed her in a bear hug and held her tight. "I have to admit, I have missed that mouth of yours." He released Sam and clapped Jake on the back. "Thanks for everything."

McComb held out a hand to Carl. "You do know not to leave town." He then shook Jake's hand. "And you both know to leave this investigation to my department and just enjoy sightseeing."

"Hey, we're on vacation. We have no plans to get in your way." Jake motioned Carl to the exit. "And I'm sure all Carl wants to do is rest."

Carl still looked unsteady, and the dark circles under his eyes hadn't diminished any; but as they left the building, Sam noticed Carl's legs suddenly appeared less shaky, his shoulders squared, and his back straightened. He had morphed into the active, take-charge FBI director Sam had first met.

"So we're really going to stay out of the investigation?" Sam asked as they approached the Cadillac.

"Hell no," the two men said in unison.

# 17

They were seated in a restaurant in a bowling alley not far from the police station. Carl chose a booth farthest from the bar and main entrance where they could have some privacy. Other than the bartender and a few stragglers at the bar and seated in booths, the restaurant was relatively empty considering it was past lunch hour.

"You look good, Carl," Sam said. "At least you didn't turn into a flabby retiree."

"I get bored too easily. Martinique is beautiful if all you want to do is jog, swim, and lounge around the pool. I actually did write a book, though."

Sam pushed her leftover fries to Jake. "A spy novel?"

"Actually, an alien invasion, apocalyptic novel. It was fun. Still needs polishing, but, who knows? May not see the light of day. Might be a best seller. Can't be any worse than the drudge I've seen lately on the best seller list."

Although the restaurant was separated from the bowling lanes, the thundering sound of balls hitting pins carried through the building. A wide-screen TV by the bar was tuned to a baseball game, and noisy beer drinkers appeared to be fans of whichever team was winning.

Carl took a sip of sweet tea, then waited for the waitress to refill their glasses.

"How can you drink that stuff?" Sam said. She and Jake had ordered unsweet tea.

"If you live here long enough, it starts to grow on you. Now, tell me how you sprung me out of jail. The guard wouldn't tell me a damn thing."

Jake filled Carl in on how they found Mossy Belden's name scrawled on a napkin in Carl's jacket pocket, how they located her, how Mossy identified the deceased as her home companion, Angela Douglas, whom Mossy hadn't seen in a couple weeks. "Either Angela wanted to point you to Mossy for some reason or she didn't want you to know her real name."

"Come to think of it, the name does sound familiar. The photo you showed me means nothing. The name, though, yeah. I think she used the name Mossy."

"What about Angie's husband? Ever meet him? He died last year." Sam turned her phone toward Carl to show him the wedding picture.

He shook his head. "No matter how many times I look at this picture, neither of them spark a memory cell. Does she live in Heyward Bluff?"

Sam explained how they found her house in a local gated community. "Someone already trashed it before we got there. They were looking for something. We picked up some prints from her bedroom and sent them to Tim."

"What about prints from the living room? Maybe the trashers weren't that careful."

"We didn't want to overstay our welcome or contaminate the evidence. Let the Heyward police spend hours checking prints," Jake said. "Camera at the guardhouse shows Angie's car driven by a male. Another man was in the passenger seat. Couldn't see the faces; and the fact that it was after Angie's body was found is proof it was after her death. So they had the keys to her car as well as her house. And obviously knew where she lived."

Carl thought about that as Jake placed cash on the table. "So whatever they were after, Angela didn't give it up. Maybe that's where they drove us, to her house while they searched. No, that can't be right. They aren't going to haul my ass out of the vehicle, into her house, then back into the vehicle, then over to the motel."

"She wasn't killed in the motel or her house. I didn't pick up anything other than the word *Montana*," Sam said. "Does that mean anything to you?"

"No. And according to what Mossy told you, Angela had a Kentucky accent. Maybe the killers are from Montana. Did you learn anything about the husband other than he's dead?"

"Obituary said he was from New York." Jake slid out of the booth, followed by Sam and Carl.

"Where are we going now?" Sam asked as they exited into the bright sunlight.

"You, little lady, are going back to my place." Carl's hand on the small of her back propelled her to the back seat. "Find out more about this Angela. Maybe your little friend, Tim, has some results. Jake and I are going to go visit that bar where you found my car keys. Someone there has to know something."

"Great," Sam mumbled. "Relegated to all the heavy lifting."

# *18*

Sam fired up the laptop and turned on the overhead fans. After making a pot of iced tea, she carried a glass out to the deck and set it on the table. She sipped her tea while admiring the panoramic scene from the first floor deck. Several boats could be seen in the distance while a trail of kayakers maneuvered through the marsh and out into the Harbor River. She wanted to see the island before they left. The reports on Hurricane Matthew last October had been all over the news back home, and she wondered if the area was still recovering.

In a way, she was glad she had the house to herself and was out of the blasted heat. Although it was warm, she felt the air conditioning drifting from the opened French doors. If Carl should complain about his electric bill, she would just say it was a way to keep the laptop from overheating.

She tapped the keyboard and brought up the pictures she had taken yesterday of the May River shoreline, tourists, as well as the interior and exterior of the church. There were several duplicates and some images that were blurry, which she deleted. The photos of the interior of the church needed the color and brightness adjusted. She thought Abby and Alex would love seeing this piece of history; and she made sure to include the picture of the sign outside the entrance.

One of the last pictures was of the house next door to the church where Mossy was sitting on the swing. "Why you little devil. You were there." Sam zoomed in on the image of the boy standing next to the swing. He had dark hair and eyes, skin the color of Alex's, sort of a dark honey. The boy was bare-chested and dressed in what looked like shorts held up by suspenders. Sam's attention had been diverted to the boats in the river after she had taken the picture. That must have been when the neighborhood boy ran off, only to be found lurking around a corner. She studied the picture of the church again, then attached all of the pictures to an email and sent them to Abby.

Her phone chirped alerting her to a text message. It was from Tim telling her to check her emails.

"Great. Hope you found something, Tim." She clicked on her emails and opened the one from her young hacker. "Angie Douglas, maiden name Angela Marie Hogan." She printed out the four-page report, then skimmed it quickly. Sam located Milla's business card and dialed her number. "Hi, Milla. This is Sam Casey."

"You mean the wife of John Doe's attorney?"

"Well, sorry about that."

"Thought you were sightseeing."

"I can multi-task." Sam heard Milla chuckle. "We identified your deceased through an international database, specifically Italy. Can you give me your email address? I'd like to send something for your eyes only."

"Okay, but you do know I'm not working the case." Milla gave Sam her address.

"Maybe we'll just have to change that. I do have a favor in return."

"Why am I not surprised?" But there was a hint of humor to Milla's comment.

"Can you get a photo of the two men in Angela's car? The one from the guardhouse?"

"I'll try. The asshole, sorry, Detective Larson, practically shoves the working file under his shirt. He did send out a BOLO on the car. The pics, unfortunately, don't show any faces. I'll see what I can do."

"Thanks. I'm sending my info now." Sam hung up, typed in the email address, attached the report, and pressed SEND. "Take that Detective Arrogant Phil Larson."

As before, Jake found the door to the Palmetto Bar and Grill open and Butch washing the floor. "Seems to me you are missing out on a lot of the lunch crowd sales by not opening until four."

"Locals tend to be my biggest customers. I'm too far off the main drag to be a draw for tourists. Learned that the hard way. Besides, locals rarely drag themselves in until after nine at night." Butch pushed the bucket against the wall. He looked toward the doorway as though expecting someone else. "Left that sexy little lady of yours home, I see."

"Yeah, she's in timeout."

"Well, my loss." He finally noticed Carl standing next to Jake. "Butch Cassidy's the name."

"Really?" Carl wished he had gone home and changed clothes. He didn't feel in charge dressed as a tourist.

"Recognize him?" Jake asked.

"Don't know the name. Then again, if it hadn't been for the hot babe hanging all over you Friday night, I wouldn't have recognized your face."

Jake asked, "How many bartenders did you have on duty that night?"

Butch scratched a hand across the stubble on his chin. "Friday night? Probably two plus four waitresses. Gets a bit crazy in here. Some regulars even lend a hand behind the bar pouring their own drinks. And with the bus bringing tourists back from the island, it gets even crazier. They dragged me out of the office when things started getting a bit rowdy. Gramps here had a few too many and she had to help him out to the car."

Carl's piercing gaze stopped the smirk from forming on Butch's lips. Even though he was retired, Carl still maintained an air of authority. "I haven't been rowdy since my college days and rarely have more than two drinks. Someone drugged me. I need the names and addresses of the bartenders who worked that night."

"Date rape drug? At your age?" This time Butch couldn't control his laughter. "You sure it wasn't a little blue pill?"

If Carl's glare had drilled Butch any harder, the guy would have been pinned to the dart board behind the bar. He had had about enough of this guy. Carl pulled out his FBI badge and shoved it toward the bar owner, being careful to keep his finger over the word *retired*.

"Whoa. Just having a little fun. That's all."

"Do you see me laughing?"

Jake enjoyed watching his former boss in action. Carl had always been a hardass until you got to know his serious side from his more serious side. Sam often accused Jake of following too closely in his former boss' footsteps.

Carl shoved the badge back into his pocket while his eyes scanned the ceiling and corners of the bar. "What about video or doesn't a swank place like this have high tech surveillance?"

Butch's smile faded and the veins in his neck started to throb. "Oh sure. We have an IT staff in the basement monitoring every move," he snarled.

"I see a camera behind the bar," Jake said with a nod at the black dome attached to the wall between the two mirrors.

"That's strictly to watch the cash registers. Won't get anything out of those tapes, though. I watch them every morning and then tape over them. Whatever might have happened Friday is only in your dreams." Butch saw a snarl forming again on Carl's face. "Let me get you the names of the bartenders that night."

"Probably shouldn't have flashed the badge. Now he'll probably tell his bartenders and they will never open up."

"Especially if they were in on the drugging," Jake said in agreement.

Butch returned with a sheet of paper. "Jon Draper and Luke Parsons worked that night. I have their home addresses and phone numbers."

While Carl reviewed the information, Jake asked, "Have you had problems with any of your employees in the past?"

"Some have been in fights or had fingers in the cookie jar. Typical stuff that gets them fired immediately. As far as for Jon and Luke, no problems that I know of. Jon's a married guy. Luke is going for his Masters in marine archeology or some such thing. He's hit on a few of the female customers which has pissed off the boyfriends in the past. Good looking guy so you can imagine the shit load of tips he makes. Brings in a lot of the local women."

Jake showed him a photo of Angie. "To your knowledge, has Jon dated this woman?"

Butch shook his head. "To tell you the truth, I hadn't seen the lady in my bar before that night, but then, I spend most of my time in the back office buried in paperwork." He looked from Jake to Carl. "Is she in some kind of trouble?"

The bar owner obviously hadn't heard about the body found in the motel room. "Other than the fact that she might have been the one to drug me and perhaps had help?" Carl said. "No."

Jake caught up with Carl in the parking lot. He was standing by the Cadillac studying the building across the street. It was a storage complex with an office in the front of an L-shaped structure. A number of cameras along the side of the building and in the front could be seen from where the two men stood.

Carl slipped his keys back into his pocket and headed across the street. Jake trailed behind; and within a few minutes, they were standing in front of a large glass window of a business called *EZ Storage*.

As they entered, Carl was already reaching for his I.D. He held the badge up to a gray-haired man who peered over his half glasses at the badge before Carl tucked it out of sight. Mac was the name on the square name badge on his left pocket.

"I need to see your tapes from Friday night and please tell me you didn't erase them."

Mac slid his gaze from Carl to Jake, then back to Carl. The two men's choice of touristy clothes did not go unnoticed by the business owner.

Jake pulled out his shield and held it up. "I've come all the way from Illinois to follow-up on a lead. We think the person we are looking for left the bar across the street some time Friday night. I think your tapes might confirm our suspicions."

Mac took longer studying Jake's shield. Carl hadn't given Mac that much time.

"Martha," Mac yelled toward the back room. A woman sporting hair shorter and grayer than Mac's charged from behind the wall. She was wearing the same khaki shirt with her name on the pocket. "Watch the desk while I show these gentlemen to the back."

She gave them the same cursory examination Mac had given them; and Jake could almost see the wheels spinning in her head. With their line of work, she was probably very good at sizing up people. Her seasoned suspicions quickly brought her attention to the bulge on Jake's right hip. "You sure you don't need help?"

"We're fine, Martha. Just gotta show these officers some tapes." Mac stressed the word *officers*. He obviously was a spouse who could read his wife's mind.

Mac led them into a room only slightly larger than a walk-in closet. A shelf above a table held rows of tapes. He checked dates, then popped a tape into a player. "Just fast-forward to the time you want. Sorry, I've only got one chair so one of you gentlemen will have to stand."

"Do you have a blank tape?" Carl asked as he took a seat in front of the monitor. "I'd like to make a copy if I find something of interest."

Mac did a sound that sounded like a tsk. "I've got blanks but don't have another recorder."

"It's fine," Jake quickly said. "We'll make do."

"Okay, then. I'll leave you to your work." Mac closed the door behind him.

Carl turned slightly and eyed Jake. "What do you mean *we'll make do*? If there's anything on this tape, I'll want a copy or just take the damn thing with me."

Jake held up his cell phone. "We'll make our own recording of just the faces we need."

"Oh." Carl turned back to the monitor and tapped a few keys. "Make me feel like a goddamn dinosaur," he said under his breath.

# 19

Sam parked the Charger in front of the church. Tourists were strolling in and out of the building with more spectators admiring the river scene. Jet skis were slapping the water near a distant pier while a pontoon boat drifted with the current. She crossed the lawn to Mossy's house, expecting to hear the whispers and feel the thrumming she had heard before. Everything was quiet. She climbed the four stairs to the porch. The back door was closed. Sam pressed her face to the window but didn't see or hear anyone inside. She probably should have called or tried the front door first. Sam moved to another window and shielded the sunlight with her hands. Still no sign of Mossy. Had a neighbor driven her somewhere? Maybe she called a cab.

A strange chill spread over her body. Sam could feel every hair on her scalp come to life. Either she was being watched or her mysticism had kicked into gear. There they were again, those three words she was sure were important. She slowly straightened and turned. A boy about five stood on the bottom stair smiling. He had a matted tangle of dark hair that touched his shoulders and wore the same shorts and suspenders he had worn the first day she glimpsed him. Bare feet were caked with what looked like years of dirt.

"Hi." Sam moved cautiously to the top stair and sat down. "Were you talking to me? Can you tell me what *hatak ome pa* means?" The boy only smiled, his eyes widened with joy as though happy to see visitors. "Is that your name? Hatak ome pa?"

The boy slowly moved up a stair, then another. His head

cocked as he appeared to study her. Sam thought he was studying her face; but when he inched closer the boy reached over and touched Sam's third earring of beads and feathers.

Does he not speak English? Sam thought. "Hanta," Sam said in Sioux. "That's stupid," she whispered to herself. "He doesn't look Sioux." No response from the boy. Mossy, or was it the docent, had mentioned that there were Civil War reenactors who took their characters seriously, eating what they ate back in the day, sleeping outside, wearing authentic clothes. Those portraying Natives would only speak in their Native language. But could a five-year-old act that authentic? And what tribes were known in this region? Sam wished she knew her history a little better.

She pointed to herself. "Samantha." Then she pointed to the boy. All he did was smile and run his gaze over her face then down to the leather pouch hanging from her neck. He looked up and pointed over her shoulder. Sam turned but wasn't sure if he was pointing to people walking toward the bluff or the property across the street. "I don't understand," she said when she faced him again. "Are you pointing at someone or the lot across the street? Do you live there?" Still no response. "Wonder if you would understand if I drew a picture." The boy cocked his head. "Let's try this again." Sam pointed at herself. "Sioux."

A slow smile spread across his bronzed face. He pointed at himself. "Yam Ossie." He climbed the last stair and sat next to Sam. Tourists continued to tour the grounds, sit on the bluff overlooking the shore, and snap pictures of the church. They were close enough to notice the attractive woman sitting on the porch stairs having an animated conversation with herself.

# 20

It took longer than they thought to run through the tape and find the exact time Carl and Angela had appeared in the parking lot. Carl had parked the Cadillac exactly where Jake had found it. She was dressed in the same clothes that had been found in the motel room, with the exception of the floral purse hanging from one shoulder.

"According to the police report, they didn't find a purse in the motel." Carl backed up the tape so Jake could record the scene on his phone.

"Now we know you didn't meet Angela in the bar. You gave her a ride there, but from where?"

"Good question." Carl fast-forwarded and checked the time on the monitor as he and Angela exited the bar. "We were in there less than an hour. Certainly not long enough for me to get drunk." Although Angela held onto Carl as they walked through the parking lot, it was obvious he was anything but sober. Carl was just about to hit the fast-forward button when he saw on the monitor a dark vehicle stop alongside the couple. A man wearing a baseball cap charged out of the passenger side, jerked open the back door, shoved Carl in, and with a gun pointed at Angela, forced her into the front seat. He slammed the back door, and with the gun pointed at Angela, forced her to slide behind the wheel. The driver stepped out, ripping the purse from Angela's arm."

"Another man in a baseball cap, but what the hell is he doing with Angela's purse?"

A few seconds later, they found out as another set of headlights appeared on the right side of the screen. The first vehicle spewed gravel as it tore out of the parking lot followed by the second car.

"Her car must have been parked at the bar."

"Can barely make out the color of the first vehicle," Jake said. "Maybe dark green or brown. Older model, maybe a 2010, 2011. Looks like a Crown Vic."

"One thing about this area, they don't believe in lights. Think it spoils the ambiance. Meanwhile, no one can see a fucking street sign let alone someone's face. We're just lucky the bar signs are lit or we wouldn't even be able to see me or the woman."

"Too dark to get a good look at either of the guys."

"Can't get a plate number either. There is something about the second vehicle, though." Carl paused the video, rewound it, then played it back in slow motion. "See the design of the headlights? That's a Cadillac XTS, probably a 2015. And I'd guess it's the metallic silver color."

"Chief Ray said the victim owns a silver Cadillac. It would probably be a waste of time to send it to CHPD to see if they could clean it up and get a better I.D. Can't see much of their faces."

Carl watched the tape for a few more seconds. "Doubt those guys are going to keep the purse. We should check the dumpster across the street before leaving." Satisfied the tape wasn't going to reveal anything more, he popped it out. "Maybe the Bureau can find something."

Jake stopped him in mid-sentence. "You really want someone at the Bureau to see you staggering out of a bar?"

"Good point."

# 21

Milla drove down a shady road past Old Town to a restaurant which didn't open until five o-clock, so the parking lot was empty. Milla backed into a spot under the shelter of tall oak trees, rolled down all of the windows, then ate a sandwich while reading the report Sam had emailed her. Dispatch had sent her out to investigate the theft of high-end purses from one of the outlet malls which kept her busy until three o'clock. This was the first chance she had to catch a bite to eat.

According to the police report from Italy, Angela Hogan had worked at an auction house when a priceless work of art went missing. All of the employees had been fingerprinted as a formality and everyone had been cleared. Milla skimmed through the police report and searched for more references to the victim. It was mentioned that Angela had attended the UK Art Institute before taking the job in Italy. In the interview, Angela had mentioned that she was from New Jersey.

"Doubt that's true," Milla said under her breath. She took a sip of her drink and contemplated turning the car back on so she could get the air conditioning going, but decided against it. She didn't plan to stay long.

Another page was an article on Angie and her sugar daddy husband. They had met on a cruise of the Mediterranean. He was close to forty years her senior. The article also mentioned that he had a terminal illness. Was that why Angie picked him? Was she a black widow of some sort? Milla picked up her cell phone and called Sam.

"The report is interesting but not exactly filling in all the blanks."

"That's why you are going to find answers before Lawson does."

"Did you find anything in the house that might help?"

There was silence on the phone. Milla figured Sam was going back over the search in her mind. "In Angie's bedroom there is a dressing table with some boxes I didn't have time to open. Jake was too antsy to get out of there for me to search any farther. What about the picture of the two men?"

"Hang on." Milla found a photo on her phone and attached it to a text message to Sam. "Just sent it to you. Can't see either of the men's faces. However, the driver does have a tattoo on his upper left arm. Other than that *I'm too lazy to shave* five o-clock shadow, there isn't enough to even hope for an I.D."

"Did Lawson talk to any of her neighbors? I'm curious if Angie coffee-klatched with any of the women, maybe spilled some secrets."

"The photo I sent you was obtained from our I.T. guy. He owed me a favor. Lawson, though, is still keeping his case folder with him. I haven't been able to get into his computer to take a peek. I did hear him tell the chief that most of the neighbors are up north for the summer and the rest would see Angie come and go, but never spoke to her."

"Why don't you take a quick trip to her house?"

"I'm not sure I can gain access."

"You're a detective. Tell them Lawson asked you to take another look, unless you think you're going to run into him."

"He's in Beaufort at the medical examiner's office."

"There you go. In and out. Easy peasy."

Milla looked at her phone after Sam hung up. "Wow, you certainly walk a thin tightrope."


Milla found one patrol car parked at the curb. Two officers immediately climbed out when she pulled up.

"Take charge attitude," Milla whispered as she exited her vehicle and marched up to the two men. She didn't recognize either one and figured they were from the substation. She flashed the detective shield on her belt and announced, "I need to take another look around. Do you have the sign-in sheet?" She pulled a pen from her pocket and waited.

"I thought Detective Lawson already searched." The officer pulled a clipboard from the front seat and handed it to Milla. His uniform was so new Milla wasn't sure if he was a recruit or had it dry cleaned daily.

"Detective Lawson is in Beaufort. When there are new developments, we have to see if there's any evidence we might have missed." She quickly scribbled her name which was about as legible as a physician's. Milla pulled latex gloves from her shoulder bag and called over her shoulder, "I shouldn't be too long," as she headed up the walk.

Whatever debris had been on the living room floor had been stacked on the coffee table and bookshelves. Either Lawson couldn't get a warrant to take everything back to the precinct or he didn't find it necessary. The thought of checking for prints in this mess was not a job she would relish.

She made her way quickly up the staircase, taking in the wainscoting lining the walls, the glistening oak bannisters, and multiple skylights. "So this is how the rich live," she said under her breath.

Milla located the dressing table and wasted little time searching the drawers. Angie's taste in makeup was a brand Milla could never afford. One drawer held brushes, combs, and a hair dryer. One bottom drawer had a variety of facial creams, scrubs, and body lotion.

The last drawer she opened held a small address book. She fanned through it quickly finding only entries for insurance, utility, hairdresser, doctors, and other routine contacts. Not one looked like a relative's phone number or even what might be a friend.

When Milla had searched the Internet for Angela Hogan, the computer had revealed over 20,000 women with that name. She had to find a way to pare it down, but how?

"Detective? Are you okay?" A voice called from downstairs.

"Shit!" Milla didn't think she had taken that long. "Just a few more minutes, please," she called out.

When she heard footsteps on the staircase, she made her way down the hall and looked over the railing at the officer.

He stopped when he saw her. "Just wanted to let you know that Detective Larson released the house so we are leaving. Patrol found the victim's car abandoned, and an anonymous caller found what might be the victim's purse in a dumpster. We're going to go check it out. Can you lock up when you leave?"

"Sure." She silently breathed a sigh of relief. "No problem." Milla checked her watch. "I will be out of here in fifteen minutes tops."

"I'll mark that down. Have a good day." He turned, hurried down the staircase and pulled the front door shut behind him.

She returned to the dressing table and sat down. "Where

was I?" She tossed the phone directory onto the surface where it skidded against the mirror. In the back of the drawer was a small box. She pulled it out and set it in front of her. Inside was a class ring with *LH* in gold lettering in the middle. Milla slipped it on her ring finger. "Definitely a man's." Next was a silver heart in two pieces on a silver chain. The last item was another silver chain with what looked like a collegiate tag with a large *KU* in the middle. Milla knew some colleges used collegiate tags in lieu of class rings.

She pulled out her cell phone and snapped photos of each of the items. She checked for any engraving inside of the ring. Not finding anything, she turned the two heart halves over and found an *A* on one half and a *T* on the other. The class ring had to be from a high school, but she would have to do more searching to figure out which high school.

She tossed the items back into the box. As she scooped the phone book into the drawer, a small envelope fluttered to the floor. Milla picked it up and took a peek inside. It contained several pictures. Lining them on the table, she snapped photos with her cell phone and sent them to Sam. As she placed them back in the envelope, she considered leaving them in the drawer, but thought better of it. These were items Lawson should have found. He probably didn't think anything in a woman's dressing table was important. She shoved the envelope in her purse, surveyed the room for a few seconds, then returned to the first floor.

Milla wasn't sure when or if she would ever return to this house so she pulled out her cell phone and took pictures of the titles on the spines of the books. She then walked over to the dining room table where framed pictures, some with the glass cracked, had been laid out. She stole a glance out of the bay window. The patrol car was gone. Now that she had uninterrupted time, she finger-walked through the items on the shelves. Various books on Native Americans, the Civil War, *The Burning of Heyward Bluff, How the South Lost the War, Pirates and Treasure Chests, The Minting of the Confederacy, Modern Era Reenactments.* Gordon Douglas appeared to be a history buff. And he hadn't limited himself to the South or the Civil War era. There were books on the Revolutionary War and the thirteen colonies. Several framed pictures had been left on the bookshelves. One photo showed Gordon Douglas with several men in Civil War uniforms standing in front of a tent. It had obviously been taken before he ended up in a wheelchair.

The wedding picture showed a beaming bride and groom in a vineyard. Milla could make out a California insignia on one of the buildings. She didn't have to know the cost of the gown. It just reeked of money with all the pearls and gemstones sewn into the dress and headpiece. She thought back to her own wedding dress, a simple ivory taffeta with beading around the collar. Her mother had made it. Considering the circumstances, her mother wasn't upset when Milla dropped it off at Goodwill.

The grandfather clock at the bottom of the staircase started clanging. Milla checked her watch. It was after five o'clock. She wondered who was going to handle the estate. Did Douglas have any surviving children? Was there a family lawyer? Not her problem. Let Phil sort it out. It was time to go. As she climbed into her car, she didn't notice the vehicle parked two houses down, nor the two occupants who were snapping pictures of their own.

# 22

The next morning Milla found herself on the couch in her apartment surrounded by a sea of papers. A mop of black uncurled from her feet and jumped from the couch. It meowed loudly, trudged in the direction of the kitchen, then hung a look over its shoulder.

"Hungry, I take it?"

Another meow from the black cat as it took three more steps toward the kitchen, then stopped to see if its owner was following.

Milla grabbed the papers and placed them in a neat stack on the coffee table. "Okay, Hoodoo. Let's fill your food bowl."

Hoodoo wove figure eights around Milla's legs as she poured dry cat food into a ceramic bowl. Milla smiled to herself as she thought of how uncomfortable people became when they learned she owned not just any black cat. Hoodoo was one of three offspring of a cat that had belonged to her grandmother. Not long after Madam Udo's death, Hoodoo started acting strangely. Milla's mother believed Udo's spirit resides in Hoodoo. Milla had laughed it off, but thought Hoodoo was a good judge of boyfriends. One long hiss was a sure sign that the man who entered Milla's apartment would never get a second date. In all of Milla's dating experience, not one potential boyfriend had received Hoodoo's approval.

"Okay, sweetie. Is that better?" Hoodoo was too busy eating to reply. While the coffeemaker hissed and churned, Milla took a quick shower, dressed, and returned to the kitchen to make two pieces of toast. After spreading cream cheese on them, she grabbed her coffee and headed back to the living room to go over the notes and printouts from last night.

The one bedroom apartment was actually a duplex on stilts near the May River in Old Town. From her balcony she could see the Oyster Factory. Luckily, she was far enough away not to smell it. The owners and occupants of the second half of the duplex were part-time residents, preferring to spend half of the year at their home in Maine. A housecleaning service came once a month to clean the owners' residence and check to see that everything was in working order. Milla had a key should she hear a smoke alarm or security alarm blaring.

The area was a mix of A-frames, singlewides, doublewides, run down shacks that hardly looked livable, and new construction, although her duplex was surrounded by empty lots. Street curbs were non-existent. Thanks to Rooms to Go, Milla was able to furnish her apartment without going into too much debt, although her taste was more *ready to go*. She had purchased the barest minimum and disregarded any knickknacks, paintings, much less plants. Heyward Bluff wasn't her first choice of cities to work. Unfortunately, it had been the first opening so she had grabbed it, as well as the first apartment she could find. A place setting for two, a large stack of paper plates, one pot and one fry pan were all her cabinets contained. It was a wonder she had unpacked at all.

She had lucked out on the apartment. The owners had painted and modernized the place, installing wall-to-wall carpeting, window blinds, new appliances as well as upgrading the bathroom. Milla thought the rent was rather inexpensive, compared to the normal high rental rates near the Old Town area. She could only assume the reason was that she was a cop. The owners probably felt they had their own person watchdog.

She sighed as she returned to the coffee table. The stack of notes was no longer in a neat pile. A fluff of black was lounging on several sheets of paper. "Okay, go find a windowsill, Hoodoo. I need to work." Yellow slitted eyes stared with complete boredom. Milla grabbed the remaining papers and shuffled through them. "All right, stay there. I'll start with these." Hoodoo rose and turned her back on Milla. With a flick of a back leg, the papers the feline had been lying on flew off the table and onto Milla's lap. Hoodoo leaped from the table and stopped, settling those slitted eyes again, and dammit if it didn't appear to Milla that the cat was smiling. With a haughty swish of its tail, Hoodoo pranced to the nearest window and leaped onto the sill.

"You little brat," Milla said under her breath, until she saw the papers Hoodoo had conviscated.

Her search on Lexington High School for the years Angela might have attended had netted a number of articles on class trips, various team championships, debate awards, and art scholarships. Milla shifted her gaze to the shiny black fur ball on the windowsill. The pages on class trips and art scholarships she was sure had been near the middle of the stack of papers, not the top. How had Hoodoo pulled these particular pages out and purposely flung them onto Milla's lap?

"No, it's impossible." And yet, she found herself studying the papers to see what clue might be buried. All three pages appeared to mention the same woman, Becky Cramer. What would she have to do with Angela? She picked up the pictures she had taken from Angela's dressing table. In one photo a younger Angie, probably college-age, was hamming it up for the camera with a female friend, tall with long, blonde hair. Where the blonde was cute, Angie was beautiful in a sophisticated way her friend couldn't pull off. They were on a beach in what might have been a spring break photo since the beach was crowded with similar aged students, some with bathing suits, some with little more than a couple strings which barely left much to the imagination. Milla could see a sign at a tiki bar which said *Pineapple Willie's*. Was Becky Cramer the blonde in the photo with Angela?

Several more pictures revealed what looked like frat parties with Angie and a group of girls. Angie had obviously enjoyed her college days seeing that she had kept a few pictures. But why hide them? Did her deceased sugar daddy not like to hear about her previous life?

She picked up the two halves of one photo that Angela had obviously torn in two. On one half was a nude Angie, her hair in an *I had a late night* mess which did little to make her less sexy. A man's arm was snaked around her and clasping her ass.

Milla picked up the other half of the photo. The man was also naked. She again studied the tattoos they had on their upper arms, each with half a heart. She picked up her phone and brought up the photo of the two men at the guardhouse and studied the man driving Angela's car. His tattoo was clearly half of a heart. "That certainly looks like a match." But something wasn't right. Didn't she hear Phil tell Chief Ray that the victim had a rose tattoo? Milla checked her watch.

As she studied the picture of the naked couple further, she noticed in the position they stood with their shoulders pressed close, it made the heart whole. She must have had her tattoo changed.

"Something tells me one of you cheated which is why she ripped up the photo," Milla said. One thing was clear—the photo showed enough of the man's face to do a facial I.D. Milla wrote an email to Sam and asked her if she noticed that the tattoo the young Angela wore was a mirror image of the tattoo on the driver of Angela's car. She also requested that she see if her computer expert had software to do a facial recognition of the man in the photo.

Milla grabbed her laptop and started checking on college graduation tags and was surprised when she saw a match to University of Kentucky. Next, Milla did a search of Angela Hogan and Lexington High which netted her zip. Then she searched Angela Hogan and University of Kentucky. Still nothing. Two things were clear—Angela either led a very uneventful life or Hogan wasn't her real name. Milla leaned back and stared at her notes. She once had collegiate tags. They were from a guy she was dating at Strayer University in Savannah. Perhaps Angela's tags were from the man with the half heart tattoo.

"I wonder." Milla slowly chewed on the cold piece of toast as her mind mulled over ideas. She brushed crumbs from her fingers onto the plate, then did a search of Becky's name and Lexington. She pressed ENTER and watched as the cyber gods found endless entries of anything with the word Becky…Cramer…and Lexington. Next, she put quotes around the entire name of Becky Cramer and tried the search again. This narrowed the list down. However, glancing through the brief descriptions did nothing to explain why Becky would have anything to do with Angela Douglas, nee Hogan.

Next Milla checked the area code for Lexington, Kentucky, then dialed information. Unfortunately, there weren't any Becky Cramers in Lexington so either she had moved away or… Milla did another search of Becky Cramer, this time adding the word marriage.

"Yes!" Milla glanced at Hoodoo who slowly yawned, then

licked one paw. "That still doesn't explain why you were so focused on this woman. She isn't even my victim." Hoodoo yawned again and stretched out.

Becky Cramer was now Becky Jamison. Her husband was an engineer for a solar panel company in Dallas, Texas. Milla called directory assistance and, luckily, Becky's number was listed. "Now the question is, how do I present this?" Hoodoo looked up from her nap with narrowed eyes that seemed to say, "And you really have to ask?"

Milla finished her toast, went to the kitchen to refill her cup, then returned to the coffee table. "How would Sam handle this?" She dialed Becky's phone number, then waited with pen in hand.

The phone was answered on the second ring. "Hello," a voice whispered.

"Becky Cramer?"

Silence for a few beats. "It's Jamison now. Who is this?" Another whispered response.

"I'm sorry. You were Cramer, I take it? This is Detective Milla Boles with the Heyward Bluff Police Department."

"Heyward Bluff?"

"I'm sorry. Should I call you back at another time? You seemed to be whispering. Do you have company?"

"No, no. I just got the baby to sleep. Let me grab the baby monitor and go outside so I don't wake him."

"How old is your baby?"

"Eight months. I also have a six-year-old boy."

Milla heard the sliding of a door, the scraping of a chair, then what sounded like water lapping in the background. She pictured Becky lounging by the pool or overlooking a lake. The solar panel industry must pay pretty well.

"Sorry about that. You said you were with a police department?"

"Yes, in South Carolina. I'm looking for anyone who might be able to give me some background information on Angela Hogan?"

"Angela Hogan. I never knew an Angela…wait. Do you mean Angela Hoganfeiffer?"

*No wonder she shortened her name*, Milla thought. "Let me send you the photo I have and you let me know if we are talking about the same woman." Milla retrieved Angie's photo from her phone's gallery and attached it to a text to Becky.

A few seconds later, it was received in Dallas. "Yes, that is certainly Angela. Is she in trouble again?"

"Again? I take it she was in trouble a lot."

"Who wouldn't with the loser of a boyfriend she had in high school."

"You don't mind if I tape our conversation, do you?" Milla put her phone on speaker, then grabbed a handheld recorder from the drawer and pressed RECORD.

"No, I guess not. Wait. Did something happen to Angela? Did he hurt her again?"

"I'm sorry, I can't divulge that information. We haven't been able to locate her relatives yet."

"There aren't any relatives so you don't have to worry about that. Angela's parents died when she was young. A great aunt raised her until she died. Angela was on her own at the age of seventeen." Sniffling could be heard on the line. "Dammit, Angie. I knew this would happen one day. He killed her this time, didn't he?"

# 23

After a quick breakfast, Jake and Carl tracked Jon Draper down at his house. They had left Sam at Carl's place reviewing photos Milla had emailed her. When Carl had inquired how Sam had been able to get Milla to share information with her, Jake only said, "Just go with it."

"Each night kinda blends together, and Friday nights are hectic."

"Take another look. I'm sure not every woman who walks into the Palmetto Bar and Grill looks like her."

Jon Draper swiped a forearm across the sweat on his forehead as he leaned on the shovel. He took what looked to Jake like a nervous glance at his wife who was planting flowers several yards from where the three men stood, while their toddler played on a blanket under an umbrella not far from her mother.

The petite blonde looked up from her planting and glared at her husband. Jake detected a bit of distrust in that glare. A bartender meets all kinds of women on the job. How much flirting goes on? He could see Carl's jaw clench. His former boss had little patience when having to pull information from a witness. Jake decided to try another tactic.

The house was a moderate-sized stucco with a wrap-around porch and at least an acre of property. Flowering trees provided abundant shade while gardens were filled with bird feeders and bird baths.

"Did you do all this work yourself?" Jake asked.

"Yeah. I've got a landscaping business. Only bartend on the

weekends for extra money. I use pictures from our yard in our ads." He tossed a glance at his wife, his smile evaporating the distrustful glare she had exhibited just minutes ago. "Susan has an eye for color and balancing the seasonal shrubs. We make a great team."

Susan looked away with a smile, her straw hat shielding her eyes.

"You could certainly use an update of your landscaping, Carl. Some of the shrubs in the front have seen better days."

Carl studied Jake for a nanosecond, then pulled Jon's clipboard from his hands and scribbled an address on the top of a work sheet. He handed the clipboard back to the landscaper. "I'm not a homebody with a green thumb so I need plants easy to maintain. I'm not even sure if every plant has a dripper hose. Can you handle that, too?"

"Sure. When's a good time?"

"What's good for you?"

He checked his watch. "Five tonight?"

"I'm taking Lacey for her swim class," Susan said.

"I can take pictures of the area, hon. Then you can make your suggestions on plants."

"He could use a decorative brick border, too," Jake suggestion.

"What the hell? You come to visit and start spending my money?"

"Someone has to." Jake knew they weren't going to pull any additional information from Jon with his wife around, which told him that the part-time bartender might have a history with female customers. He explained as much to Carl on their way to search for Luke Parsons, the other bartender on duty the night Carl was drugged.

\* \* \*

It wasn't easy to track down Luke Parsons. It was summer break for the local college, and the address Butch gave was off campus. A cloud of foul-smelling smoke drifted from the apartment when the roommate opened the door. "Yo, dudes." Sloven was too kind of a word for the guy standing in the doorway. The movie, *Animal House*, came to mind as Jake ran his gaze over the stained wife-beater shirt, ragged shorts that weren't zipped all the way, and hair that stood on end in what looked like an attempt to detach itself from any knowledge of being part of such a degrading piece of humanity.

"Oh, shit." Pothead stumbled back and waved at the plume of smoke circling his head. Neither Carl nor Jake needed to be dressed as law enforcement. It literally emanated from their bodies. "Uh, you dudes have a search warrant? What do you want?"

"Luke Parsons," Carl barked. He did little to hide the disgust at the future of America.

"Luke?" He scratched his crotch, then looked at the joint between his fingers as if wondering how the stub of marijuana got there. "Uh, beach or golfing, I think. I don't keep track of him."

Jake had to laugh when Pothead tried to hide the joint. "We don't care what you do here. We only need to talk to Luke."

"He hardly stays here. It's been weeks since I've seen him."

"Do you know where we might find him?" Carl took a step back for fear the odor was seeping into the fabric of his suit.

"Find any hot woman in town and check her bed."

"Any females here he might hang with?" Jake followed Carl's lead and took a step back. They'd have to hang their clothes in Carl's walk-out to air them out.

"It's summer, man. Hardly anyone on campus. Like I said, check the beach, golf course or any hot chick's bed."

Pothead was of little help; and although Jake claimed they could care less what he did in his apartment, that all they wanted was to talk to Luke, it didn't stop Carl from making an anonymous call to the police department claiming he was a neighbor and thought there were drug deals going down in the building, especially from apartment 2B. Now they would just have to wait until Luke worked again to catch him at the bar.

# 24

Milla arrived at the police station late. She had spent time at home typing up her notes starting with what she had found in Angela's home and culminating with her one hour conversation with Becky Cramer. She felt as though she was finally making headway.

"Milla," Kate called out from the doorway to Reception. "Today is Foley's last day. There's cake in the breakroom."

"Is Chief Ray in?"

"On the phone."

"Can you let him know I need to see him?" She pulled the papers and tape recorder from her red grain leather laptop case, a purchase she had treated herself to when she was hired.

Milla forgot today was Bud Foley's last day. He had been in charge of the department garage for eons, she had heard. She glanced at the chief's closed door, then headed to the breakroom passing work stations where some staff members were already digging into cake. Streamers hung from the ceiling and clusters of balloons had been placed on each table.

Bud looked despondent, but Jilly, his wife, was beaming with images of cruises and European tours. It was always harder for a man to get acclimated to retirement. Bud was a beloved member of the department. Always cheerful, always helpful, with never a harmful word about anyone.

"How exciting, Bud." Milla wrapped her arms around the balding man. He stood ramrod straight dressed in his uniform. "It will take some adjustment, I'm sure, but you won't believe how busy you will be."

"Jilly already has my itinerary for the rest of the year," Bud said with what looked like a forced laugh.

Milla reached out her hand to the demure woman standing next to him. "I'm Milla Boles. I've only been here a year, but believe me, Bud is one of my favorite people."

Jilly's grip was strong for such a petite woman. She smelled of Dolce and Gabbana, one of Milla's favorites; and, unfortunately, strictly out of her price range. Jilly's white cotton candy hair had a hint of pink in it; and as she leaned in and whispered, Milla detected a British accent. "Bud is all talk and no trousers. Keeps agreeing to all the travel I want to do, but I just know I'll be flogging a dead horse."

"Nah, sweetie. You know I want to go to England with you. Maybe one or two trips a year till I get used to retirement."

"Right. I've seen the classifieds on the floor next to your chair. You are already looking for a part-time job." Jilly turned to Milla. "Please, help yourself to some cake. I'm going to go freshen up."

Milla felt sorry for Bud. She remembered when her father retired he had been at a loss on how to fill his day. Her parents couldn't afford to do a lot of traveling, so her mother found odd jobs to keep him busy, got him interested in gardening and bike rides with her in the mornings. She interested her friends' husbands to start fishing once a week and playing cards. Now he complained that there weren't enough hours in the day.

When there was a lull in well-wishers, Milla took the opportunity to pull Bud aside. "I know you have a reputation for being closed-lipped. Being your last day, maybe you can help me understand Phil better. Why would someone who was a lead detective in a big city like Miami, suddenly move to a town with fewer than fourteen thousand people?"

\* \* \*

Stunned at Bud's revelations, Angela returned to her desk to find her briefcase as well as her tape recorder missing. Her red case was now sitting on her chair. Milla panicked as she looked under her desk, then over at Phil's empty desk.

"Milla!"

Chief Ray was standing in his doorway holding a stack of papers and a tape recorder. Milla felt her heart do a drumbeat. Then Phil appeared behind the chief with his fists jammed on his hips.

There wasn't a long enough walk from her desk to the chief's office to tamp down her anger.

"Why the hell are you working my case?" Phil yelled before Chief Ray had a chance to close the door.

"What are you doing stealing items off of my desk?" Milla countered.

"Take a seat, both of you, and keep your voices down." Chief Ray closed the door, then pointed at another chair in front of his desk. "Milla."

"I can explain."

"Oh, please do!"

"Phil, clamp it." McComb sank into his seat and clasped his hands over what looked to be the folder from Milla's briefcase. He opened his hands briefly as if to tell Milla she had the floor.

"I played a hunch and searched through the victim's personal items in her bedroom."

"You went to the house?" Phil looked to Chief Ray for support. "First those detectives from up north and now Milla who isn't even working this case?"

"Let her talk, and I don't want to have to tell you again to keep your voice down. Now, Milla, continue."

"You already have the photos I found. It was the high school and college items which led me to search the high school on line, which led to a school friend, which led me to Angela's real name. The friend, Becky Cramer, filled me in on Angela's boyfriend through high school and college. I'm sure, since you have seen my stolen notes," she leveled a glare at Phil, "you know Travis Goodwin is the ex-boyfriend. You saw the pictures."

Phil jammed a finger on the desk. "I want to know why you injected yourself into my case."

Milla turned dark eyes on him in much the same way Hoodoo did to her. How nice it would be if her pupils were as slitted as Hoodoo's. "My cat led me to it." Her voice was as close to a hiss as she could make it and it had the desired effect. Phil slid back into his chair. She turned her attention back to Chief Ray. "The case wasn't moving fast enough, in my opinion. One of the photos showed a younger Angela with a tattoo which matched the one on the suspect driving her car."

"The victim's tattoo was a rose, not half of a heart," Phil sneered.

"Becky confirmed that Angela and Travis Goodwin had a tumultuous relationship…couldn't live with each other or without. Angie had altered the tattoo after discovering Travis had cheated on her multiple times. I had to call in a few favors and finally saw the picture from the guardhouse at Heron Lakes. The driver just happened to have a matching tattoo on his upper arm."

"Chief." Phil said the word as though it were an admonishment.

McComb sighed heavily. He had needed a top notch detective on his team, not knowing Phil Lawson would be a royal pain in the ass. "Why didn't you uncover any of this, Lawson?"

"I've been to Beaufort and back several times with the medical examiner, a mound of trash in the victim's house I had to sift through. Luckily, we found the victim's purse, which did not contain any cash. Then there's the only suspect who wouldn't even give me his real name, who, by the way, you released. I'm only one person."

"Watch it. Don't forget who you're talking to. You are the one who insisted on working alone when I explicitly said I like my people working in teams. You now have a partner. And until Brayburn is back from medical leave, you and Milla are the only two I have. I don't care what you two have to do, just make it work."

"Fine." Phil grabbed the folder from the chief's desk. He stormed out of McComb's office with all of Milla's notes as several heads at work stations suddenly jerked their attention back to their work.

Milla was too shocked to respond. He had all of her notes. Here she was with a degree in criminal investigation and Phil was treating her like a rookie. She took a deep breath. It was better than nothing, and as her mother would say, "there's no sense arguing in an empty house."

She clasped her fists, feeling sharp nails digging into her palms as she stood.

"Sit down."

Milla eased her way back down and leveled her best in-charge glare at the chief.

"They aren't letting this case lie, are they? One of them, probably Sam Casey, told you about the items in the victim's bedroom. Am I right?" He waved a hand to cut her off. "I already know they were in the house, and women do have a tendency to stick together. She isn't too fond of how Phil has been treating you. I understand that. But this isn't their case, it isn't their town, and you are not part of their police department, unless you'd like to be."

Milla took that threat loud and clear. Overstep her bounds and she will be out on her ass. "May I leave?"

McComb made a shooing motion. As Milla reached the door he said, "You did good work, Milla. Mighty fine work."

She smiled as she left the chief's office. Not so much from the compliment, but from the knowledge that she had a copy of all of her research back in her apartment.

# 25

"Hi, Mom." She waved at the images on the monitor. "Hi, Dillon. It's Mommy. Are you having fun?" Dillon brows furrowed with confusion. All he did was look up at Abby.

"How is Carl?"

"Out of jail. He has been told not to leave town and to stay out of the investigation."

"How's that working out?"

"Take a guess." Sam stood and lifted the laptop, turning it to show the view from Carl's deck.

"Look's beautiful. Is that the ocean?"

"No, it's the Harbor River. It is so nice down here. Wish you guys could see it." Sam set the laptop back on the table and sat down.

"How's the weather?" Alex appeared behind Abby, a potted plant in his hands, then disappeared from view again.

"You know how hot it is in July on the reservation? Well, take that and double the heat index. I'm tempted to shave my head."

"Other than the weather, what else is going on? Were you able to help Carl? You have that look in your eyes." Abby could tell Sam's moods and concerns just by looking in her eyes.

Sam told her about the condition of Angela's house. "Someone was looking for something. Although the wall safe was open, the cash and jewelry was untouched. Even if there was one piece of jewelry he was looking for, that wasn't a reason to trash the living room. Drawers had been opened, the bookcases emptied. Given all that, I still couldn't pick up one vibe. I really feel useless."

Abby studied her daughter's face, familiar with every subtle change. "Don't be impatient, my daughter. The spirits will reveal the clues you seek in good time. Now, did you find out anything more about the boy on the porch?"

"Other than he isn't real?" Sam added with a laugh. "Not really. He didn't seem to understand English so I pointed to myself and told him I was Sioux. When he replied, I think he said his name was *yam ossie*."

Alex's voice boomed from somewhere in the kitchen. "Do you mean Yamassee?" He suddenly appeared behind Abby, then pulled out a chair and sat next to her. "It's pronounced YAM-uh-see." He spelled Yamassee for Sam. Dillon averted his attention to Alex, reaching for one of his pigtails. "The boy was telling you his tribe, not his name. They were in the western part of Florida until the Spanish drove them out in the late 1600s. They fled east then north into the Carolinas." Alex was a walking encyclopedia of Native American history.

"Why is it I've never heard of them?" Abby asked.

"The government does not recognize them as an official tribe. They had splintered, joining up with a number of different tribes after the Yamassee Indian War of 1715."

Sam asked, "What war was that?"

"One of the bloodiest wars in history. The Yamassee joined with other tribes, like the Cherokee and Catawba against the British settlers. There was a trade dispute. Seemed the settlers would demand payment, and when the Indians had no way of paying, the settlers took the Indian women and children as slaves. After the war the Yamassee split, some going back to Florida, some to other areas. They integrated into a number of different tribes. One of them was the Seminole tribe."

"But they were no longer in this area?"

"Not to my recollection. After all of the splintering, the actual Yamassee tribe just didn't exist anymore, at least as it was originally known. In its prime, they were one of the most important tribes."

"He did say three words. It sounded like *hatak ome pa*. Any idea what language they spoke?"

Alex shook his head. "I'd have to do more research. Pretty sure their original language is extinct now."

Sam thought back to the coin that the boy had held in his hand.

"What are you thinking, Sam?" Alex asked.

"He was holding a coin that had the year 1861 imprinted on it. I'm pretty sure not all of their tribe fled to other states, not if some were here during the Civil War."

# 26

Phil didn't let her into the conference room when he made the call to Goodwin's parole officer. However, Milla made damn sure she was in Chief Ray's office when Phil gave him the details of the call.

"What does the P.O. think?"

"He was surprised Travis would be involved in a murder. He was strictly small stuff, check forging, burglary. But here's where it gets interesting. He gabbed a lot in prison about his wife, Angie, although there's no record of them ever marrying. He pimped her out to rich, old guys. Not for sex. More like escort service, eye candy at parties. Travis and his brother, Tyler, would gain access to the houses thanks to Angie leaving a patio door or window open and disarming the alarm. They had a good scam going until Angie found out Travis was poking a lot of women on the side. Angie fled to Europe to pursue the art world."

"He just happened to reveal all this to complete strangers in prison?" Milla asked.

"Guess you could call it crying in his beer. Rumor is she had set him up which is why he ended up in prison."

"How's that?"

"There had been an armed robbery at a local cigar store. Cashier was tuned up pretty bad. Officers found a gun on a shelf with Travis' prints all over it. The P.O. said Travis never used a gun. Guns weren't his thing. The cashier even said the thief didn't use a gun, yet a gun was found. Four years into his sentence, Angie returns to the states and visits him, practically confesses that she set him up. Pressed his fingers to the gun while he slept, gave the gun to some guy and told him what to do for a nice tip of ten grand. Travis was furious. He had to tamp it down or he'd screw up his pending parole."

Chief Ray was scratching notes of his own. "How did Travis track her down?"

Milla jumped in. "According to Angie's friend, Becky, Tyler was devoted to his brother. Since Becky had been Angie's closest friend, maybe Tyler knew where to start his search."

"Seemed as though the friends were estranged. Let's assume Tyler has half a brain. Guess a smart guy would check online newspapers, maybe search wedding announcements. Out of all the states and cities, someone had to clue in Tyler where Angela was living." McComb pointed his pen in Milla's direction. "Maybe you can give her another call. Get her to confide in you." McComb turned to Phil. "Did you find anything in that mess the brothers left on the living room floor?"

"Nothing so far. Bunch of books, pictures, expensive vases and artwork. Appeared more like trashing for the fun of it."

"The personal photos, though," Milla added, "were smashed, like Angela's wedding photo. Whoever damaged them had real anger issues. Someone that angry could have easily strangled the victim. Travis has been letting that build since Angela's visit to the prison."

"And what about Director Underer?" McComb directed his question to Phil.

"Wrong place, wrong time. This isn't the first domestic abuse case I've worked that turned into a homicide. Angela latched onto someone with a gun who could protect her. My guess is those brothers are long gone. We sent out their pictures and vehicle description in the APB. They already dumped Angela's car and were careful to wipe the car clean."

Chief Ray's phone beeped. "Yeah, Mike." He listened for several seconds, then said, "send them in." He hung up and rose from the chair. "We have company." He opened the office door and watched the two guests approach.

Phil turned and grimaced.

Milla followed his stare to the outer office where Carl Underer and Jake Mitchell stood. Carl was in a dark suit, white shirt, tie, and dark sunglasses. Jake wasn't dressed as formal, opting not to wear a tie or suit jacket. They looked every bit like FBI agents. A far cry from how Carl looked when he was released.

Carl ripped the sunglasses off and strode across the room to Chief McComb. Phil stood and told Milla, "Why don't you go make that call to Angela's friend."

Even Milla was surprised at the difference between John Doe, the drugged suspect, and Carl Underer, former FBI Director. And although the chief had ordered Phil to take Milla under his wing, he was dismissing her. Phil will probably even take credit for all of the information she had gathered this morning.

She gave a nod to the two men as she left, hearing the door close behind her.


"Detective Lawson, no hard feelings, I trust." Carl stuck out his hand. Phil stared at it then reluctantly shook hands.

"Depends on how much you are going to interfere."

After McComb closed the door, everyone took a seat. "I had hoped you would take my advice to let my department handle this case. So what can we do for you, Director?"

Carl didn't waste any time. "Normally, I would never intrude. Hell, I'm retired, but I'm also the victim here and I don't like it one damn bit. Now, you may not want my help. You may not need it. Being the victim and originally the suspect has me hell bent on getting to the bottom of it. The only thing I will promise is that I will share everything I find."

Carl had thrown down the gauntlet. McComb was hard to read so Jake wasn't sure if Carl had made a friend or an enemy.

"What have you got?" McComb asked.

"I spoke with Travis Goodwin's P.O."

"I already have that," Phil snapped. "Do you have anything else to offer?"

Carl paid little attention to Phil's blunt attitude. Jake handed Chief Ray his phone, explaining to McComb how they had watched surveillance video from the storage facility on the night that Carl and Angela were abducted. "Although it's too dark at times to see clearly, watch when the driver pulls up behind the Crown Vic in the Cadillac. You can see the half heart tattoo on the driver's arm." Phil walked around behind McComb to view the recording.

They watched as Angela and Carl were shoved into the Crown Vic, how her purse was ripped from her arm, and less than a minute later the Cadillac appeared behind the Crown Vic. McComb paused the video, then zoomed in.

"You're right. It confirms they were the ones who abducted you and the victim." McComb handed the phone back to Jake.

"The suspects aren't stupid," Phil said. "They wiped their prints from the Cadillac."

"And neither brother is on record with the DMV as owning a car," Jake added. "No one has reported a Crown Vic being stolen.

Anything come back on the BOLO?"

"Nothing." Phil crossed his arms and remained standing behind McComb. "We found an old friend of Angela's who gave us background information on Travis and Angela and the scam they were pulling on…"

Carl dismissed him with a wave. "That's okay. We don't need that."

McComb's eyebrows shot up. If their guest didn't need it, that meant Milla already shared everything she had with them, probably with Jake's wife, Sam.

"My wife believes Angela was dead before they went to the house."

Phil drilled Jake with a stare. "Your psychic wife? Really?"

"Makes sense," Carl said. "As you can see from the video, I could barely get to the car. They aren't going to drag both of us to the house, kill her, trash the place, then put both of us back into the car and drive to the motel."

Jake agreed. "Besides, they would have never gotten past the guardhouse with Carl incapacitated and a reluctant Angela in the car. They went to the house after dropping Carl and the body off at the motel."

"After the motel, they headed to the house to find whatever it was they were looking for. They had the house key from the victim's purse to gain access. Makes sense." McComb looked to his detective.

"It wasn't enough to kill Angela." Phil spoke as though he were educating the two men. His slow cadence broadcast that he felt they needed help following his brilliant logic. "Travis wanted to strip her house of anything of value. Sure, he left some money and jewelry, but that was smart on his part. Leave just enough behind to throw us off. None of us were in that house when the victim was alive so we have no idea what kind of artwork or collectibles she had."

"Maybe." If Phil was waiting for Carl to challenge his assessment, he had a long wait. "Right now, my focus is on who drugged me."

"Well, we can put you in touch with our Special Investigations Unit. They handle drug and gang cases." Phil moved toward the door, dismissing the chief's guests as if Phil had been the one to invite them.

Carl and Jake smiled, so in sync it was as though it were practiced. "That's okay. We don't want to take them away from their genuinely serious cases." Carl stood. Jake followed suit. They shook hands with both men and left.

# 27

Sam walked along the frail wire fencing along the property across the street from the church, feeling the slight vibration in the ground. It wasn't as strong as what she felt in Mossy's yard. Beyond the thicket and scattering of trees was a dilapidated structure that was hardly habitable. It was on a prime piece of real estate overlooking the May River. A sign on the fence read, *Squire Pope Carriage House 1850.* Why would this interest the boy? Was he possibly telling her his name? She turned back to the church. She knew of one person who could possibly know.

"Come back for a proper tour?" Jerry Nolan was standing in the vestibule of the Church on the Bluff straightening pamphlets when Sam walked in.

"Actually, I have questions."

"Ask away," Jerry said as he grabbed his cane.

"It's about the property across the street."

"Ahhh. One of the handful of buildings not burned in 1863." Jerry led Sam outside and down the brick path to where Sam had parked the Cadillac. "It's an historic landmark so what's left there certainly won't be torn down. Squire Pope owned the Coggins Point Plantation on Hilton Head. It was used as an officers headquarters during the war. The carriage house across the street was sometimes used by Jefferson Davis as an office. There were a number of outbuildings, too, but all destroyed."

"How many people died?"

"Not one. They had all fled. Usually residential buildings were never touched. Word is the Union got pissed after the Confederate raid on Pinckney Island where the Union had set up camp. So they burned through Heyward Bluff leaving a handful of buildings, our church being one of them. That and two of the Pope houses. After the war, Missus Pope and her daughter returned, a hell of a lot poorer than before. The two buildings that survived were pieced together."

"And who was this guy, Pope?"

"Squire William Pope was a member of the South Carolina House of Representatives for years, also the Senate. Owned a number of plantations, not just Coggins Point. They abandoned the place when 10,000 Union soldiers took over the island. Pope family never returned to Hilton Head."

Sam wondered if William Pope had a son. Then again, the boy was Native American. Had the boy been a slave?

"What's going to happen to the property?"

"The city is turning it into a park."

Sam looked at the cars crammed along both sides of the street. "I trust they will add more parking."

Jerry chuckled at that. "You're not the first person to suggest that, not just this area, but the whole Old Town area."

"What will happen to the house?"

"Oh, it's staying."

"Anyone buried on the grounds, like servants or slaves?"

"The Historical Society would have documented it. They've combed through it numerous times. Course, back then, they sometimes didn't use grave markers."

"With all this history, it's a wonder the whole town isn't haunted."

The old docent chuckled. "Who's to say it isn't?"

\* \* \*

Jake set his cigarette down and studied the picture of Mossy on her porch with the boy standing behind her. He and Carl could both see the boy. It hadn't been Sam's imagination.

"They are big on Civil War reenactments down here," Carl said, ever the skeptic.

"He disappeared, Carl. My spidey senses were on high alert when he magically appeared." She told them what Alex had said about the Yamassee tribe. They were sitting on the back deck watching birds diving into the water. It was high tide so most of the shore grasses were hidden. Jake's pledge to only smoke two cigarettes a day had been broken since his ordeal. He was now up to six a day that she knew of. He never smoked in the car or the house and definitely not around Dillon.

"Unfortunately, I'm not up-to-date on the history of this area. Kids that age are fast, though." Carl looked to Jake for help, but was met with silence.

"And what about the coin?"

"A souvenir fake. They printed thousands of them."

Carl's unyielding logic sometimes drove Sam crazy. He was still as stubborn as when they had first met. She grabbed the picture and shoved it in her purse. "I'll show it to Mossy tomorrow. Now, what did you find out today?"

Carl told her about their visit to the precinct and the information Becky Cramer had given to Milla. He in turn told the chief what they had discovered after watching the film from the storage facility.

"Wow, Carl. You, in a sharing mood?"

"I'm learning, Sam, although I can't say the same for Detective Lawson. He's practically closing the case as a domestic dispute while I'm spinning my wheels trying to find out who drugged me. The ass had the audacity to try to pawn me off on their Special Investigations Unit."

They were interrupted by the doorbell. "That should be my landscaper."

Carl and Jake met Jon Draper at the bottom of the front porch steps. The landscaper grimaced at the overgrown shrubs and weeds growing from between the rocks.

"See what you mean," Jon said as he nodded toward the eyesore substituting for a landscaped garden. He proceeded to snap several photos with his cell phone, some close up, others from a distance, in order to capture the entire front of the house. He jotted down notes on a clipboard. "You really should have mulch instead of rocks. We get hurricane winds and those rocks will be like bullets whizzing through the air. A lot of your perennials appear healthy, but they are in the wrong place. Taller ones should be in the back and the shorter ones in front." Jon pointed a pen toward the three foot high cobblestone wall separating Carl's property from the declared nature preserve adjacent to his property. Vines were zigzagging across the wall. "Those vines need to be removed, rocks replaced with mulch, and some perennial shrubs planted, something with color. He walked closer to the carport where a bougainvillea snaked up one side and across the roof. "That should be relocated. If it gets any bigger or heavier, it's going to pull your carport down. If you want, I do know someone who can build you a garage."

"Of course you do," Carl sneered. "A carport is sufficient, thank you very much. Where would you move that climbing killer?"

"Side of the porch. I'd cut it down which won't kill it. Then stake a fifteen foot trellis against the side of the porch and replant it there, let it climb up and provide some shade on that side to block the afternoon sun."

The screen door opened and Sam stuck her head out. "Why don't you bring Jon in for something cold to drink."

The men huddled around the dining room table with cold beers. Sam set out a platter of cheese and crackers, placed a few on a small plate for herself, then retreated to the deck with an iced tea. She had kept the French doors cracked open just enough to listen in on the conversation inside.

"So you don't want landscaping? You just wanted to grill me?" Draper growled.

"Let's face it," Carl said. "You didn't want to answer our questions in front of your wife so we brought you here, not on the pretense of needing landscaping work, though. I do plan to have you do it. What I need now are some honest answers." He slid a photo of Angie across the table. "She was in the bar Friday night supposedly with me. I say supposedly because someone slipped me something. I have no idea where I met this woman, how I got there, nor how I left. I need you to fill in the blanks."

"Whoa." Jon held out his hands as though pushing the words back across the table. "We do not drug people in the bar and if we see anything like that going on we report it. Butch doesn't go for any of that shit."

"And her?" Jake tapped the edge of the photo. "You appeared a little nervous in front of your wife to admit you knew Angela."

"I'm just trying to get her to trust me again. She walked in the bar near closing once to find me in a..." Jon cleared his throat. "One of the waitresses had been coming onto me for some time. I admit it was flattering and I almost reciprocated. Susan still thinks if she hadn't shown up it would have gone farther." He nodded toward the photo. "But her? Beautiful and way out of everyone's league. She was friendly, flirted, but had this unapproachable air about her." He studied Carl a little closer and nodded. "I do remember you being there Friday night. You looked very uncomfortable, as though she had to drag you in. I take it it's not quite your place to unwind. She, on the other hand, looked nervous, kept searching the door as though she were being followed."

"Did it sound like we had joined the bus tour, that we came back with them?"

"No. The bus tour came back a couple hours later. Besides, when most of the people were in the bar waiting to take the bus, you were not with the group."

"Angela was?" Carl asked.

"Yes. I heard her mention she planned to look at a couple houses on Daufuskie Island. She joked that it was a great place to hide out." Jon thought about that for several seconds while studying her picture. "Funny thing is, I remember someone asking her if she found a house. She said she never made it to the island. Changed her mind."


"What do you think?" Jake asked Sam after Jon had left. They were seated on the front porch as Carl grumbled about the estimate Jon had written on the quote.

"Well, we know Carl drove his own car because we have him on video driving himself and Angie to the bar where her car was parked. Maybe Carl planned to go to Daufuskie and Angie latched onto him when she thought someone was following her."

"And whoever was following her happened to get onto that

ferry so she hopped off and convinced Carl to give her a ride."

Carl blinked back images. "Yes."

Jake asked, "Do you remember something?"

"Angie saw the gun. Don't know how. I always have a jacket on or wear my shirt untucked. Just now I remember her saying something like 'I hope that's loaded.' She was frightened. Asked if I had a car and could I drive her back to Heyward Bluff. Yes. I remember that."

"Why didn't you show him the pictures of Travis and Tyler to see if he ever saw them in the bar? Sam asked.

"Thought of it for a second," Carl said. "However, I wasn't sure if Jon or one of the other bartenders might have been working with the Goodwin brothers.

"And don't forget, Sam," Jake said, "Angie could have been part of it. You heard what the parole officer said. Travis and Angie were a team. They could have been a team again. Along with Tyler, they got Carl to the motel to rob him, but something went horribly wrong. Maybe he discovered Carl didn't have a wallet on him, Travis got pissed and hit Angie a little too hard, then decided to put the blame on Carl and hightail it out of there."

"We need a fuckin' break in this case." Retirement had not made Carl more patient. "What we need is to speak to Mossy's son. Angela may have confided vital information to him that might give us the break we need. I'll find out which department is closest to his church retreat and have them drive out there and direct his ass back to Heyward Bluff."

# 28

When Becky Cramer still hadn't returned Milla's call by the next morning, Milla tried again. She was sitting in one of the conference rooms, the half wall of class enabling her to see who was in the outer office. She had thought about Tyler Goodwin all night. Milla had been unable to find a marriage announcement of Angela and Gordon Douglas. Smart on her part if she wanted to make sure Travis didn't find her when he was released from prison. Travis appeared to be the smarter of the two brothers, Milla thought. He had a lot of time on his hands in prison. However, any attempt to search the computers for Angela's whereabouts would have sent up a red flag to the prison officials.

It seemed like such a long shot for Tyler to track Angie to a small town like Heyward Bluff. In their previous conversation, Becky had mentioned that she also had a six-year-old son. What if? Milla's thoughts where interrupted when Becky finally answered her phone.

"You just aren't going to take no for an answer, are you?"

"I'm sorry, Becky. I promise, this will be the last time you hear from me." Milla saw Phil enter from the break room. She waved for him to come in, then she put the call on speaker. "Can you talk?"

Phil entered the room and closed the door.

"I don't know what else I can tell you. I'm through talking about Travis."

"It isn't about Travis. I want to ask you about Tyler. I know this is a sensitive subject so I need you to be as forthcoming as possible. We wouldn't bother you if this wasn't important."

They could hear Becky sigh, then the sliding of a glass door. It had to be around seven in the morning in Texas.

"Are you alone?"

"Yes, my husband's out of town and the nanny is with the kids."

"We have a rather small town here and I was curious how Tyler located Angela so quickly. Did he pressure you in anyway, maybe blackmail you?"

"Blackmail? I have nothing he could blackmail me with."

Phil's attempt at looking relaxed was to sit back in the conference chair. Unfortunately, the starched shirt and tie looked anything but laid-back.

Milla waited her out, then said, "Is your older son Travis'?" She heard a gasp from Becky. With that, Phil sat up straight, elbows on the table. Milla quickly filled the silence. "I can understand how you wouldn't want Travis near your son, or more importantly, for your husband to know he isn't your son's father." Now Milla heard a muffled sob. "This won't go any further, I promise. It just seems that with all the towns in this country, that Tyler would head right to Heyward Bluff. I have checked newspapers. It seemed Angela made sure there wasn't a wedding announcement or pictures, absolutely no publicity. You told me you hadn't spoken to Angie in years. Was that true?"

Becky could be heard blowing her nose and sniffling. "I didn't lie. I just omitted that detail, especially after you told me Angie was dead. If I did or said something that contributed to her death, I wasn't sure if I would be in trouble."

"You won't be."

Phil's eyebrows slowly arched.

"Angie called me after her marriage. I wasn't sure if she was just gloating or what. Thing is, I never heard her happier. And it wasn't about the money. Her husband already had plans to donate his estate. Angie didn't seem to care, which really surprised me. After all, what woman wouldn't want to make sure she would be taken care of after her husband's death? There was a life insurance policy of about a hundred thousand, no more. And that was all Angie would receive. She didn't seem concerned at all that she wouldn't even get to keep the house. Strange."

"Did she give you any indication why she didn't care about his money? Do you think she was running some other scam, like what she and Travis used to do?"

"You mean the escort service?"

Phil's brows crawled up further.

"Yes."

"I doubt it. She seemed perfectly happy."

"How so?"

"Travis, Tyler, and Angela had a pretty lucrative deal going on. She used to brag that they had made several million in one year. Angela might have set hers aside for a rainy day, but the Goodwin brothers spent it as fast as they made it."

Phil pulled Milla's notepad over, scribbled a note, then turn it around and shoved it back. Milla nodded. "Becky, do you know if either brother owned a 2010 Crown Victoria?"

"Gosh, it's been so long. Last I heard, Travis had a truck. I think Tyler sold it while Travis was in prison. Those two changed cars more often than they changed girlfriends."

"Did Travis have much of a temper? You mentioned before that he and Angela had a tumultuous relationship."

Becky scoffed at that. "To them it was foreplay. All the reason for make-up sex. The one with the temper was Tyler."

Milla thanked her for her time and hung up.

"Interesting," Phil said. He grabbed his cup and headed for the door, then turned back. "What made you think that Travis was the father of her baby?"

"A hunch. Sometimes your closest friend is the one who's the first to betray you."

Phil studied her for a few beats, then walked out.


"Nice quiet place. How did you find it?" Sam had to laugh at her own comment. Of course it was quiet. They were seated at a picnic table overlooking the May River. Behind them were tombstones. They were in a small cemetery where dates on the tombstones were no later than 1942.

"I went out for a walk one day about a mile from my house and took a private gravel road. It seems they started a cemetery but then something happened. Ran out of money. Sold land for development. Who knows. It isn't a family graveyard because all the names are different. Sometimes I come hear to clear my head, be where I know I won't be disturbed."

Sam had made sandwiches back at Carl's and packed a lunch for the two of them after Milla had called to meet. The area was surrounded by trees, the gravel road practically hidden by underbrush. White flowers covering a row of hedges emitted a wonderful fragrance. The area was on a bluff almost as high as the one Mossy's house sat on.

"How did you meet your husband?"

Sam had to smile, remembering that first encounter and still wondering if she had cracked any of Jake's ribs. "Jake was working security at a local politician's house. I was undercover as a blackjack dealer at the illegal game. I was actually there to break into the politician's safe and steal back some incriminating photos said politician was using for blackmail."

"Really? Are you kidding me?" When Milla saw Sam's shrug, she broke out laughing. "What happened?"

"I got the photos, Jake got a few bruised ribs. Then I found out he and his partner were transferred to my department and he suddenly knew who the thief was. Then he did some blackmailing of his own when he found out the police chief didn't exactly sanction my little escapade."

"Oh my god. He doesn't seem like the type to blackmail. He seems so…."

"Straight-laced? By-the-book? Logical? All of the above. He's Mister Logic to my Miss Woo Woo."

"And yet you are married. Strange."

"That's Mom's doing. She saw the good qualities in him and eventually I started to see him through her eyes. Mom always looks for the good in people. She would probably find some redeeming quality in Phil, some flaw in his shell or his past that would help her understand why he is so defensive and hard to get close to."

"Interesting you should say that." Milla explained what Bud had revealed about Phil's past in Miami.

"So he probably feels guilty his lover died, lost his wife and custody of his son. The superintendent threatens to fabricate his own version of how things went down leaving Phil with no choice but to quit and get lost in a small town."

"No reason to make everyone's life around him miserable."

"Guess Mom would see the pain in his eyes and say he was

telling the truth, that he covers up the pain with being a hard-ass."

They ate while Milla explained her phone call with Becky where she confirmed that her six-year-old son was Travis'.

"Sounds like a secret she didn't tell her husband. How did you know?"

"A hunch. She mentioned having a nanny, I could hear what sounded like a pool in the background. She latched onto a goldmine so I was curious if her husband knew about her fling. I suspected she was sleeping with Travis while dating her soon-to-be-husband. When she said Travis had slept around a lot, I didn't think it was that much of a stretch to suspect some of the women might have been Angela's friends. Tyler pressures her to reveal any information she might have on Angela or he would tell her husband."

Sam watched several yellow butterflies hovering over the hedges while a woodpecker pounded away in one of the trees. She wadded up the empty aluminum foil and tossed it in a bag, then finished her can of Pepsi while mulling over the timeline. "These brothers were pretty smart not to use credit cards or register anywhere using their real names. However, Tyler had to stay somewhere while he searched your small town for Angie and while waiting for Travis to be released. Carl didn't find any apartments or houses being rented out by anyone with the name of Goodwin. He could have false I.D.'s. Not hard to get these days."

"So Tyler picks up Travis when he's released and they drive down to Heyward Bluff to check it out. Angie thinks she spots one or the other, she's not sure, but she's panicking anyway, so she latches onto Carl before they went to the bar. The brothers wouldn't approach her in the bar with all those witnesses around so they couldn't have been close enough to slip the drug into the drink." Milla finished her can of Pepsi and dropped it into the paperbag.

"Tyler may have befriended someone here, maybe staying at his or her place."

"Not sure how much driving around you have been doing in our town. Just like this cemetery is tucked away from prying eyes, there are a number of vacated single and doublewides in surrounding unincorporated areas. It's not a stretch to think they may be holed up in one of them."

Sam pondered that theory. "No running water or bathrooms? Something tells me those two aren't the camping out types. And I would nix the idea Tyler latched onto a woman. Women tend to gossip more and would be curious about Tyler, asking too many questions." She gathered up the garbage and they headed back to their cars. How Milla ever found this place was a puzzle, although if she had been walking in the winter when the trees and brush weren't full, it might have been easier to spot.

"Phil thinks there's still a chance these two took what they could and left town. Travis wouldn't want to be suspected in a murder."

"True, however, they were looking for something in that house more than money and jewelry. My gut tells me that they didn't find what they wanted. I don't know why, but they just don't seem finished."

Milla was nodding her head even before she spoke. "My gut is telling me the same thing."

# 29

Alma Goodwin had once said that with his bedroom eyes and sexy swagger, Travis would get into more trouble than Tyler, yet could sweet talk his way out of it. Tyler, on the other hand, was recklessly impulsive and wouldn't see trouble coming from all sides until he was nose first in a pile of shit.

It had been a mistake to have Angie drive the Vic while Tyler held a gun on her. All she did was taunt him, tell him he didn't have the balls to pull the trigger. When her driving became erratic, Tyler was afraid the cops would pull them over. So he had her pull off the isolated road and onto a dirt road with Travis close behind driving Angie's sweet ride. She no sooner put the car in park then Tyler shoved the gun in the small of his back, opened the door, grabbed her by the hair, and dragged her across the front seat, tossing her onto the dirt like a bag of garbage.

Tyler's rage had been all about jealousy. He had grabbed Angela by the throat, lifted her off of the ground and throttled her. Travis had tried to pull him off, but Angela's words kept ringing in his ears. "You'll never be as good as your brother. You're a loser. You bring everyone around you down. I had to pretend you were Travis when we were in bed." He knew she had only slept with him to get back at Travis. In that one moment, all he could think of was they were both better off without Angela in their lives.

As usual, Tyler had screwed up. Angela died without telling them anything. Travis always cleaned up his messes. It was Travis' idea to break into one of the flimsy door locks at the motel and place Angela's body in bed, let the old fart take the blame. Without identification on her or him, it would buy them time to find what they were looking for.

"What are we going to do?" Tyler asked for the fifth time. He watched Travis continue to pace. They were in a cabin located down a dirt road off of one of the back streets running parallel to 278. The owners were in Canada half of the year. It wasn't swank but it would do.

"Quit your damn whining and let me think." Travis wasn't surprised he didn't feel anything after Angela's death. Retribution was what he had wanted, although not quite that final. And he couldn't fault Tyler. After all, it was through Tyler that they had met Montana. And through Montana they had use of the cabin while laying low. Not quite his taste in décor. Ruffled curtains and lace doilies? No thanks. It needed some bear and deer heads mounted on the wall, maybe a bearskin rug.

"I don't trust Montana," Tyler said, just to try to fill the silence.

Travis stopped pacing and looked at his brother. "On that we agree. I knew a lot of guys like him in prison, strutting around, playing the role of big shot. And who's taking all the chances? Us, you and me. The only good thing is that he doesn't know Angela is dead."

"We already checked the house, Travis. It wasn't there."

Travis started pacing again. What were they missing? There had been little publicity. Leave it up to the city fathers to keep a lock on bad publicity during tourist season. At least they had that going for them. "What about the guy she was with at the bar when you picked her up?"

"She latched onto him when she saw us," Travis said.

"That was smart, getting seen."

"And we already searched him. She would have been stupid

to keep it on her."

Tyler snapped his fingers. "The woman, the one we saw carrying items from the house. She must have been a friend. The cop car wasn't there when I saw her come out of the house. Angela may have told her exactly where to look."

"That's a good place to start. We need to find the woman."

"How nice of Carl to give us some alone time." Sam wrapped her arms around Jake's neck and snuggled closer. The scent from his aftershave was intoxicating. One dimmed light by the bar was the only light on in the living room while Keith Urban crooned *break on me*.

They slow-danced to the tune as Jake's lips touched the nape of her neck. "Wonder if we have time for another shower before Carl gets back."

"I am definitely ready for round two," Sam whispered. She had learned not to touch or stare at the scars on his neck. When he came home from the hospital, he would pull away whenever she touched them, interpreting her look of concern as pity. Now she did her best to ignore them. His lips found hers as he pulled her in close.

Like a needle scratching across a forty-five record, the melodic tune was abruptly cut off. "Don't start anything you can't finish." Carl flipped the lamp on by the end table. "We have work to do."

"Oh, damn," Sam moaned. "I knew we should have kept that hotel room."

"What? And miss my wonderful hospitality?" Carl opened the French doors revealing a sky of orange and blue hues.

Jake extricated himself from his wife and joined Carl on the deck. "Learn anything at the dock?"

"Nothing. No camera footage from last Friday. The captain doesn't recognize me or Angie. At least I had a great dinner at the Poseidon restaurant. What did you two do for dinner?"

Sam stepped onto the deck hoping her cheeks weren't turning red. "We had leftovers from the fridge."

"Uh huh." Carl turned to Jake. "I think we need to check out the bar again. This is about the time I was there on Friday night so I might remember more."

"What time do we leave?"

"We…" Carl wagged his finger from Jake to himself, "…are the only *we* I'm referring to."

Sam bit back a retort while a plan started to form in her head. "And you are going to go dressed like that?"

Carl fingered his dress shirt and slacks. It was bad enough his military hair cut screamed cop. "What's wrong with the way I'm dressed?"

"Everything. You two couldn't camouflage what you do if you were covered in mud. Put on some shorts and golf shirts. And wear visors. Stick a golf tee behind one ear. And would it kill you to put some grass stains on your clothes?"

"Now you're pushing it, Sam." He tapped Jake's arm. "Come'on. I've got some golf shirts you can try on."

"And wear gym shoes, not those four hundred dollar loafers," She yelled at their backs as they climbed the stairs. Once they were out of ear shot, she tapped a number on her cell phone. When it was answered, she said, "It's me. Are you free tonight?"

# *30*

Jake surveyed the pool tables where scantily clad young women, some he didn't think looked old enough to drink, were clustered in groups ogling the pool sharks. Waitresses weaved through tables carrying trays of food and drinks. It was past dinner hour so there were empty tables as well as empty seats at the bar. They claimed one corner of the bar by the door.

Eight wide screen TV's broadcasted a variety of sports programs, all with the sound turned down. Jake removed his visor and set it on the bar. Sam was right. He and Carl looked like tourists who just finished a round of golf and dinner and were stopping off for a nightcap.

A tattooed bartender with a mound of flesh spilling over the top of a sleeveless top strolled over. "What can I get you two?" They ordered two draft beers and watched her saunter over to the beer taps.

"Anything look familiar?"

"Definitely not her." Carl slowly swiveled the bar stool so he could study the pool sharks in the adjacent room, then the faces of locals seated at the tables and booths. "Nothing. Anyone curious about us?"

Jake scanned the faces in the room, then the few people seated at the bar. Two seats from him, an aging senior with a long ponytail snored loudly, his head resting on his arms. How he managed to keep one hand wrapped around a beer bottle was puzzling.

The bartender returned and set two glasses of beer in front of them. "Did you want to see a menu?" When they refused, she said,

"My name is Lola if you need anything."

"Made up name if I ever heard one," Carl whispered.

Jake pulled out his phone and thumbed through the photos of the Goodwin brothers. One photo showed Angie standing between the two brothers, one arm around each of them. Tyler wasn't as tall as his brother, nor as good looking. Both wore their hair collar length and shaggy. Where Tyler looked like a choirboy, it was Travis who had the steely look in his eyes, the half grin that bordered on a smirk.

"One thing is for sure, I remember the noise. Other than gramps snoozing by you, there aren't that many people here my age. I was probably as out of place as a pastor at a motorcycle rally. You would think someone would remember me from that night."

"I remember you," came a muffled slur.

The two men turned to the snoozing senior citizen who lifted his head just high enough to reveal a grizzled beard. His hand tipped the beer bottle to his lips and he appeared to inhale rather than swallow a sip. "Ahhh. Yep. I thought, man, that guy is banging one sweet piece of meat. I mean, we're about the same age right? You just dress nicer." A gravelly cough, half laugh, erupted from the old man's throat.

Carl couldn't help but smile. Besides, it wouldn't do him any good to flatten the guy in front of so many witnesses. "Anything else you remember besides my taste in women?"

"Hard to look at anything else."

"Do you remember who was bartending?" Jake asked. "How long he was here? Anyone else he talked to? Anyone hanging around who might have put something in his drink?"

"You mean like Viagra?" Another phlegmy cough erupted from the old man.

"Oh, hell. Hold me back if I go for my gun," Carl whispered.

"We're serious here, gramps," Jake said, finding it difficult to hold back his own amusement. "What about the bartenders? Any of them engaged in anything suspicious?"

Gramps raised up on his elbows and studied them both with red-rimmed eyes. He tipped the beer bottle to his mouth, then belched. "Like what? You talkin' about dealing drugs or something?"

"Or something." Carl wasn't sure he could trust the old drunk's memory. "See anything unusual that night?"

Gramps scratched his head, then eyed the twenty dollar bill near Jake's glass. Jake slid the twenty in the drunk's direction, but kept his hand on the money. "What exactly do you recall?"

"You and the lady came in, were here less than an hour. Then you staggered out. Figured you two had been partying someplace else first."

"Did I walk in or stagger in?"

The rheumy eyes blinked. He tipped the bottle to his lips again. "You walked in, staggered out."

"Anyone else help him out?"

"Just the lady."

Carl wasn't buying it. "You seem to be asleep more than you are awake so how can we trust you?"

"Not sleeping. Just don't want to talk to anyone so I pretend to sleep. Do hear a lot, though."

"This was Friday night when they are packed, according to the owner. That and the TV sets and all the banging of pool balls, how can you hear anything?" Carl made a point of checking if the old fart had a hearing aid.

"Nothing wrong with my hearing. Alls I know is the lady was

nervous and was practically draggin' you out the door."

"Did you see if anyone followed us?"

"Nah. At that point, I just kept my head down." With that the old guy plopped his head on his arms and started snoring, one hand wrapped around the beer bottle, the other gripping the twenty dollar bill.

Carl stabbed a glare at the old man and just shook his head. The twenty bucks didn't get him anywhere.

Jake turned his glass in a circle, studying the pattern from the condensation.

"What are you thinking?"

"Sam didn't put up a fight about coming with us."

"Yeah. That was unusually nice of her."

"Right. The operative word being *unusually*. Normally, she would have pulled the car up to the front of the house and laid on the horn, refusing to take no for an answer."

"Like I said…pretty nice of her."

"Which makes me highly suspicious."

Lola returned with a large glass mug filled with pretzel rods and set it in front of them. Jake studied the old man again who appeared to be snoring, or was he faking it?

"Salt. That's all drinkers need to keep them buying drinks." Carl couldn't resist and quickly pulled one out. It wasn't so much the movement by the door that caught his attention as the sudden drop in ball banging from the pool tables. He could see in the mirror behind the bar that every pool player had straightened and turned their attention to the entrance. Carl swung his gaze to the doorway. "Well, one thing I can say with absolute certainty, Jake. You definitely know your wife."

# *31*

Sam strode past the two men without acknowledging their presence. Jake was pretty sure she had not packed a sleeveless top and calf length skirt for the trip. She had obviously done some shopping. The ankle-wrap espadrilles were favorites of Sam's. And when she walked a lot of thigh flesh was exposed. Sam had a habit of only fastening the top three buttons on her skirts when she had an ulterior motive. Tonight was no different. She slid onto a barstool, and when she slowly crossed one leg over the other, Jake was sure he could hear an intake of breath from every guy in the place. Women, on the other hand, appeared curious about the feathered earrings and elaborate turquoise and coral necklace. Sam was definitely overdressed compared to the other women.

Carl stabbed the air with the stub of a pretzel. "Gotta say, your wife has got the best damn legs of any woman I ever met. Let's go say hi."

Jake clamped a hand on his ex-boss' forearm. "Let's wait and see what she's up to."

Sam was seated four barstools away from them. A male bartender appeared from the backroom and grabbed Lola's arm before she could approach Sam. He lasered a stare as he strolled over and leaned his forearms on the bar, exposing chiseled muscles. "Luke at your service. Let me guess. Wine spritzer? Something with an umbrella."

Sam smiled, remembering that Luke was one of the bartenders

who had worked Friday night. "Sorry, wrong. Vodka tonic with a lime."

"I'm rarely wrong." Luke let his gaze drop to the coral stone in Sam's necklace that was nestled in her cleavage. He placed a coaster on the bar and winked. "I'll get right on it."

Another figure breezed past Jake and Carl. It was Milla, dressed in shorts and a tank top. She sat two barstools away from Sam and motioned toward Lola. She quickly ordered a beer and started checking her phone, not acknowledging that she knew Sam. The noise from the pool tables slowly returned to life.

Luke set the drink in front of Sam and resumed his muscle-flexing position. "So, what's your name? I haven't seen you in here before so you are obviously vacationing. How long are you in town?"

Sam cut him off. "Actually, I'm looking for a friend. I'm about fifteen minutes late so I'm afraid she may have left." She made an attempt to quickly check the faces of women in the room. "She's about five foot six, auburn hair. Name's Angie."

"If she dresses like you, I haven't seen anyone in here tonight that fits that description."

Sam pulled out her phone, flipped through pictures, and turned the phone toward him. "She usually isn't that hard to forget."

A pool shark in a wife beater shirt strolled over and made an attempt to claim the seat next to Sam. She slapped a hand on the stool. "Sorry, I'm waiting for someone."

Casanova took the hint and slinked back to the pool table. Sam was definitely out of his league.

"Take another look, please. I don't want to waste time here if she already left."

Luke grinned. "Trust me, it wouldn't be a waste of time to

stick around. My shift is over at midnight."

"I remember an Angie," Milla said, then quickly apologized. "Didn't mean to eavesdrop." She pointed at Sam's phone. "May I see?" Milla moved over one stool as Sam handed her the phone. "Yeah, I saw her here Friday night." She looked up at Luke. "You were bartending Friday, right?"

"Friday nights are hectic. I can't remember all the faces. Besides, she's asking about tonight." Luke motioned Lola over. "Do you remember seeing her tonight?"

Lola took a quick look and shook her head. "No. And I didn't work Friday night, but why is anyone bringing up Friday night?"

"I only mentioned that I have seen her here before and I'm pretty sure it was Friday night," Milla clarified.

"What's her name?" Lola asked.

"Angie Hogan. Well, it's Douglas now."

"She does look familiar."

Luke took another look at the picture. "Not someone, though, that you'd see in this bar."

"That's for sure," Lola chimed in.

"How can you tell?" Milla asked.

"Her hair, jewelry. I have a friend who works on the Island. This woman's hair was definitely done at a high-end salon." Lola turned to Sam. "You're not from around here, are you?"

"On vacation."

"Gotta confess," Luke started, "I certainly wouldn't have forgotten that face, anymore than I could forget yours, so I'm pretty sure she wasn't here tonight." He checked his watch, then gave a nod toward Lola. "Can you cover while I take a break?"

"Sure."

"Want to bring your drink out back, have a cigarette?" He

flashed a smile at Sam.

"Don't smoke and I prefer to finish my drink here."

"If you change your mind, I have a white van out back. I'll keep the air conditioning running."

Lola shook her head as Luke made a retreat. "Sorry ladies. He never passes up a chance to flirt." A pool shark caught her attention at the end of the bar. Lola excused herself.

Sam looked over and saw that Carl was no longer seated at the bar.

"The minute Luke said he was going out for a smoke, Carl headed toward the bathroom which is right by the back door." Milla took a pull from her beer bottle. "Not sure if I believe Luke. If he ever met Angie, he did a good job of covering it up."

# 32

Luke tossed a wet match into the gravel and tried another. A flicked lighter loomed in front of his face and he gratefully accepted it. He smiled broadly as he turned, expecting the blonde from the bar to be standing next to him. His smile eroded as he saw the man from Friday night.

"Thanks." He inhaled deeply, gathering his thoughts. Who was this guy? How should he play it? He already acknowledged that he didn't know the woman whose picture was on Blondie's phone.

"You recognized me. I can read people pretty well so don't deny it."

Luke shrugged. "You obviously have a better memory than me since you know I worked that night, even though you could hardly see straight."

Carl didn't smoke and had grabbed Jake's lighter before leaving the bar.

"Something tells me I'm being set up. You show up the same day the blonde shows up asking about someone named Annie."

"Angie."

"Whatever. In my line of work it pays to play dumb, keep your head down, don't admit when you see some guy in here with a woman not his wife and vice versa. I rarely go home alone any night I work. For all I know, you're Angie's husband." He took another long drag, then flicked an ash onto the ground. His shirt was starting to cling to his skin like Saran Wrap from the humidity.

"I assure you, I'm not anyone's husband."

Luke took another long drag from his cigarette, collecting

his thoughts. "Yes, Angie and I had a very short fling. I knew her husband was older and ill, but could swear she told me her husband died. You certainly look alive and kicking so you can't be her husband. What is Angie accusing me of?"

"Angie's dead." Carl figured there was no sense sugar-coating it.

The cigarette dropped from Luke's fingers. "Dead? How? When?"

Carl felt Luke's shock was genuine.

"I didn't see anything in the paper."

"That's how the police chief wanted it, at least until she could be identified. She had given me a fake name, didn't have any I.D. on her when she was found in a motel room bed next to me. Besides wanting to know who killed her, I'd like to know who the hell drugged me here in this bar and dumped me in that bed. My guess is that's the person who killed her."

"Whoa. That shit doesn't happen in this bar. Butch would fire anyone dosing someone's drink let alone dealing."

"I stopped by your room on campus. Your roommate could barely focus through the haze of pot smoke."

"Hate that shit. That's why I always crash at a girl's place or a friend's."

"Where were you Friday night?" Carl could sense Luke's guards going up.

"Who are you to ask? You're no cop."

"The police here have their hands full trying to solve a murder, especially during tourist season. They don't exactly have my case of being drugged high on their to-do list."

"So why aren't you their number one suspect?"

"I've been cleared." Carl left it at that. "But I'm pissed and

I'm not going to drop this until I get answers. I already spoke with Butch."

"Oh, shit." The bartender raked fingers through his sun-bleached hair. "Listen, I don't need any more trouble. Disgruntled boyfriends have started fights in this bar so I'm skating on thin ice as it is. Unless you can show me a badge, I'm not saying anything else."

Carl almost reached for his FBI badge, but thought better of it. Luke tossed the butt onto the gravel and returned to the bar.

"Maybe I can get more information out of Luke if I went home with him," Sam said.

"Hard to walk with two broken legs."

"He can carry me." Sam wrapped her arms around Jake's neck and kissed his cheek.

"You two like this all the time?" Milla asked. She and Sam had moved to the two seats near Jake. Luke had yet to return to the bar area.

"He just hates to share." Sam pulled out her phone again and flipped through the photo gallery. "Isn't he the cutest?"

"Awwww. This your little guy?"

"Dillon. He's not quite two."

"Definitely the spitting image of his father."

Carl emerged from the backdoor and returned to his seat. A ruckus started by one of the pool tables. Butch appeared like a specter and stopped one pool shark from skewing another with a cue stick.

"What about you? I didn't see a wedding ring. Do you have a boyfriend?" Sam asked Milla.

"No. I'm either too busy or Hoodoo doesn't approve."

"Hoodoo?" Sam asked.

Milla sighed and then told them about her relative and how her mother believed Madam Udo's spirit resided in Hoodoo. "That damn cat has yet to like one man I have brought home. They last about ten minutes before she digs her nails or teeth into their ankle, then it's out the door they go." She gave a reluctant shrug. "It's just as well. I'm too busy to have a relationship."

"A possessed cat." Carl shook his head. "Sam, you attract the strangest people."

"What does that say about you, Carl?" Sam asked with a coy smile.

"Someone has to be the sane one in the crowd." Carl stared in the direction of the back door in search of Luke. "So, our happy bartender hasn't returned yet." Carl signaled Lola for another round.

"Not for me." Milla rose from the barstool and turned to Sam. "I have to be at the precinct early tomorrow. Keep in touch."

They watched her leave, then turned their attention to their drinks just as Luke returned to the bar. He glared at Sam as though he had been rebuffed. She had chosen a sweaty golfer over him.

"Learn anything useful?" Jake asked.

"Just like Butch, he claims they know nothing, saw nothing, heard nothing when it comes to drugs." Carl shoved his empty glass to one side. "Seemed genuinely surprised that Angie is dead. And he had slept with her and half the female population."

A snort came from the old-timer several seats away. Gramps raised his head, ran his gaze over Sam's body. "Damn," he breathed, "sure wish to hell I was younger."

"You'd have a heart attack trying to handle her," Carl said.

"I may be old, but I ain't done yet." Gramps gave another careful look at Sam's jewelry, and especially the medicine bundle. "You Native?"

"Sioux," Sam replied. "That and Scandinavian but my mother's our tribal medicine woman."

He lifted his head higher and maneuvered the beer bottle to his mouth. "Not from around here."

"The reservation is in South Dakota, although we now live in a suburb of Chicago."

He pointed the beer bottle at Carl. "Get what you wanted from Romeo over there?"

"Not much. Still denies anyone does drugs in this place."

Gramps gave a disinterested shrug then resumed his napping position.

# 33

"Where the hell did you go?"

"I needed air, Travis."

"Don't tell me you are showing your face in public."

"No one knows us. Have you seen our faces on TV or in the papers? No. Besides, I needed a beer and guess what? I found the woman who was at Angela's house. She was at the bar."

"No shit?"

"I'm tailing her now."

"Just get her address. We can go together in the daylight and search the place. Don't screw this up, Tyler."

Tyler hung up. He wasn't upset that Travis thought he was a screw-up. All Tyler wanted was his big brother's approval. Here was his one chance to make it up to him.

One block ahead the car turned into a driveway and parked in a side carport. If this woman was a close friend of Angela's, why didn't she live in an upscale neighborhood? She was obviously a trusted friend since she had a key.

Tyler drove past the house, noting the address, then turned the corner into an empty lot. He sent Travis a text telling him the woman's street address. But he wasn't about ready to leave. He was going to find out exactly what she had. Why wait until daylight where there might be witnesses?

Milla stood under the hot water, letting the pulsing showerhead ease the tension in her muscles. Ever since leaving the bar, she had felt uneasy. Had there been someone in the bar watching them? Sam and her husband were getting nowhere in finding the person who drugged their friend. If Phil was right and the brothers had left town, why was she so on edge?

Phil had been unable to find a storage facility or safety deposit box in Angela's or Gordon Douglas' names, not even under her maiden name. And what woman doesn't carry a cell phone? It wasn't in her house and they had been unable to trace it. If the brothers were as smart as Phil thought they were, they probably smashed it and tossed the pieces in a lagoon.

Milla turned off the water, slid open the shower door, and grabbed the towel. Details of the case clogged her brain, shutting out the faint noise from the living room. She shook her head, dismissing it as Hoodoo knocking something over. "Little brat," she whispered. A scraping sound shoved the case details out of her head. The noise stopped. Hoodoo couldn't have moved a table. She wasn't even that talented enough to open a drawer. That's exactly what it sounded like. No, not quite. Milla froze. It sounded like the squeaking of a floorboard.

She listened for additional sounds while pulling on undies and slipping a Carolina Panthers jersey over her head. Slowly, she turned the doorknob and eased the door open. Silence. This case was making her jittery. Not knowing if the suspects were still on the loose was playing on her nerves. No, not nerves…adrenaline. Her senses were on high alert. Why her, though? Sam had been the one who showed the bartender Angie's photo. So why not Sam? Did Milla claiming she had been there Friday night and saw Angie, garner the attention of the person who drugged Carl? That would mean that person was in the bar tonight. Maybe he had followed her.

What kind of cop am I? Milla thought. Scared of every noise. She relaxed a little. Silence was the only thing that filled the house. She cautiously walked down the hallway to the living room. The front door was closed, dead bolt in place. Windows were closed, not that anyone hauled a ladder around to climb into a building on stilts. Nothing had been knocked over, drawers were closed, CDs were stacked neatly on the shelf under the television set

Squeak. Another floorboard. The blow came too quick for her to respond as her body slammed against the floor. The weight on her back made it difficult to breathe. All Milla could think of was how glad she was that she had purchased an area rug.

"What did you take from the house?"

"What?" A blast of stale beer and cigarette odors hit her face.

"The house. What did you take from Angie's house, bitch."

"I've never been..." Her words were cut off as her head was slammed against the floor. "This how you killed her? Slamming her head on the floor?" Milla jammed an elbow into his body hoping he would release his grip. Instead, he slapped a hand against her forehead. The guy probably hated the fact that her hair was so short. She suddenly felt the sharp end of a blade and something running down her neck. Milla froze.

"You have one minute to give me everything you took."

Milla thought of screaming for help, if only her landlord was back. She was too isolated for anyone to hear, and by the time help came, she could be dead. "All right. All right."

He released his grip and rolled off of her, standing quickly and taking a step back. "Make it quick."

Milla slowly rose and pressed fingers to her neck. She pulled her hand away and saw blood. "Why don't you tell me exactly what you are looking for. If I don't have it, maybe I saw it in the house." She had seen pictures of both brothers and almost called him Tyler. That would have assured her death, though.

"I'll be the judge of that. Now get it."

Milla grabbed her purse from the coffee table.

"Empty it out."

"What?"

"On the coffee table."

Milla ignored him, reached in and grabbed the photos. "Pictures. That's all I took."

Tyler ripped the purse from her hand, sending her wallet, gun, and badge skittering across the floor. "Shit." Tyler wrapped an arm around Milla's neck. A cry like a screaming banshee erupted, and it wasn't coming from Tyler. Tyler's scream was more like a howling hurricane wind. When his grip on Milla was released, she saw Hoodoo riding Tyler's neck, sharp nails digging into his scalp.

Tyler howled again, dropped the knife, reached back and tossed Hoodoo off of him. The feline landed on all fours while Tyler made a run for the back door, almost ripping it off the hinges.

Milla picked up the gun and took pursuit. Tyler was in the car so fast he forgot to turn the headlights on until he was a block away. "Damn." Milla stood at the bottom of the stairs feeling her heart hammering. She slowly smiled. She had Tyler's knife and proof the brothers were still in town. She climbed the stairs, closed and locked the screen door, then closed the back door. After turning the lock, she braced a kitchen chair under the doorknob and cursed herself for not installing a better lock. The ball of black fur was licking its paws when Milla returned to the living room. "You took your sweet time." Hoodoo gave a screech and looked toward the kitchen. "I know, I know. I've been saying for weeks I need a dead bolt on the back door." She swiped a hand across her neck again, coming away with more blood. Using an edge of the newspaper, she grabbed the knife from the floor, carried it to the kitchen, and placed it in a paper bag. Wetting a paper towel, Milla pressed it to her neck. Once she was assured it had stopped bleeding, she poured a shot of bourbon, sat at the kitchen table, and made a call.

# 34

"I thought I could do something on my own, something to make up for my screw-up."

Travis eyed his brother through the veil of cigarette smoke. He had been the only one he could count on while in prison. Tyler was the one who visited him, had been the one to track down Angela, and had been the one to meet Montana. Travis could care less how many men Angela had slept with. The fact that her pillow talk with Montana confirmed what that old fart of a husband had told her was worth the five years he spent incarcerated.

"We have bigger problems," Travis said. "I told Montana we would have it tonight. Whatever you do, don't tell him we were following a cop. He doesn't need to know."

"So what do we tell him?"

He thought about that for a few seconds while he stubbed out his cigarette butt in the ashtray. "The truth, with a little embellishment. Stall him. Say she had company so we are going back tomorrow to search the place."

"Okay, sounds good, if he buys it. The guy's an ass."

The back door opened and a figure climbed in. He set a twelve pack of bottled beer on the floor. "I trust congratulations are in order." He handed opened bottles to the two men, then opened a bottle for himself and raised it in a toast. "Where is it?"

"Shit, Montana. Not even a hi, how are you?" Travis snarled, then took a long pull from the bottle.

"Hi and how are you. Now tell me what happened." He turned steely eyes toward Tyler. They were parked by a lagoon in an unincorporated area off of 278, away from prying eyes. Didn't matter much. Seemed every street off of the main roads was cloaked in darkness. And right now, this location served Montana's purpose.

Tyler glanced at his brother. God how they hated this guy. Travis always said they should work alone. Course, then there was Angie. They had been a trio and it had worked until it all went sideways.

"I followed her home, but she had company. I waited a while until it looked like these people were never going to leave. Thought it better if we go back tomorrow, wait until she leaves the house. Not too many houses close by so we won't be seen."

"Tomorrow, huh?" Montana's eyes twinkled.

Travis watched him closely. This guy could never play poker. He knew something and was broadcasting it with every twitch of a smile. "That's what he said. You have a problem with that?" The Crown Vic was running, air conditioning blowing, almost too chilly. Close to midnight and it was still eighty-five degrees. The silence was only broken up by the sound of guzzling. Travis eyed him with disdain. "Seems to me you would have engaged in a lot more pillow talk with my ex. I'm surprised she didn't clue you in on who her friends were."

"We didn't do a lot of talking, other than about her rich husband. She actually did love the old man."

"Angie didn't love anything but money. She may have admired him, loved sex with anyone, but actually love someone? Hardly." Travis took a long pull from the bottle, then stared at it. These beers were hitting him hard. "If this friend was close enough to have a key to Angie's house, I'm surprised you didn't know her."

"Trust me. If Angie had any close friends, I would have known. She kept everyone at arm's length. Didn't trust a soul, and for good reason. Always looking over her shoulder, looking for you two." His eyes drifted to Tyler, then back to Travis. He took another long swallow, then pointed the bottle at Travis. "Can't much worry, though. As my daddy used to say, 'Worryin' is like a rockin' horse. It's somethin' to do that don't get you nowhere." He eyed the two beer bottles, gauging how much was left in them and how long he would have to keep stalling. "My guess is she played all three of us. Her dead husband talked a good game, but he never found it. My uncle is sure of it. But Angie? I could read her like a book. I know she had it cause she waived it in our faces." He placed his empty beer bottle down, and rested his arms across the back of each of their seat. "Think we're at a crossroads here. So let me ask pointblank—which one of you assholes killed her?" When neither answered, Montana said, "Doesn't matter now, does it? She took it to her grave. However, now you two have a bigger problem." He watched them suck down the last of their beers, their eyes looking everywhere but at him. "I followed you, Tyler. You went into the house, let her see your face. And you know why that's a huge problem?"

Tyler turned in his seat and glared at Montana, a cocksure punk he'd love to shove his knife into, if only he hadn't dropped it at the bitch's house. He looked at his empty beer bottle, then shook his head. Something wasn't right.

"The lady's a cop, you assholes."

"What?" Travis' head whipped from Montana to his brother. "What the hell's he talking…" The car suddenly felt as if it were tilting and he was finding it hard to focus.

"He's bluffing, has no idea who she is or where she…"

Tyler braced a hand against the dashboard as he, too, felt like the vehicle was moving. He raised the bottle and stared at the contents, expecting to see some telltale remnants. The bottle fell out of his hand and clattered to the floor.

Travis swung his gaze back to Montana. "You son of a bitch."

"You two have managed one cluster fuck after another. That woman is a detective and now she knows you two are still in town." He turned to Tyler who was blinking furiously, trying to focus. "You've unleashed a shit storm of trouble." Montana continued to unleash his anger even though the Goodwin brothers were no longer hearing him. He opened the rest of the beer bottles and poured them out. He climbed out of the back seat carrying two of the empties. After wiping off his prints, he tossed one on Tyler's side of the car, then walked around to the driver's side and tossed one on Travis' side. He opened the door and pressed the button to lower the driver's side window. Once he positioned Travis' foot on the gas pedal, he closed the door, reached in, and shifted the vehicle into DRIVE. The Crown Vic lurched forward as Montana rushed around to the back and helped push it into the lagoon. He watched as the car hit the mucky bottom, leaving the hood of the vehicle exposed, which was good. He wanted it found, wanted the cops to feel the case was closed. The killers had too much to drink and drove down an unfamiliar road into the lagoon. Case closed.

# 35

"You really didn't have to do this."

"I talked you into going to the bar last night," Sam replied. "It's the least we could do."

"We?" Carl balked. "It's Jake and I who are doing the work." The power drill whirred, installing the dead bolt into Milla's back door. Jake worked on the screen door, fixing a loose handle.

"But we don't mind. Ignore Carl. His bark is far worse than his bite." Jake tried jiggling the handle, satisfied that it was secure.

"I made iced coffee if anyone is interested." Milla set two glasses on the kitchen table. She and Sam opted for iced tea. The kitchen was cozy offering a nook where a square table was surrounded on three sides by cushioned bench seats. Milla hadn't bothered with decorating, although, after last night, she wished she had curtains on the windows.

Once the tools were put away, they assembled around the table where Milla had also set out cinnamon scones from a local bakery.

A flash of black fur peered around the entry to the living room. "Is that Hoodoo?" Sam snapped her fingers and called out the name. Hoodoo shrank back a couple steps.

"It isn't unusual for her to be shy," Milla said. "I bet she's curious about the vibes you're emitting."

Carl balked again. "Right. Your possessed cat meets Native American mysticism."

Hoodoo crept closer, made a tentative sniff at Sam's ankle, then leaped onto Sam's lap. "Whoa. Hey there."

Hoodoo sniffed at Sam's medicine bundle, then peered up at

Sam. The cat took a swipe at one of Sam's feathered earrings.

"Get down Hoodoo."

"She's okay." Sam stroked the shiny coat. Hoodoo turned in a half circle, then settled on Sam's lap.

"Unreal," Milla said with a shake of her head. "She's rarely that friendly."

"She did kind of save your life last night." Sam studied the bruise on Milla's forehead and the cut on her neck. "Could have been a lot worse."

Milla touched the knot forming on her forehead, thankful again that she had purchased a thick area rug. "He must have been in the bar last night and followed me. Did any of you see one of the Goodwin brothers?"

"No," Carl said. "I am curious, though, why you were on their radar."

Milla thought about that. Why would they even think she knew anything? "The house," she finally said. "I went to the house when Sam told me to check Angela's bedroom for pictures. The police had left so Tyler had no way of knowing I was a cop until he saw my badge at the house."

When Jake's phone rang, he checked the screen. It was a local number he didn't recognize. "Hello." His eyes flitted to Sam. "Yes, Mossy. I remember you." He listened for several seconds, then checked his watch. "How about a half hour...good. See you then." He hung up and looked across the table at Carl. "Mossy's son is back in town."

Sam turned to Milla. "Want to come with?"

"Sure. I have nothing else to do. Besides, I'd feel safer surrounded by three other members of law enforcement." Milla stirred sugar in her iced tea while she stared at the side yard that was in desperate need of a green thumb. There was hardly any grass for the landscapers to mow. The duplex was surrounded on three sides by trees and brush and empty lots for sale at a premium. How could it not with the view of the May River.

"Milla, did Phil ever talk to Mossy?" Jake asked.

"Only by phone. She didn't tell him anything more than what you found out."

Milla grabbed her phone from the center of the table. "I feel obligated to let Phil know that the Goodwin brothers are still in town." The call was answered on the second ring. "Hi, Kate, is Phil there?" She listened for several minutes, her gaze dancing to the three faces at her table. "Did he confirm it?...okay...no, no problem. I'll talk to him when he's free."

"What's up?" Sam asked.

"A guy walking his dog earlier this morning saw the hood of a vehicle in a lagoon off 278. When they towed it out, there were two male victims inside matching the description of the Goodwin brothers."

# 36

Phil watched as a black SUV carted the brothers off to the medical examiner's office. Chief McComb exited his car and walked over to his lead detective. A woman dressed in all white looked more like a beekeeper than a forensics expert. She strolled over carrying a clipboard. "Good thing this place is isolated or we'd have a ton of onlookers." She pulled the white cap off releasing strands of gray hair from her ponytail. Betty Murphy had been with the county sheriff's office for over twenty years. She had been on her way to a sale at the outlet mall when the call came in. A firm believer in being prepared, she always kept her kit and uniform in the back of her van.

"Hey, Betts. Hope we didn't screw up your day off."

"Nah, chief. You saved me money." The scowl didn't leave her face as she gave a nod at Larson. "You again."

Phil said nothing.

Betty pulled her gloves off as she spoke. "We can tow the vehicle to our garage on the island. It's closer. Found hair and blood on the driver's side door. Hair is too long to be from either of the deceased so could be tied to your victim from the motel room. Empty beer bottles in the car, two on the grass. Both had burner phones."

"Cause of death?" McComb asked.

"No signs of foul play, no noticeable wounds. They haven't been dead for more than eight or ten hours. I'd put time of death around midnight."

"They aren't familiar with the area, had too much to drink,

flew the curb and lost control. It can happen." The police chief was a happy man. "Send us a report. Phil, if you can match the motel victim's blood and hair to the samples in this vehicle, I'd say we have our crime scene. If you match one of the victim's to the skin samples found on Angela Douglas' neck, I'd say we have solved our case." He clapped Phil on the back. "Good job."

"I'll send my report over to Detective Lawson pronto."

"Thanks, Betts." The chief watched her stroll over to her van. Great lady," McComb added as the van and accompanying squad cars left the area. He pulled on the fabric of his tan shirt, feeling the dampness. The only saving grace was that they had changed department uniforms last year from dark blue, which held onto the sun's heat, to the light tan color. The officers on bike patrol were the lucky ones, getting to wear shorts.

Phil squatted down and studied the grass between the gravel and the water. Ground was dry so it was difficult to see any other tire tracks much less footprints. "Was there a full moon last night?"

"Nah. It was overcast. No skid marks, dark, unfamiliar area."

"Right. I'm still trying to maneuver myself around this town. Can't tell you how many times I passed up Lowe's. Not only is the sign buried behind bushes, it's also past the entrance to the store. Makes no sense." Phil straightened and the two walked back to their vehicles.

"Let me know when Betts sends you her reports. Should this shake out the way we hope, I'll draft up something for our press release."

# 37

"I really didn't know Angela that well. I'd see her on rare occasions when I'd stop by to see my mother, make sure she was treating her good." Jonah Belden took a sip of sweet tea. He had a warm smile and a voice like liquid honey which reminded Sam of a young Denzel Washington. He was around Milla's age, yet when she glanced at Milla, the detective didn't seem as impressed. Instead, Milla had skepticism down to a science.

They were seated on the porch; and although the overhead fans were on high, it did nothing more than circulate hot air. Carl didn't appear bothered by the humidity as he sat in a short-sleeved shirt that had enough starch in it to stand on its own. Not a bead of sweat on his forehead while Jake was dabbing his face with a handkerchief and Sam could feel a trickle running down her back. Poor Mossy didn't have air conditioning in her house, something her son said he would install the moment he had a little extra money, after paying for her cataract surgery. Mossy seemed to love the heat. "You could roll up a map of South Carolina and squeeze out a cup of water," Mossy liked to say.

"Did she ever say why she was working as a home companion when she lived in a gated community?" Milla asked. It didn't go unnoticed that her question was more like an interrogation.

"Who are you again," Jonah asked. "Mother said nothing about four people stopping by, only three."

"I'm Detective Milla Boles, and I'll ask you again." Milla felt a hand on her shoulder and looked up to see Carl's stern expression. She tried hard not to shake off his hand. After all, it was the same hand that installed a dead bolt lock on her back door.

"What the detective is trying to ascertain," Carl started, "is if Angela seemed like the type of person who would go around drugging someone."

"Drugging? Absolutely not."

"But you just said you didn't know her that well." Milla felt Carl's hand lift from her shoulder.

Jonah looked at his mother. "You think she drugged my mother?"

"No. She latched onto me on the Island, and we went to the Palmetto Bar and Grill where someone drugged me. It could have been Angela, since I can't find any other likely candidates. I'm sure you've heard of women drugging tourists and then robbing them."

Jonah was shaking his head before Carl even finished his sentence. "This is Heyward Bluff, not Vegas. Besides, Angie wasn't like that. She was a decent person helping others. And you said so yourself, she lived in a gated community. Why would she need to rob someone?"

"What about you, Mossy?" Sam restrained from pressing the cold glass against her chest. A fleeting shadow by one of the hedges caught her attention, but it was gone by the time she turned her head. Was the young spirit listening in on their conversation? "Did you ever notice anything missing after Angela was here? Did she ever borrow money?"

"Never. I have even given her money to do some shopping for me, and she always returned the change."

"She isn't the squeaky clean apostate you make her out to be. She was accused of theft in Italy several years ago and before that she and her husband ran quite a scam," Milla countered, hoping the revelation had the expected effect on the pastor.

"Husband." Jonah looked noticeably disturbed. "He was elderly and disabled."

"Her first husband." Jake said it so quietly, most everyone forgot he was even there. "At least they led everyone to believe they were married, though we haven't been able to find any records." He had decided beforehand to only sit and observe. Now he could see Jonah was visibly upset. Angela wasn't exactly who or what she had led him to believe.

"Oh, my." Mossy turned to her son, her eyes searching his face as only a mother could. Was it disappointment that he didn't see Angela for what she was or was it something else? Mossy didn't say anything more.

"Well," Jonah appeared to collect himself, "it isn't like she sought out my counsel. We exchanged pleasantries and she certainly seemed like a polite and giving person."

"Giving in what way?" If Milla had a voodoo doll of Jonah in her hand right now, she would have ripped its head off.

"I beg your pardon?" The good pastor was become incensed. He braced his hands on the back of Mossy's swing.

Sam stood. "We won't take up any more of your time. If either of you think of anything else that might help us, you have Jake's number." She turned to Jonah. "No one deserves to die the way Angela did. We need…" Sam stopped and turned to Milla. "The POLICE need all the help they can get in solving her murder."

Milla pressed her business card into Mossy's hand. "I apologize for the intrusion. If you think of anything that might help, please give me a call." She was down the steps and walking toward the church parking lot before Sam could catch up to her.

"You were a little hard on him."

"He's hiding something. He knew her far better than he is letting on."

"How can you tell?"

"A guy that good looking meets a woman who looks like Angela and you don't think there was more than just a hi and how are you? More like *hallelujah* and *good gawd* moments."

"You certainly didn't give him the benefit of the doubt," Jake said.

"I've known guys like him. Pastor or no, he's still a man." Milla slammed into her car. The three of them watched Milla's car spew gravel as she sped off.

"What do you think?" Sam asked no one in particular. "Someone cheated on her?"


Milla had calmed down by the time she reached the precinct. Chief McComb was coming out of the breakroom when he saw her. He stopped a few feet away, his eyes staring at something over her head.

"Something wrong, Chief Ray?"

"I should ask you the same thing. What the hell happened to your head?"

Milla's hand reflectively touched her head. The two Tylenol she took had taken the pain away, but she forgot the bruise and knot on her head were still quite visible. "Oh, that. I had a visit last night from Tyler Goodwin."

The chief sighed. "In my office." He closed the door, then took a seat behind his desk.

"I hear they found the Goodwin brothers this morning. Was it an accident?"

"Looks like dumb luck. No sign of foul play, bunch of beer bottles. The vehicle is being processed now. Found hair samples on the upper part of the driver side door that don't match either of the brothers so that could be where Angela was killed. Betty will compare forensic evidence on Angela Douglas' neck with the DNA of the brothers and see which one killed her."

"Then case closed. Guess Phil was worth all that money."

"Careful." Chief Ray stared at her for a few beats, then shook his head. "Now your turn."

She sank against the chair back and let out a puff of air. "I think they returned to Angela's house when I was there and were curious what I had found. There wasn't a patrol car out front; and for all the brothers knew, I was a friend of Angela's and took something from the house, which I had. You know about the pictures."

"But you came to the precinct afterward. How would they know where you lived? They wouldn't have been that stupid to wait for you to leave work and chance being seen."

Now what? Milla thought. She had to step lightly. "I stopped for a drink last night. I went to the bar where John Doe, I mean Director Underer, thought he was drugged. As long as I was there, I thought I'd see if any drug action was taking place. I only stayed for one drink and went home. Didn't see anyone there that looked like Travis or Tyler Goodwin, and the female bartender knew nothing about drugs in the establishment. I did happen to show both bartenders Angela's picture to see if they recognized her from Friday night. The female bartender thought she might have been in there, but the guy said it was too busy for him to remember. Personally, I don't believe him. I think he knew the victim. He's a good looking guy. May have done more than serve drinks when it came to Angela."

The chief jutted his chin in the direction of Milla's forehead. "And that?"

"Tyler followed me home and was waiting in my house when I got out of the shower, demanded to know what I took from Angela's house, got me down on the floor and pounded my head into the rug. When he grabbed my purse, my badge and gun fell out and he went ballistic."

"Jezzus, Milla. What the hell were you thinking? You could have been killed?"

"He was worse off, believe me. My cat attacked him and Tyler went running out the back door like a scared sissy. Where he went after that, I couldn't tell you."

Chief Ray started scratching notes on a notepad. "Do you remember what time that was?"

"Around ten I think."

He sighed again, his gaze returning to her forehead. "You took a chance. They might have both come back to finish the job because you could have identified Tyler."

"Guess it's a moot point now."

Chief Ray tossed his pen down and pushed away from his desk, propping his legs on the desk. "He give you a clue what he was looking for?"

Milla shook her head. "Maybe she took something from Travis before he was arrested."

"What could be that valuable that they had to spend years tracking her down?"

"She had what looked like expensive artwork. They could have taken her jewelry and cash but didn't. And she might have taken something when she was overseas that the Goodwin brothers thought they should have been cut in on. Guess we'll never know."

"I trust you're going to get some better door locks."

"I had dead bolts put on."

# 38

"So, you're the new guy." Betty circled the Crown Vic where it was parked in the garage bay, aware that Phil was tailing a little too closely. Did he doubt her ability to do her job?

"If you consider one year new, but hardly new to the job." His hand wandered to his nose, pretending to scratch.

"I heard. You certainly made a name for yourself in Miami." The footsteps behind her stopped.

She straightened from her note-taking and directed her assistant to turn on the overhead fans.

"You are going to let the interior dry out first, aren't you?"

Betty faced the detective, whose fingers now appeared to serve as a shield. "How long have you been a detective?"

"Ten years."

She tried not to laugh and instead continued her walk around the Crown Vic. "I've been doing this for thirty years. I've inspected boats that have been buried in pluff mud for six years, bodies dined on by alligators, ripped apart by buzzards and every type of carnivore. Sometimes all that's been left are a few organs and bones, yet I'm still able to make an identification. Well, most times," she added with a chuckle. She could swear he was holding his breath. "That smell is pluff mud. Comes from the decaying of fish, creatures, vegetation. Creates hydrogen sulfide. It's leftover from a boat that was hauled in last week with an old fisherman on board. He had died of a heart attack, and the boat attempted to drift back to shore only to be stuck in the mud. Authorities thought it was caught up in Hurricane Matthew. They tried locating the owner to get it removed, not knowing the owner was on board."

Phil looked up at the ceiling and walls where large exhaust fans were doing little to help with the ventilation. Betts followed his gaze. "Believe me, it smells much better in here than it did a week ago."

'Hate to get stuck in that shit."

"Some have. Many a person has lost a boot or two to the grey-black muck." Betty inspected the detective's crisp, short-sleeved shirt with sweat stains, and floral tie knotted with precision. You'd do best to toss the tie and buy some of those climate control shirts before you drown in your own sweat. No one will think less of your professionalism. Matter of fact, they won't think of you as a pompous know-it-all from the big city." Now she did laugh at her own comment.

Phil unconsciously stuck a finger behind the knot and loosened the tie. "That's what people think of me?"

"Course, you strike me as someone who doesn't care what people think." Betty lapsed into mother-mode. She couldn't help it. It was her nature. She knew Phil's history through the grapevine. Who didn't have a history? She knew men like him who put up their guards like giant shields. "Word of advice?" Betty didn't wait for a reply. "You don't have to make friends but it helps to be friendly. My guess is you have a lot of expertise to share with your fellow cops. Drop the wall you've built around yourself. You'll be amazed at how people will start to give you the benefit of the doubt."

If Phil was incensed, he didn't show it, unless one looked at the way his jaw was grinding. "When do you think you'll know more about the vehicle?"

"Know as much now as when it will dry out. We're processing

the hair and blood samples as we speak. That part of the vehicle never made it under water. The M.E. should be starting on the bodies today."

"Best guess?"

"Don't like to guess. I like to wait for the evidence. That said, the hair looks similar to the hair found in the motel room. If we can match the skin samples found on her neck to one of the brothers, then I'd say you've just cleared a murder case. Good notch on your belt since we don't have that many murders here."

As he exited the garage and made his way to his vehicle, Phil ripped the tie from his neck and tossed it in the back seat. He already felt twenty degrees cooler.

"You have been very quiet tonight, Jonah. Actually, ever since our guests left."

Jonah barely smiled at Mossy as he sipped his wine. Several lights blinked out on the water, probably boat running lights. Tree frogs barked like rabid dogs. Mossy had two floor fans placed on each side of the porch to circulate the humid air and discourage flying insects. She sipped her own wine, positioning her head so she could study her son from the working part of her right eye. He had been quiet at dinner and barely touched his dessert.

"That detective was pretty rough on you."

"I think she could tell I wasn't quite truthful."

"I know." Mossy could hear the anguish in his voice. "Angela had a way of getting you to talk about your fianceé's death and how her loss is still painful. I didn't mean to eavesdrop, but could hear you talking down here."

"We didn't just talk."

"I suspected as much. Even before this whole thing happened. I'm not one to pry, and for the first time in a long time, you were smiling more."

Jonah heaved a long sigh and opened a picture album which he had placed on the coffee table. "When our guests told me about Angela's past and her history of crime, something hit me. Don't know why I hadn't checked before. Guess I was too blinded by intimacy. Thought she was genuinely interested in me and our family history." Jonah fanned through the album. Not convinced, he fanned through it a second time. "It's gone, Mom. She took it."

"But why? It's just a silly piece of paper, a pipe dream your father chased."

Jonah pressed his palms together, prayer style. "What if that is why Angela was killed?"

Mossy shook her head. "It could have been misplaced. No sense stirring up anything."

"Still."

# *39*

What are you doing here?" Milla looked over Jonah's shoulder, expecting to see a vehicle. "You walked?" She stood behind the screen door, not about ready to let in any creatures, whether two-legged or four-legged.

Jonah shrugged. "Needed some air and just kept on walking."

"And you just happened to know where I lived?"

A tired smile lifted one corner of his mouth. "You're not the only detective."

Milla had to give him credit. Course, it helped that her address was in the phone book. The chief had warned her when she moved here that it would be best if all police personnel kept their addresses and phone numbers unlisted.

"What do you want?"

Jonah started swatting at hungry mosquitos. As soon as one swarm left, another would start. "I don't suppose I could come in for a minute."

Milla sighed and turned on the porch light to divert the insects. "Make it quick before they follow you inside."

Jonah slid inside, closing the screen door behind him. Milla closed the front door, preferring to keep the air conditioning inside. He stood for several seconds taking in the décor, or lack of, the television set that was tuned to a cooking show, and a laptop sitting in a scattering of papers. Milla folded her arms and waited. Without saying a word, Jonah handed her a small storage container.

"Mossy made apple pie."

Milla looked at the container as though it contained snakes

and not the wonderful odor that was seeping into the room. "You walked all the way over here to bring me dessert?"

"That, and to apologize for lying."

"Well, now we're getting somewhere." Milla jerked the container from his grasp and carried it to the kitchen. She returned with the opened container in one hand and a fork in the other. The aroma had gotten the best of her. She plopped down on the couch and said, "Talk."

"I didn't kill Angela."

"Didn't say you did, but now that you mention it." Milla thought she'd knock him back on his heels a bit.

"I only lied about my relationship with Angela."

"You were having an affair."

"No...I mean yes...I mean."

"Which is it?"

"My mother was sitting there. I didn't want to admit that one time, just once, Angela asked me over to her house for dinner and things got a little heated. I'm not proud of it. It just had been a long time since my fiancée died, and Angela seemed to really care."

"Spare me the details. What else?" Milla thought about asking Mossy for her recipe, but who was she kidding? Milla had yet to turn the oven on in her own apartment.

"She stole something that has been in our family for a long time. Mom and I never removed it from the scrapbook, but after your visit today and the revelation about Angela's past, I started to wonder if she had played me. After all, I was vulnerable. She had a way of getting me and my mother to talk about our family history. We just thought she was being kind."

Milla finished the pie and set the container and fork on the coffee table. She tried desperately to hold back a belch. The pie had been inhaled rather than eaten lady-like. "What exactly did she steal?"

"A map."

"Map? Like a map of Heyward Bluff?"

"No, a treasure map."

Milla handed Jonah a beer and took a long swig from hers. Jonah had moved to the couch and they each claimed a corner, turning so they faced each other. "Let me get this straight. Your great-great-grandfather was a Yamassee Indian?"

"Easy to mistaken. Our tribe is a little darker than what you normally know as Native American."

Milla shoved her beer bottle into a koozie as her mind conjured up visions of a pirate treasure. "Something tells me apple pie and Angela aren't the only two subjects you wanted to discuss."

"No." Jonah set his empty beer bottle on the coffee table. "I wondered if you saw anything that looked like a map in Angela's house."

"It was pretty trashed. If her killer was looking for the same thing, and I'm beginning to think he was, there's a chance it wasn't found because the brothers never left town." *Except in a body bag*, Milla thought. To her knowledge, Chief McComb wouldn't issue a press release on the Goodwin brothers until tomorrow morning. "What makes you think the map might be the real deal?"

"I don't, neither does my mother. My grandfather had spent far too much time with my late father trying to decipher it. Allegedly, my great-great grandmother had received the map from her husband. She had fled to Florida during the Civil War with a daughter and infant son. The map was passed down from ancestor to ancestor so I'm sure each generation embellished its significance."

"Have you researched it at all?"

Jonah shook his head. "Never had the time. Besides, Mom was so upset that Dad had spent his life looking into it, neglecting his family in the process, that she tucked it away vowing never to bring it up again."

Milla took another swallow of her beer as she thought about Angela and the Goodwin brothers. Had Angela's death really been the result of domestic violence? "Was the map easy to decipher?"

"It doesn't look like an actual map. I mean, it didn't have a pirate ship on it or skull and crossbones nor a picture of a chest of gold coins. There were squiggly lines, a tree, and an X."

"As far as I have heard, there aren't any relatives, and Gordon Douglas left everything to a number of charities. An attorney is supposed to be settling the estate and putting all the paperwork in order. I'm sure I can get in there and take another look around, but I don't hold out much hope. Forensics and Detective Lawson combed the place ad nauseum, as well as myself and..." Milla stopped herself from admitting that the contingency from Illinois had also been in the house.

A shadow crossed under the coffee table and stared at their guest. Good, Milla thought. Hoodoo should be biting Jonah's ankles about now and getting rid of this guy. Sam was right. Milla had been engaged one time. Unfortunately, the jerk had used her credit card as though it were his personal bank account. A few dollars here and there didn't bother her at first, until she found out he purchased a ring, for another woman. Said jerk skipped town the morning of their wedding, leaving her with a debt of five grand which took her two years to pay off.

Hoodoo was now at Jonah's feet. Milla hoped he was afraid of black cats.

"Hey, who's this? You don't take me for a cat person."

"No?"

"More like a pit bull."

He had an easy smile and Milla was beginning to feel bad that Hoodoo was seconds away from drilling her teeth into his ankles. Just when Milla was about to warn Jonah, Hoodoo leaped onto Jonah's lap and planted her front paws onto his chest.

"Hey, what a beautiful shiny coat you have."

Milla was too flabbergasted to speak.

"What's its name?"

"Hoodoo," she finally spit out. "It's a she."

Jonah's hands stopped in mid-stroke. "Hoodoo?"

"Long story."

There was that easy smile again. "I don't suppose I could bother you for a cup of coffee." Hoodoo looked at Milla and blinked. If she could talk, the damn cat would have said, *Get to it. You heard the man.*

Other words came to mind as Milla popped a pod into the coffeemaker, like *don't you have to get home? Isn't it too dark to be walking alone? And no, don't even think I'm going to drive you home. Are you used to overstaying your welcome?*

"He's getting it black," Milla whispered to the empty kitchen. "What does he think this is, an all-night diner?" She carried the cup into the living room only to find the pastor lying on the couch, fast asleep, Hoodoo curled next to him. She was just ready to yell un-Christian type words when Hoodoo raised one eyelid in warning.

"Damn," she whispered, and carried the cup into the kitchen, spilling the contents into the sink.

A quarter moon slid behind a cloud, transforming nightfall into ink black. Beyond the twisted wire fence and thick undergrowth, a hooded figure bent in concentration. Slowly, he moved the detector over a grid area he had marked off earlier, just one of many tracts he had scanned with the metal detector. The display screen was state-of-art, lighting up whenever it detected coins, relics, and other artifacts on the monitor so as to avoid unnecessary digging. His uncle had spared no expense.

Black clothing helped to conceal his presence and limit the number of bug bites. But it was hot as hell, and itchy. He pulled a marker from his pocket and swiped it across the branch of a tree, one of several he had marked each time he visited.

Lightning raced across the sky. Although the darkness hid his presence, the lightning might not be as kind. He had even worked on the island for a few months, taking a job with a private security firm, choosing to work nights so he could search the grounds. When he realized how much ground he would have to cover, he decided it was useless, even with the Goodwin brothers helping.

He worked his way back down the bluff, away from prying eyes and the impending storm building in the distance.

# 40

Detective Lawson was on the news the next day, reporting on the death of Travis and Tyler Goodwin and their ties to Angela Douglas. He downplayed the revelation of a murder in Heyward Bluff, citing that he had needed confirmation of her identity first before saying anything to the press. The hair and blood samples in the vehicle matched Angela's and the skin samples found on Angela's neck were a match to Tyler Goodwin. He played up the history of the three as well as Angela and Travis' Bonnie and Clyde checkered past.

"That's how I would have played it." Carl scooted his chair back so he was under more shade from the table umbrella. The shirt he wore over his swim trunks was unbuttoned. Although he had said before that he didn't wear shorts much because of his knobby knees, he looked unusually tan for a man who claimed to never go to the beach.

"Short and sweet, never took questions, and left the reporters to scrounge around for details to fill in the blanks." Jake thanked the waitress for the refill on their iced teas. He also wore swim trunks and a short-sleeved shirt whereas Sam had thrown on a knee-length cover-up and shoved her hair under a straw hat.

They were seated on the patio of an outdoor restaurant in Sea Pines on Hilton Head Island, one of Carl's favorite places for lunch. He often walked the beach at sunset and sat at the outdoor tiki bar. Sam thought he looked absolutely at home in South Carolina.

"How long are you going to stay?"

"Trying to get rid of us?" Sam asked.

"Not at all. Just need to know if I have to join Weight Watchers. You guys are dragging me to just about every restaurant on the coast."

"Not true. We eat breakfast in and you made steak the other night," Sam said. "Besides, we're on vacation. Eating out is part of travel."

Beach umbrellas were lifeless in the distance. They dotted the beach in a myriad of colors. Swimsuit-clad bathers moved from the beach to the sandwich bar, changing rooms, and restrooms. It was a public beach and wall-to-wall people this time of year. The inside restaurant was filled and there was a line waiting to be seated on the outdoor patio.

"Don't forget to give me that list of gift shops to visit. I want to buy souvenirs."

"Ka-ching," Jake said under his breath.

They were silent while the waitress cleared the table and placed the bill in front of Jake. He shoved cash in the black folder and nudged it toward the edge.

"At least the chief was kind enough to instruct his detective to withhold my name from the entire investigation. Would have been nice, though, to find out who the hell drugged me. Angela just didn't seem like the type."

"Really? You knew her all of twenty minutes," Sam said. "Besides, now that we know her background, I think it's quite conceivable that she did."

"Still."

Jake raised the binoculars to check out the object on the horizon. There were a number of barges and freighters out on the ocean in addition to sailboats and fishing boats. He lowered the binoculars and eyed his former boss. "Guess it will be another mystery in your long line of mysteries, Carl."

A flash of light caught Sam's eye. While most people studied the ocean with their binoculars, Sam could swear someone had directed their attention toward shore, toward their table.

Milla tried not to glare at Phil. At least he took his success with a smidgen of humility. Now he was behind closed doors with the chief while Kate was kept busy handing out press releases to the media who were lined up at her window.

All Milla had to show for her efforts was a folder containing the items she took from the Douglas house. The chief had informed her that the Douglas family attorney would be in town today. She also had to come up with a good excuse for having the items since they had been retrieved without a search warrant. That was the easy part. After all, they used them to help verify Angela's identity. The hard part was to prove her usefulness to the department since Phil had managed to solve the case completely on his own.

Her thoughts returned to last night. She liked Mossy, a crusty old woman, although not much older than Milla's own mother. Her son, on the other hand, the good reverend, or was it pastor? Didn't matter. He had immediately gone on the defensive. It was a wonder Milla hadn't found any pictures of Angela and Pastor Jonah among the photos in the Douglas house.

She stared at the chief's door, still closed up tight. They were probably deciding her future. She could imagine Phil telling Chief McComb that he could handle three towns on his own. No sense having two detectives. Good thing she wasn't settled into her apartment.

Pastor Jonah Belden. Without thinking, her fingers started typing his name into a search engine. What other secrets was he hiding? She expected to find a Facebook page with two thousand followers, all female, claiming to have found Jesus once he crossed into their lives. Instead, nothing. Not a Facebook account, MySpace, Twitter, or even a website. Only the Church on the Bluff website showing his photo along with a number of visiting pastors. She found numerous articles on news sites praising his work with the area youth and the summer youth camp. His father, Calvin Belden, had died in his forties of lung cancer when Jonah was fifteen.

"Of course you graduated high school at sixteen, and second in your class at Duke University," she whispered. Then she saw another photo...an engagement announcement. Nicole DuMorney. They were the perfect couple. Young Denzel meets young Halle Berry look-alikes. Milla skimmed the announcement, taking in the French Quarter reference, how the bride-to-be's mother was an interior designer and Nicole followed in her footsteps. Her father was an investment broker and her brother a PGA golf instructor. Perfect teeth, perfect family. Milla bet the family name was pronounced *Doo mor NAY*. Why was jealousy spreading through her body like a January flu bug? She didn't even know Jonah Belden that well and never knew the fiancée.

She had Phil to blame for that. She had been shoved aside by one man. Now she was already considering herself shoved aside by a man she had never even dated. Jealousy or self pity? She wasn't even in the same league as Nicole frickin' *Doo mor NAY*.

Milla silently admonished herself while her finger clicked on another article from less than a year ago, describing the car accident that killed Jonah's fiancée. She had been returning from

Savanah in heavy fog when her red Prius skidded off I-95 into an embankment, flipped over several times, and slammed into a tree. "Oh my god," she whispered.

"You okay?" Chief McComb was standing in front of her desk. She hadn't heard his door open.

"Yes. Sorry, Chief Ray. Did you need something?"

"Attorney Derek Collins is at the Douglas home now. Why don't you take your illegally confiscated items over there and get on his good side so he doesn't sue the hell out of us."

# 41

Sam clutched the list of gift shops in her hand. Carl and Jake had seemed too eager to get rid of her. Shopping store-to-store just wasn't in the male genome. Instead, they were waiting for Jon and his crew to arrive to tear apart the landscaping and prepare it for new plants. She pitied the crew. Carl will probably sit in the shade of the porch and bark out orders.

They had taken two cars to lunch. Carl insisted she drive the Cadillac when she went shopping. Her guess was he wanted to drive the Charger. It was just as well since she was a bit intimidated by the power under the hood of that monster. The Cadillac was more to her liking.

Since the shops near the beach were crawling with tourists, Sam opted for the quaint little shops along the main road. Wexford and Shelter Cove took up most of her time. There was so much to look at that she found it impossible to try to remember where she found the perfect gift in order to go back and buy it. She ended up just buying on first sight rather than trying to remember which store she saw the perfect gift for family and friends. Her favorite was the three foot plush alligator. Sam just hoped Dillon wasn't afraid of it.

It was near the Poseidon restaurant that Sam felt it. A tingling that slithered over her body, giving her a chill in the ninety degree temps. She strolled past the outdoor seating and stood in front of the window in the store next door, trying to catch something out of place in the reflection. Maybe she shouldn't have made two trips to the car to unload purchases. With the number of shoppers and witnesses, she doubted anyone would try to steal something from parked cars in broad daylight. No, this was something different.

Sam crossed the street to the ice cream shop. After purchasing a single dip of caramel ripple, she sat on a bench in the shade. Behind her dark sunglasses she studied, not the shoppers, but anyone standing still or sitting down. Someone was watching her. Jake would say that wasn't unusual, seeing that her best assets, her legs, were exposed. Sam always dressed conservatively. No *Daisy Dukes* for her or plunging necklines. That was how Abby had raised her, except, of course, during her undercover days.

Cars passed slowly in the crowded street. Sam unfolded a map of Shelter Cove and pretended to read it while her eyes searched behind dark sunglasses. Was it the man leaning against the building by the jewelry store? No. A woman exited the store and he obediently followed. Two guys sitting at the outdoor bar staring in her direction? No. Just oglers. There were benches up and down the street, all occupied. Women with children, teenagers, couples, an array of shoppers. Not one piqued her interest, yet the tingling kept crawling.

Sam folded the map, shoved it in her purse, and made her way toward the sidewalk by the water. According to the map, there were more shops by the King Neptune statue. The harbor and marina had a number of beautiful boats. She stopped to finish her ice cream and checked for anyone following her.

The sidewalk looped around restaurants and an outdoor concert area. She ducked into one of the stores and studied items on a display, which gave her a clear view of the outside. Not one person looked suspicious.

This is ridiculous, Sam thought. She was wasting time. There was only one more stop she had to make and it was back in Hayward Bluff. Markel's was a must place for shopping, according to Carl. How strange that a guy who hates to shop knows all the best places.

Keeping her eyes on the reflections in store windows as she made her way to the parking lot, Sam still couldn't shake the feeling that she was being followed. Was it her imagination? Was it just an ogler? She knew better when she again heard that word in her head—*Montana.*

# *42*

Milla followed the attorney into a living room filled with stuffed boxes. She had expected a stoop-shouldered lawyer around the age of Gordon Douglas. Although he had a full head of gray hair, Attorney Derek Collins barely looked fifty.

"My father was the Douglas family attorney," Derek Collins said. "I ended up with all of dad's clients after he passed away."

"You've certainly cleaned up a lot."

Collins stared wistfully at the sea of cardboard around them. "That's my wife's doing. She's the organized one. According to the will, anything relating to the Civil War is being donated. The house, furniture, and fixtures are being sold and the money given to a list of charities. My wife, Elaine, is upstairs going through the clothes in the closets."

Milla spied the photo albums and photo boxes on the coffee table. She retrieved the photos from her purse. "When we needed something our medical examiner could use to make a positive I.D., I borrowed these photos." She expected to be lectured on a litany of laws she had broken.

Instead, the attorney said, "Just add them to that box."

Milla took a seat on the couch and lifted the lid on the box. "What's going to happen to these since there aren't any relatives?"

"Probably get tossed."

"Did you know Angela or Gordon Douglas?" Milla noticed several current photos of Angela. While she kept the attorney engaged in talking, she quietly sifted through the miscellaneous photos.

"I met Gordon years ago. It was right after his first wife died. Very interesting guy." Attorney Collins read the spine of several books and smiled. "I don't think I ever met anyone who knew more about the Civil War. He was a walking encyclopedia."

Milla lifted one of the photos. "It looked like he also participated in reenactments."

"Oh, yeah. Big time. Dad told me Gordon would go away for weeks on end just practicing for the reenactments, living in tents, cooking by campfire."

"Who's this guy with him?" Milla held up a picture of Douglas standing next to an old codger in a long white beard and long white hair, dressed more like someone you would have found on an old cattle drive.

Collins walked over and peered at the photo. "Never met him. There were all kinds of characters at those reenactments. Could be portraying a cook. Looks more like someone you'd see panhandling for gold. But don't let the costumes fool you. He's probably a clean-shaven banker." He found an empty box and started to fill it with more books from the shelves.

Milla kept sifting through the photos. "What about Angela? I take it you never met her."

"Heard about her. Dad said Gordon found his soulmate, someone who was just as passionate about history as he was."

How strange there weren't any photos of Angela and her wealthy husband, nothing from the cruise where they met or vacations. It seemed Gordon liked to take pictures of his wife, though, and she was beautiful. Not one bad hair day or a rotten pose. Milla's fingers stopped. There were a couple photos of Angela with another woman. They were standing in front of a cobblestone building Milla recognized as one of the restaurants on

River Street in Savannah. Another showed them leaning against the railing of a ferry boat. The date handwritten on the back of each was a year ago. There was no mistaking that the friend of Angela's in the photo was none other than Nicole DuMorney, Jonah's dead fiancée.

Milla's mind raced. Was Jonah lying about not knowing Angela before hiring her? How long had Angela known Nicole? If Jonah knew Nicole and Angela were friends, why wasn't it disclosed? What else was Jonah not telling her? The doorbell grabbed the attorney's attention which gave Milla the chance to slip a photo into her purse. A woman dressed in crop pants and a sleeveless top came down the staircase just as Collins opened the door. A young man in a damp white shirt and long pants shifted a briefcase in order to shake hands. Milla heard Derek introduce Stu Ballard, a realtor, to Derek's wife, Elaine. Milla stood when they entered the living room.

"This is Detective Milla…"

"Boles," Milla said, and reached out to shake hands. Elaine had a friendly, but suspicious look on her face. "I was just returning some items we needed to identify the deceased. I'm not here to purchase." She let her gaze sweep up the staircase. "The department doesn't pay me enough."

"The, uh, owner didn't die here, did she?" The realtor dabbed a hanky across the perspiration on his forehead. By the looks of his shirt, Milla thought he should toss it in the dryer while he was here.

"Oh, no. Not at all," Milla assured him.

"Where would you like to start?" Elaine waved a hand as if directing the realtor to *door number one*.

"Upstairs, then we can work our way down."

"Great." Elaine led the way; and without a backward glance or "nice seeing you, show your way out," they climbed the staircase.

Milla waited until they were out of sight. She was certain there weren't any other photos of Nicole upstairs, and the attorney had already pretty much torn apart the downstairs. There wasn't any way she could ask the attorney if he had seen anything that resembled a hand-drawn map without arousing suspicion.

She walked into the kitchen and scanned it quickly. Flat boxes were standing against one counter waiting to be assembled. Cabinets were opened, some of the contents stacked on the counters. She backed out and opened a door to her right. It led to the garage where a motion sensor tripped the overhead lights. There was a workbench on one wall, a golf cart to her right, and a tarp-covered car against the other wall.

She closed the door and walked past the pristine workbench. Not one tool on it, just a thin layer of undisturbed dust. There was an empty pegboard on the wall, not one long-handled or hand tool displayed. It was as though when Gordon died, Angela removed anything she had zero use for. Curious, Milla lifted one edge of the tarp. The car was baby blue in color; and by the shape, the double hood ornaments, or did those have something to do with air intake? Milla wasn't sure. She wasn't an expert on classic cars, only that her father had always wanted a 1957 Chevy Bel Air. He used to save pictures of those cars and go to every classic car show.

She lifted the tarp further. "Oh wow," she gasped. "A convertible, too." The last car show her father went to this car sold at a hundred thousand dollars. How many years ago was that? Why on earth didn't Angela sell it? She appeared to have sold every tool in the garage and she had been driving her own

Cadillac. Milla kept lifting the tarp as she walked around to the passenger side. "What?" The entire right side of the car was damaged, as if someone had driven too close to a guard rail, scraping and denting the entire length of the vehicle, leaving streaks and flakes of red paint. Guardrails, to her knowledge, were not painted red. How did an officer not catch this? Did they only lift the tarp high enough to check the license plate and verify it was registered to Gordon Douglas?

Milla folded the tarp back onto the hood and took out her cell phone. She heard voices coming from the house so she quickly snapped several photos, then replaced the tarp. There was a side door to the garage. Fearing the entourage would walk into the garage and wonder what she was doing there, Milla quietly unlocked the door and slipped out.

# *43*

Sam stuffed the last of her purchases into the back seat and slammed the door. She was in the parking lot at Markel's and had to mentally drag herself out of the store before she maxed out her credit card. Carl had been right. Markel's was right up at the top of places to shop. They had even wrapped several of the gifts in the most unique way, something Sam would have never been able to accomplish.

Having taken various side streets, Sam was sure she lost any tail had there been anyone following her. Her main problem with driving Carl's retrofitted car was figuring out what all the buttons and dials were for. She had no idea what she touched on the dashboard; but while driving over the bridge from the island, she noticed a side panel on the passenger side door had popped open.

Sam opened the passenger door, and upon seeing the handle of two guns, she quickly climbed in and closed the door. "Well, looks like I found one of your secret compartments, Carl. I trust there isn't a trick to closing it." Just as Sam was about to push the compartment closed, she noticed something white near the bottom of the panel. She pulled it out and unfolded it. At first glance it looked like a drawing someone might doodle on a piece of paper after too many drinks. There was a straight line, an X, a squiggly line, and two short parallel lines. Carl was too much of a clean freak to use a secret compartment as a garbage can. And it didn't look to Sam like anything Carl would have drawn. She decided to fold it up and put it in her purse. She would ask Carl about it later when she asked him how to connect Blue Tooth since that was the button she thought she had pushed. The panel closed with a snap.

Sam exited the passenger side then climbed in on the driver's side. Satisfied she wasn't being followed, she got back onto 278.


A team of workers swarmed the front of Carl's house. All of the old bedding, vines, invasive creepers, and rocks had been removed. The carport no longer looked as though it were being held hostage by an errant perennial. Two trucks filled with plants were parked on the side of the drive. Black dirt had been hauled into the planting beds while some workers had already started to position some of the plants.

One vehicle looked familiar. Sam could swear it was Milla's. Leaving her purchases in the trunk of the Cadillac, Sam climbed the front steps and entered the house to find Milla pacing the living room.

"What's up?" Sam tossed her purse on the couch.

Jake glanced at Sam's empty hands. "Wow. You didn't buy anything?"

"There were too many to carry in. Thought it would be easier just to move them from the Caddy to the Charger."

"Let's go outside." Carl had morphed into FBI mode. He led them to the back deck. After retrieving sodas from the refrigerator, they assembled around the table.

Milla wasted no time telling them about her online search for additional information on the pastor and how she had found the article about their engagement and Nicole's subsequent death. She segued to her trip back to the Douglas house to return the photos to the attorney settling the estate, and how she had found several photos of Angela with Jonah's fiancée. She concluded with the description of the damaged Chevy Bel Air in the garage.

"I checked the accident report from Nicole's death. She was driving a red Prius. With the number of times the vehicle flipped, it would have been very easy for the police to not be suspicious of all the damage done to the car. I want to go back to the house tonight and take some of the paint flecks to have analyzed."

"I don't think that's wise, Milla," Carl warned. "You can't break into the house. Any proof you find would be inadmissible in court."

"I left the garage door unlocked, provided, of course, that the attorney didn't check it before leaving. And I heard him say he wouldn't be back for a couple days."

"Still, you don't have a search warrant."

"But I don't need one," Sam said with a sly smile.

Carl sighed heavily. "Jake, you keep her on a short leash and she still manages to gnaw right through it."

"I can go after dark, quick in and out," Sam said. "Besides, the closest neighbors are part-timers and currently out of town."

"No," Jake said. "You aren't going. WE are going. You and I, together. We can tell the guard at the guardhouse that we are going to the restaurant for dinner. Carl and Milla can drop us off near the house where we can check the garage, take some quick samples, pick us back up, then go to dinner."

"Did you notice if there's an alarm system on the house?" Sam asked.

Milla shook her head. "There wasn't a sign in the yard nor anything posted in the windows. And I didn't notice a control panel anywhere."

"So, if the attorney did lock the back door, I'll just borrow Carl's pick gun."

They were quiet for several minutes, sipping their drinks, and looking out over the water. The overhead fans were on high which added to the pleasant breeze drifting in, carrying with it the scent of a flowering groundcover from the adjacent lot.

"This was never about retribution or domestic abuse. Travis and Tyler were after something else," Milla surmised.

"I don't think their deaths were an accident either," Sam added. "Those guys were too desperate for whatever they thought Angie possessed to do a stupid thing like get drunk and drive off the road."

"Well, Carl, looks like these two ladies have the case all but solved."

"My memory is still of little use. If Angela had anything or stole anything the brothers wanted, she took the knowledge to her grave."

"Unless he's covering it up, Jonah had no idea Nicole and Angela knew each other," Milla said. "If I have the timeline right, Angela just happened to offer her services to help out his mother after Nicole's death. Nicole must have said something to Angela which prompted her to get close to him and Mossy. I remember he said there was a map that has been in his family for generations. After our visit, he checked the scrapbook where it was kept. He remembers showing it to Angela and now it's missing."

"It couldn't be." Stunned, Sam excused herself. She returned with her purse and retrieved the piece of paper. "I was punching a few too many buttons on your car's fancy dashboard, Carl, and your side panel where you keep some of your toys popped open. I found this inside. I knew you weren't one to install a weapons compartment and use it as a trash can." Sam unfolded the paper and everyone leaned over to study it.

"That's it, I think. That's what Jonah described."

"What the hell is it?" Carl asked.

"Jonah said it was a treasure map."

# 44

"We'll be fine. If we see a security vehicle, we will just ask them for directions to the restaurant. It's easy to get lost in this place, especially at night. Now go. I'll be in your ear the whole time." Carl dropped Jake and Sam off at the mouth of the gravel drive Jake had parked on the first time they had visited the Douglas house. They were clad in black with Jake wearing night vision goggles to make their way through a tangle of brush and backyards and around to the garage's back door.

"How do you think the map ended up here?" Milla motioned to the side panel.

"The one thing I remember about Angela was her fear and anxiety. I probably showed her I could handle any trouble that came her way by popping open the side panel. She must have known what her ex was after and slipped it into the compartment so she didn't have it on her should Travis cross our paths."

"The question is, what was Angela planning on doing with it? It certainly doesn't look like a decipherable map."

"When I lived on Martinique, there was a lot of pirate history and I saw a number of pirate maps. The idea was to not make them decipherable. They were only to be understood by the person drawing them."

"Makes sense. Maybe I'll have to look for someone who can make heads or tails out of it. I can ask around and see who might have some knowledge about these things."

"Take a copy. You don't want to give him the original. But first we should show it to Mossy and Jonah to make sure this is what was stolen from them."

Milla thought about the press conference Phil just had, slamming the door on Angela's murder case. Nailed shut. Case closed. "This is going to kill Detective Lawson. Here he thought he had the case solved." Her smile slowly faded. "Great. Phil will probably take over the case again."

"Not if it's a simple robbery," Carl said. "We can have Mossy call it in, just say a family heirloom was stolen. That small of a job, your hotshot detective wouldn't touch with a ten foot pole."

"Love the way you think."


"Quick in and out," Jake cautioned as he opened the unlocked garage door. They slipped inside and then realized they tripped the motion sensor, turning the overhead lights on. "Shit." Jake took off his black baseball cap and slipped it over the sensor. Sam ran to the entry door to the house and did the same. After a few seconds, the garage was pitch black again. "Milla did say there was a motion sensor, but I didn't know it was on both doors."

"Security car just turned down your street," Carl said through their ear buds.

Milla shook her head. "How does someone retired keep all his toys?" she whispered.

"We timed that right," Jake replied. "There was a damn motion sensor on the second door. We covered both so the lights are off."

"Now he's coming our way." Carl unfolded a map of Bluffton in front of him as the headlights from the security van washed over them. When the van pulled up alongside, Carl lowered the window. The window on the security van slid down revealing a beefy guy in a grey uniform. "Boy, are we glad you showed up. We must have missed a turn for that restaurant. I think it's called Heron's Point."

"No problem. Go to the end of the street and turn around in the cul de sac. Go back the way you came, take the second right and it leads you right there."

"Thank you very much." Carl closed the window and took his time refolding the map while keeping an eye on the van's taillights.

"Is he gone?" Jake asked Carl as he held the tarp up so Sam could gather paint flecks into an envelope.

"Yes. I have to turn around so get your asses out of there. I'll pick you up on the way back."

Sam and Jake retrieved their hats which turned the lights on again. They slipped out the same door and returned the same way they came. They made a quick change out of their stalking clothes in the backseat of the Cadillac as Carl drove to the restaurant.

"I need this." Sam took a healthy swig of her martini. "Been a while since my adrenaline went into overdrive."

"Feels good, doesn't it?" Carl winked as he raised his glass in salute.

A hefty tip to the hostess warranted them a corner booth by a window and away from the crowded tables. The outdoor tiki bar was filled while only a few customers preferred the indoor bar. Two men were a few decibels too loud as they flirted with the bartender. The hostess walked over and whispered to the two patrons who immediately toned it down, paid their bills, and left.

The four studied the menus in silence, their gazes slowly

drifting around the room looking for anyone suspicious. When Carl noticed Milla's eyes widen at the menu selections, and more importantly, the prices, he announced, "Everyone order what you want. I'm buying."

"Wow. Take advantage everyone. Carl doesn't do this often."

Jake folded his menu. "Great. King filet for me."

"Lobster for me," Sam said.

"I'm with Jake."

"I'm with Sam."

"That's settled." Carl gathered the menus to the corner of the table. A college-age waiter came over with a wine list. Carl noticed that Milla hadn't ordered a drink. "How about white wine with your lobster, Milla?"

"I'm not really a wine drinker. I usually drink beer."

Carl took the wine menu and studied it briefly. "I will have the merlot with my steak and the young lady will have a pinot grigio with her lobster." He turned to Milla and said, "You will love it." Carl's face suddenly lost its color. While everyone gave the waiter their dinner order, Carl had to be tapped on the arm to return to the present.

"What just happened, Carl?" Jake said after the waiter left.

"When I said, 'You will love it,' I recall saying it to Angela. She hadn't wanted a drink at Butch's place so I ordered her a glass of wine, more to settle her nerves. I remember telling her, 'You will love it.' She didn't and I ended up drinking it."

"So someone was trying to slip her the drug, not you." Sam picked the orange from the rim of the martini glass and ate it while thinking about the case. "If it wasn't the bartender, then someone distracted both of you."

"It was pretty crowded in there, that much I remember.

Anyone could have leaned over and dropped something in her drink."

"Or the bartender was lying," Milla offered.

"What about the problem at hand?" Sam patted her purse where she had placed the evidence bag. "Where do we go to get the paint chips analyzed?"

"The SLED office is in Columbia," Milla said.

"Well, you're State Law Enforcement Division is overloaded with cases and understaffed. I'll send it overnight to the Science Unit at Quantico."

"I don't understand why Angela didn't get the car fixed, provided her car is the one that was involved in that woman's death."

"For one thing, Sam, the best body shop in town is run by a retired cop," Milla said. "He would have reported the car to our department if he suspected it was involved in a hit and run. If it had been a normal collision, the customer would have the insurance paperwork."

"She could have lied and said someone sideswiped her in a parking lot, and she didn't want to notify her insurance. After all, she has enough money to pay cash for the work."

"No, Sam. He would still have reported anything suspicious. I've heard in the department that the guy is a real hard ass."

"And a sweet ride like that," Carl said, "word would get around that someone smashed up a 1957 Chevy Bel Air. If I were her, I would have kept it under a tarp until the heat died down."

"Jake still has his Bel Air," Sam said.

"The red one?"

"Candy apple, Carl. It was my dad's. He and Alex baby it, polish it, I swear, once a week."

Their food arrived and all talk ceased, except for Milla's compliments to Carl for the selection of wine.

They refused dessert as well as after dinner drinks. "We can have nightcaps back at my house."

"Thanks, but I think I'll just retrieve my car and head home," Milla said.

"How do you plan to follow through, Milla? Your star detective will probably throw a hissy fit, as some men with bruised egos often do." Sam was speaking from experience.

"We already discussed that in the car while we waited for you and Jake. You should have Mossy call the police department and report a theft. There's a good chance they will toss such a menial task to Milla. If it piggybacks onto Detective Lawson's case, then so be it."

Milla nodded as she thought about the repercussions. "Boy, if I'm right, Lawson's going to make my life miserable."

"Been there, done that," Sam said. "However, the thorn in my side ended up being a close friend."

"How did you accomplish that?"

"My mom likes to quote something Lincoln once said, something about the way to eliminate an enemy is to make him your friend. I ended up working a murder case he was implicated in. He had been set up and I proved it. Jake had to drag me kicking and screaming to work it, but it really felt good solving a decades-old crime."

"I would say even I at one point wasn't one of Sam's favorite people." Carl gave a casual glance at the bill, then slipped a credit card in the slot and handed the bill folder back to the waiter. "Now she just loves me to death." He looked across the booth at Sam. "Right?"

"Anyone who picks up the tab is always my BFF."

"Thanks for dinner, Carl. For a moment there, I thought I'd have to stick to breadsticks. Can't believe this place is so expensive."

"I take it you don't eat out much, Milla?"

"No, sir."

"You don't have to sir me. I'm just a private citizen now."

"Yeah. Right, Carl." Milla sighed heavily. "I've learned so much from you guys. Don't know what I'll do when you go back home."

"Hey, I'm just a text message away," Sam said. "And if he's in a good mood, Carl might even give you his phone number."

"Well, if those lab results come back the way I think they will, I'm not sure how to present it to the chief. After all, I don't have a chain of evidence, I wasn't even the one to collect it, didn't have a warrant, and what if the attorney sells the car or junks it?"

"Got a point." Jake thought about that for a few seconds. "No matter how nice of a car it is, with all that damage, the attorney would be lucky to get ten grand for it."

Carl mulled over Jake's comment as he signed the bill and slipped his credit card back into his wallet. Then he slowly smiled and said, "Maybe someone will just have to buy it."

# 45

Milla was in the office early the next morning. Carl was sending the paint flakes by courier so the Science Unit would have it today and, hopefully, results by Monday. Course, if Carl had the influence she assumed he had, the results might be in by the end of the day. In the meantime, she wanted to be in the office when Mossy's call came in. It also would give her a chance to find out who would be an expert on pirate maps, although she would have to find a way to word it so as not to make people suspicious.

"Where is everyone?" Milla looked around at the empty desks and cubicles.

Tay Kyner, who usually worked weekends, was manning the reception desk. T.K., as he was affectionately known, was a strapping ex-college football player who blew out his knee in the last game of the playoffs. At the suggestion of the grandmother who raised him, he went into law enforcement, but a second knee operation side-lined him so he opted for desk duty rather than patrol.

"Taste of Heyward is going on. Most everyone is at the Town, checking wristbands, keeping the peace. Got a skeleton crew here, and ya got me." T.K.'s deep rumble of a laugh made Milla smile. T.K. was a family man with two twin daughters. Southern gentleman all the way so she knew there wasn't any harm in his flirtatious comments.

"I hope you aren't here alone."

"Nah. Two rookies are in the breakroom. They will be heading over to the substation after lunch." A call snared Tay's attention.

Milla checked her watch. It was too soon for Mossy to call so she headed to her desk and started searching through drawers. She grabbed the yellow page directory and looked up thrift shops, pawn shops, and any other business she thought might be a dumping ground for century-old memorabilia. Her mind also drifted to Jonah and how she was going to break it to him that his fiancée was killed, should the analysis of the paint flakes prove her theory. She heard Tay explaining to a caller why some streets had to be closed for the weekend's event. Her hunt was getting her nowhere. Tay finished the call and looked over to see what all of Milla's drawer slamming was about.

"Lose something?"

Milla studied him as she mentally categorized cities, pirates, centuries, and treasure. "You studied history in college, didn't you?"

"Uh, yeah. Didn't do too good, though. You know us jocks. We paid other students to do our homework." There was that rolling laugh again.

"Did your history professor cover anything about this area during the days of Blackbeard?"

"Pirates? No. Not that I remember. What are you looking for?"

Now Milla had to tap dance. "You know I have some pretty crazy relatives. One uncle bought a painting at a garage sale and took off the backing. He thinks he found some old map from Blackbeard or whatever pirates were around back then."

"You're going back to the 1700s. Blackbeard, Charles Vane, Stede Bonnet, god knows how many people have looked for their maps and buried treasure."

"Thought you didn't do well in History?"

"I sat in on a lecture one of the visiting retired professors gave. He talked about the Civil War and I recall he seemed to know a lot about the history of this region. Matter of fact, he opened an antiquities store in Old Town last year. If anyone knows the early years of the Carolinas, it's him. Webbing is his last name, if I remember correctly."

"Thanks." Milla jotted notes as another call came in. This time she knew it was Mossy by the way Tay was asking for details about a stolen heirloom.

Tay put the call on hold and turned to Milla. "Hey, want to take a ride over to talk to a lady who thinks someone stole a priceless heirloom? Her words not mine. Sounds like a sweet lady. Maybe just misplaced it."

"Sure. Give me the address."


Milla appeared at the screen door. "I'm sorry. I parked in the front. Guess you didn't hear me knock."

"It's a wonder anyone ever finds that dirt road," Mossy said. "Come pull up a chair."

"We're just waiting on Jonah," Carl said.

"Do wish I knew what all the fuss was about. It's just a pipedream my father had. His itch rubbed off on Jonah's father, may he rest in peace." Mossy started the swing moving as she focused on Sam who was still standing at the foot of the stairs.

Sam could swear she saw him again, the Indian boy she had seen the other day. The pull she was feeling had started the moment she climbed out of the Cadillac. The thrumming sounded as though the wind were playing a song through the leaves. And from the ground the rhythmic pulse appeared to keep pace. She moved to the corner of the house and stopped in front of a large blooming azalea. This was where the vibration was the strongest. She looked down at her feet. Nothing but grass. Then she saw him lurking around the corner. He smiled and a sudden thought came to Sam's mind. She said it in thought only. *We're close, aren't we?* The boy nodded. Now all Sam had to figure out was what exactly she was close to. Then he did it again, stretched out his right hand displaying a shiny coin. With his left hand he pointed over her shoulder. "Are you pointing at the carriage house?" She turned back to the boy. He was gone. She slowly climbed the stairs, continuing to glance at the azalea.

"You see him, too, don't you?" Mossy asked.

"See who?" Jonah asked as he climbed the stairs behind Sam.

"You know about him, Mossy?" Sam wondered how someone with failing eyesight could see so clearly.

"Here we go again," Carl scoffed.

"A boy, about five years old. Native American. He's a Yamassee." Sam wasn't surprised to see the skepticism on Jonah's face.

"I don't see anyone," Milla admitted, "but I feel something. An energy, a tingling. And unless that's an Encore Azalea, it shouldn't be blooming in July."

"That plant blooms twelve months out of the year. It's the damndest thing."

"But you have seen him, Mossy?" Sam asked again.

"Fleeting, out of the corner of my eye. It appears, though, that he is revealing more to you."

"You're at it again, Mom?" Jonah shook his head with a smile. "She's been telling me about a little boy for years. As long as he stays outside and doesn't roam over to the rectory where the visiting clergy stay, I'm fine. Course, I wouldn't want him floating over my bed at night either. Now, what's so important?" Jonah sat down on the loveseat next to Mossy and was soon joined on the porch with the rest of Mossy's guests. Sam and Milla each claimed an Adirondack chair. And although there were additional chairs on the other side of the porch, Carl and Jake preferred to lean against the railing.

Sam pulled out her phone and brought out the photo she had taken the first day. She handed the phone to Jonah. "Does that look like your mom and I are ready to be committed?"

Jonah grabbed her phone and stared at the translucent image of a dark haired, dark skinned boy. "You sure it isn't a shadow from something else?"

Milla leaned over his shoulder and stifled a gasp. "Doesn't look like a shadow to me."

"We wanted to talk about the map Mossy mentioned was missing," Carl explained. "We believe Angela stole it and that's why she was killed." He pulled the map from his pocket and unfolded it. "Was this the map that was in the scrapbook?"

Mossy turned her head to view the map better. "Yes, yes. Where on earth did you find it?"

Carl handed it to Jonah. "That's the map we kept in the scrapbook."

"Angela hid it in my car. I think this might have been what her ex-boyfriend and his brother were after. She must have told someone about it and then the Goodwin brothers found out. So why don't you tell us why this map is so valuable?"

Jonah and Mossy exchanged glances. When Mossy nodded, Jonah said, "It's a map to a pirate chest of gold coins."

# 46

"Pirate gold? Wow!" Milla studied the map. "Wish I knew my pirates better."

"Wish I could read the damn map." Carl snapped a gaze at Jonah. "Sorry, Pastor."

"No problem. I'm right there with you. We've never been able to make heads or tails of it and thought our ancestor was spinning a wild tale. But someone must think there's some truth to this."

"Pirates raided Spanish ships," Jake said. "That's where the gold was."

"That can't be right," Sam said. "All I know is the boy I see is from the Civil War era. Not the pirate era. That's about a century or more apart. Why would he be hanging around if he isn't part of this mystery?"

Carl shook his head. "Doesn't mean the gold wasn't discovered in the 1800s, Sam."

"Actually, our ancestor was a bit of the black sheep of the family," Mossy explained. "Word is he sold his son to the Confederate soldiers and then took off with the gold and hid it somewhere. When the Union soldiers were planning to burn the town, he sent his wife, daughter, and infant son to Florida. He gave her the map for safekeeping. It's been passed down ever since."

"So he found the chest of gold." Milla poured a glass of iced tea from the pitcher on the coffee table. "Had to weigh too much for one man to carry."

Sam asked, "I take it your ancestor never joined his wife in Florida?"

"She probably wouldn't have him, not if he sold his other son as a slave to the Confederate soldiers." Jonah accepted a glass of iced tea from Milla.

Sam thought back to the coin the young boy had showed her. It wasn't gold and nothing about it screamed Spanish. And if the father had sold the boy, why was she still seeing him in Heyward Bluff? Wouldn't his spirit be wherever he died?

"What are you thinking, hon?"

Jake's question shook Sam out of the thoughts swirling in her head. "That we're out of our element."

"I found an antiquities store in Old Town," Milla said. "Maybe we should show him the map, if that's okay with you."

"What do you think?" Mossy asked her son.

"Someone must think it's worth killing over. One person is already dead."

"Actually, four, if you count the Goodwin brothers," Milla said.

"I thought the news said they took a wrong turn in the dark," Mossy said.

"Wait." Jonah looked at Milla. "That would be three. Who's the fourth?"

Milla looked away and caught Carl's eye. Carl said, "I haven't heard anything yet. Doesn't hurt to show him the picture."

Milla pulled the photo from her purse. "Jonah, you said you hired Angela about six months ago."

"That's right."

"And your fiancée died in a car accident around eight months ago."

This time Jonah didn't say anything. He just looked puzzled.

"To your knowledge, did Angela and Nicole know each

other?"

"I would have known if they had. What are you getting at?"

"So Angela just happened to see you at the church and overheard you saying you were looking for a home companion."

Jonah leaned forward and placed his glass on the coffee table. "Is this headed somewhere?"

Milla handed him the photo of Angela and Nicole. Jonah studied it, his face a mask of confusion.

"What does the picture show, Jonah?" Mossy couldn't make out the details.

"It's a picture of Angela and Nicole together, which doesn't make sense. Nicole never mentioned meeting Angela and Angela never mentioned knowing Nicole."

"May as well lay out all the facts," Jake said. "Even though we don't have confirmation from the lab yet."

"Lab?" Jonah looked even more confused than before. "What's this about?"

So they did. Jake explained how Milla found photos in Angela's house when she was returning the photos she had borrowed. Then she found the car in the garage, and he and Sam had taken paint flakes to have analyzed.

"No, no, no." Jonah kept shaking his head. "This is all wrong. You'll see. Nicole didn't own the only red Prius on the planet."

"But she did know Angela," Sam said. "Did Nicole know about the map?"

Jonah washed his hands over his face. "Yes, I told her. We had a good laugh about it. That's it."

"She might have casually mentioned it to Angela. Maybe Angela wanted her to steal it and she refused, or Nicole was going to forewarn you and they thought she was a threat," Carl said.

"You keep saying *they*. Who are they?" Mossy asked.

"Obviously, someone other than her ex-boyfriend and his brother. If their deaths weren't an accident, then we have other players here so you two are still in danger. We already made a copy of the map. I would suggest you keep yours in a safety deposit box. Don't keep it in your house," Carl said.

Mossy handed it to Carl. "You keep it. We don't have a safety deposit box and I doubt anyone would steal anything from you."

"Are you okay with that?" Carl asked Jonah.

"Sure." Jonah took another look at Nicole's picture, how happy she appeared. How long had she known Angela? Why hadn't she said anything? What else didn't he know about his fiancée? He stood and thanked them for coming. "Not quite the information I cared to hear, but thank you for sharing it with me. I need to attend to things back at the church."

They watched him descend the stairs and make his way around to the church.

Sam asked Mossy, "Were you and Nicole close?"

Mossy shook her head. "Not really. Women tend to be closer to their own families and men closer to their own. She came from a good family, and I think she truly loved my Jonah. If you want to know if she confided in me, no. She didn't. She was what you call high-maintenance. Was already picking out a house in Palmetto Bluff, as though Jonah could afford that. She said her daddy was going to buy it as a wedding gift. That was probably the only serious fight the two had. Jonah would never let her parents buy them a house, especially one in Palmetto Bluff. But Jonah loved her, or so I thought."

"What do you mean?" Milla blurted out the words faster than necessary.

"He was in love with the idea of being in love. He wasn't expecting a spouse who would teach Sunday school and plan retreats with him. The church is his thing. A wife could have her thing. Besides the house, she wanted Jonah to take a job at her father's firm, said he could make more money. Nicole had a ten thousand dollar engagement ring picked out. Jonah told her he couldn't afford it and wouldn't buy it. They were actually engaged in name only because he hadn't purchased a ring yet. Jonah became disillusioned each day. Nicole loved money so, forgive me for saying so, but I wouldn't doubt for a minute that she was taken in by that whole story about a pirate chest of gold."

# 47

"Thanks for coming with me. There are so many tentacles to this case, I feel like I'm out of my element. I'm sure the chief won't like my involving you; and I hope I don't give you the impression I'm as dumb as a bag of boiled peanuts."

"Not at all, Milla. Each case makes me feel the same way until all the pieces start falling into place." Sam had agreed to accompany Milla to the antiquities store. She was just about shopped out and her curiosity about the boy and the history of pirate gold was intriguing. "Have to tell you, we have never had a case like this in Chasen Heights, at least nothing involving pirate treasure." Sam smiled as she thought back to when she had met Jake. "We once had a case of a semi hitting the side of an overpass. All this concrete crumbled revealing mummified remains."

"A mummy? A real mummy?"

"Perfectly preserved, and that's usually when I can hear the dead more clearly. If the person just dies, or in the case of the mummy, it was as though he had just died. The accident released his aura." Sam laughed remembering Jake's incredulity. "Jake and his partner, the look on their faces was priceless. Course, they thought I was nuts."

"What exactly did the mummy say? I mean, he didn't actually speak."

Sam shook his head. "Just words would echo in my head, clues, like with Angela. I keep hearing the word Montana. Does that mean anything to you?"

"No. The Goodwin brothers and Angela are from Kentucky. Is

that why you think they weren't working alone?"

"That and my gut."

They had walked from Mossy's house after checking the location of Old Town Antiquities on Sam's phone. The building looked like a renovated gas station. It sat on a corner lot several blocks from the Church on the Bluff.

"How do you plan to play this?" It was Milla's case, so Sam was going to let her decide.

"I don't want to show him the map yet. I want to see how knowledgeable he is about pirate treasure. He might even remember others who have picked his brain about the same subject."

They entered the shop and immediately detected a certain mustiness blended with metallic and acidic odors. The concrete floor was surprisingly clean as were the surfaces of the glass and wood surfaces. It was obvious the owner took great care of his collection.

A suit of armor stood watch near a glass display which claimed to contain items from the Titanic. Other glass cases contained axes, arrowheads, old muskets, and bearskin. Native American war shirts and buckskin dresses hung on one wall. An Egyptian headdress of blue and gold lame was on the head of a mannequin displayed on a corner podium. Bookcases had locked glass doors, and a glass case of elaborate jewelry was also under lock and key.

Luckily, they were the only shoppers since it was early. It will be easier to question the owner without a hoard of tourists interrupting them. Sam stopped in front of the case with Native American jewelry. "My mom's squash necklace looks similar to that one."

Milla studied the silver necklace of coral and turquoise.

"Exquisite. Do you have one like it?"

"Similar, but Mom's is more elaborate."

"You're Native?" The shop owner peered over his bifocals at Sam. "Coulda fooled me. Curly blonde hair, blue eyes?"

"That's my dad's side of the family. Mom is one hundred percent Sioux."

The gray-haired owner straighten and pulled off his glasses. Clean-shaven, crisp white shirt, hair short, and sporting a gold earring in his right ear, he resembled a jeweler rather than an antique shop owner, much less a former professor. His gaze appeared to linger over each of their faces, as though he recognized them but not sure from where. "Really? South Dakota?"

"Yes. Eagle Ridge Reservation."

"You live there?"

"No. We live in a suburb south of Chicago. We try to make it up there at least once a year, although Mom goes whenever there is a Council meeting she wants to attend."

"How rude of me. Dover Webbing at your service. I own this nostalgic emporium." His eyes drifted to Sam's chest. "Don't suppose you'd like to sell that medicine bundle you're wearing."

"Not a chance. I've had it since birth."

Milla located a glass case in the corner filled with, what looked like, log books along with goblets, a tattered skull and crossbone flag, candles, tarnished kettles, coins that were too worn to identify, some knives, and a sword.

"Can I help you ladies find anything special?"

"I thought pirates used large curved swords?" Milla pointed at the single blade sword.

"That's a cutlass. Very popular with pirates. Could cut through just about anything." He gave a little chuckle. "I don't think you ladies would be looking for weapons."

Sam joined Milla at the display case. "What about an old pirate chest? Would be a nice conversation piece for your living room, Milla."

"Only if it were filled with gold."

Webbing chuckled again. "Purely folklore. Most bounty confiscated by pirates consisted of food, medicine, liquor, kettles, stuff you see in that case."

"Who you'all trying to kid?" Milla said with a laugh. "I'm from Savannah. I've heard all kinds of pirate stories growing up."

"And that's all they are, little lady…stories."

"What about the Central America, the ship that sank during a hurricane in 1857? Wasn't there something like $150 million in gold, in today's dollar?"

Sam slid her gaze to Milla. Had she been doing some research on her own? Smart girl.

"Sure, and close to forty insurance companies claimed a right to it. It was all recovered. Treasure hunters and divers have been looking for all kinds of wrecks off the coast." He rubbed his chin as he leaned his elbows on the glass case of pirate memorabilia. He eyed the two women curiously, although Sam thought it bordered on suspicion.

"What about that French shipwreck from the sixteenth century that was in the papers recently?"

"The Le Prince. Last I heard, they were still searching. The waters off the coast have a number of vessels from the Civil War. Some were sunk on purpose as the Union Navy tried to block supplies from being delivered to the Confederate states. But as far as pirate ships? Nah."

Milla wondered if the professor was being purposely evasive.

"And the Queen Anne's Revenge, Blackbeard's ship?"

Webbing grinned. "Once a professor, always a professor. Just testing you. Yes. It got caught in a sandbar off of the North Carolina coast."

Sam half-listened as she walked over to a wall where several Civil War uniforms were displayed. The exhibit case in front of it contained Civil War collectables. There was a crudely drawn map of Heyward Bluff along with buttons from Union and Confederate soldier uniforms and strange-looking bullets that were labeled Minie balls. Sam still thought the young Yamassee boy figured into it somehow. Had the treasure map been handed down for a century before Mossy's ancestor found it? How could a paper not have disintegrated after so many years? Or had Mossy's ancestor redrawn the map so it wouldn't get lost?

"No treasure?"

"Cannons and other artifacts, no pirate chest of gold and silver, if that's what you're asking. Now if you want to talk treasure, the San Jose was found in the Caribbean a couple years ago. It was a Spanish galleon carrying close to $17 billion in gold, silver, and emeralds. Again, that was in the early 1700's."

"But it wasn't a pirate ship."

"No, little lady."

Milla pointed to a map that was laid out like a scroll under one of the swords. " Has anyone ever tried to decipher the treasure maps you have here?"

Sam studied the bookcases against a side wall. One of the bookcases had several shelves of books on the Civil War as well as a number of framed newspaper articles on recent reenactments. She could swear one man on crutches in the photo was Gordon Douglas. The article was dated four years ago. The photographer caught a side view of another man, also with a camera, but he wasn't dressed for the reenactment. The man was Dover Webbing.

"You're involved in Civil War Reenactments?" Sam asked.

"Used to be. Don't have much time now." He showed the back of his hand, displaying a ring on his finger. "It's one of the Confederate buttons I made into a ring. The button was from my great-great-grandfather's uniform. Much of the memorabilia in the exhibit case has been in my family for decades."

Sam caught Milla's eye. It was time to show their cards.

"You seem pretty knowledgeable, Mister Webbing." Milla reached into her pocket, pulled out the map, and unfolded it on the counter top. "Do you have any idea what this means?"

Webbing put his bifocals on and studied the crude drawing. "Where did you get this?"

"I was cleaning out a relative's bookcase after she passed. It was between the pages of an old scrapbook. I didn't want to toss it until I found someone who might be able to decipher it."

Sam thought the shop owner did a superb job of hiding his shock. She could swear he had seen the map before.

"Please, don't tell me this is one of hundreds sold in Savannah in souvenir shops," Milla said. "That would kill the thrill of finding an authentic treasure map."

Webbing carefully rotated the map. "It certainly looks like X marks the spot. Hard to tell how far off the coast a ship sank, that is…" Webbing cleared his throat, "…assuming it is a shipwreck." He carefully turned the map over. "No date so it's hard to tell what era it refers to."

"That was my problem, too."

"It actually looks like an unfinished replica. Not enough information on it. It's as though the person who drew it was interrupted. Are you sure there isn't a piece missing?" He carefully pushed the map back to Milla, then pulled out his cell phone.

The front door opened and two women walked in carrying bags from one of the neighboring stores.

"I'll be right with you ladies." When they said "no hurry," Webbing returned to the map. "Do you mind?" he asked Milla. "I'd like to take a picture of it and show it to some colleagues."

Milla hesitated, but Sam quickly said, "Sure." Webbing took a picture as Sam wrote her phone number on the back of one of his business cards. He checked the picture he had taken. Satisfied that it was adequate, he placed his phone on the counter. "Give us a call if you find out anything. The realtor wants the home emptied within a week so everything goes." She smiled as she handed him the card. "Thank you for your time."

"Okay, what was all that about?" Milla asked as they left the shop.

"That framed article from the reenactment that Webbing was in? Gordon Douglas was in it, too. They knew each other."


Dover Webbing parted the drape separating the store from the backroom. "Did you catch that?"

"They have the map. The blonde was the one interested in the carriage house property. The other is the cop who was in Angela's house. The damn map must have been in there all along."

"Follow them. See where they are headed."

Dover watched as his nephew exited the back door.

# 48

"People are big on reenactments down here, Sam. And you heard Webbing. His ancestor fought in the Civil War. I'm not sure I'd read that much into it." No matter how much Milla wanted it to be true, she, too, wasn't convinced. She pulled into the circle drive and parked near the front steps. Carl and Jake were sitting on the porch.

"I believe Carl is liking his new landscape. He has started spending more time on the front porch. I think he's becoming a girly man. Pretty soon, he'll be buying pruning shears and knee pads."

"I heard that, Sam. Fat chance. Jon's crew will be maintaining the plants."

"She's right, Mister Underer. It looks great."

"No *Mister* and I don't want to remind you."

"Yes, sir."

"Hell, no *sir*, either, dammit!"

Milla couldn't help it. She had never met nor worked alongside a former FBI agent let alone the former director.

"Come up out of the heat." Carl held the door open for them.

"I take it no word from Quantico?" Sam asked.

"They promised they'd have results tomorrow."

"What about the Bel Air?" Milla asked.

"I bought it," Carl said with a grin. "Had it towed to a temperature-controlled storage facility off of the Parkway. Have a friend who knows a friend who knows your Forensics expert, Betty Murphy."

"Of course you do." Milla filled a glass with iced tea and took a seat on one of the white rockers.

"Anyway, she came to the storage place and picked the car over with a fine tooth comb. Gordon Douglas was already deceased so he couldn't have driven the car. And I just don't see Angela running someone off the road. I'm not sure Betty will find their DNA in the car after it's been submerged. I'll keep my fingers crossed."

Sam poured herself a glass of tea, then sat on the love seat next to Jake. "You two look like matching bookends in your shorts and floral shirts. My honey is getting into this island life." She gave Jake a kiss on the cheek.

"This isn't an island, sweetheart. You have to go over the bridge."

"Close enough."

"So spill it. What did you find out?"

"Always impatient, Carl." Sam told the men about Dover Webbing and the antiquities shop. "He seemed pretty knowledgeable about shipwrecks, but the curious item was the photo of him with Gordon Douglas at a civil war reenactment. I didn't want to ask him how he knew Gordon. It might have tipped our hand."

"When we showed him the map, it seemed like he dismissed it too quickly," Milla commented. "Certainly didn't stop him from taking a picture of it, though."

"Interesting." Jake wondered exactly how the shop owner fit in. "Have you ever heard of this guy, Milla?"

Milla shook her head. "I'll run him through our database. His great-great-grandfather fought in the Civil War. It would really be strange if he knew Jonah's ancestor."

"Stay for dinner?" Sam asked Milla.

She shook her head. "I need to type up a case report on the theft I was called out on. It's a very important case," she added with a smile. Then her smile slowly faded. "I think I'm eventually going to have to clue in the chief and Phil."

Dover Webbing studied the map he had printed off of his phone. It was the same one Angela had shown them. Still vague, very few details. Why had Angela been so coy about knowing more?

The shop had been closed for hours. Now they had the luxury of time. The police found Angela's killer and the demise of the Goodwin boys had been ruled an accidental drowning.

He took out his key, unlocked the floor safe, and brought out a copy of the letter from Anchor Webbing. The original had been too fragile to handle.

The cop, what was her name? Milla. She and her friend had left the shop and walked to their car parked at the church. Then the young pastor came out and talked to them. Why?

He studied Anchor Webbing's notes again. Why did he mention 140 paces? 140 paces from where? One thing was certain—they were just as much in the dark as he was. But that was going to change.

# *49*

"How your weather?" Sam could see the sky through the patio doors behind Abby.

"Warm, blue sky. Typical Chicago summer. How about you? Still humid?"

"Can't you tell by my hair?" Sam touched the tangle of curls that fell past her shoulders. "Can't wait to jump in the shower so I can put a ton of moisturizer on this mop."

"How is the case going?" Alex's voice was somewhere in the background. He appeared behind Abby holding Dillon against his hip like a sack of potatoes. He set him down and Dillon ran for the patio doors, no longer interested in the computer monitor nor seeing Sam's face.

Sam filled them in on how one murder and the drugging of Carl now morphed into four dead bodies and a treasure map.

"You attract trouble, Sam," Alex quipped.

"Are the spirits helping?"

"Not quite, Mom. Other than the Yamassee boy and the word, Montana, I'm basically useless down here. Mossy Belden did tell me a little about her ancestors. The story passed down was that her ancestor sold his son into slavery and took off with some kind of buried treasure he had found. He sent a drawing of its location to his wife who had fled south before the town was burned down.

"Do you think it's pirate gold?" Alex took a seat next to Abby at the kitchen table while keeping one eye on Dillon.

"Not according to an antiquities shop owner and expert on just about anything pirate as well as Civil War. He said pirates rarely found gold and were mainly after food, medicine, liquor, kettles, you name it."

Alex asked, "You couldn't see any details on the coin?"

"A date of 1861 which is why I know it isn't part of some treasure chest from the 1700s. Did you look up those words, Alex?"

"Yes. It either means *can you help* or *we are here*. It was difficult to find an authentic translation from the Apalachee language so I also looked up Choctaw. Take your pick."

"You may have to stay there another week." Abby turned around to see what Dillon was into. He was trying to open the door.

"I hope not. We need to give ourselves three days to drive home. I'm sure Jake can do it in two the way he drives, but I hate to sit that long. What are you guys doing on this beautiful day?"

"Alex and I are taking Dillon to the carnival at the park. I'm going to pack a picnic basket."

"How fun. I'm going to do some computer research while Carl waits on a report from Quantico and the county forensics lab. Then I'll talk the guys into taking me to lunch at the Skull Creek Boathouse.

"Good luck with that."

"Never underestimate me, Alex." Sam was sure they weren't going to be in Heyward Bluff for another week and wanted to buy Milla a gift. "Hey, Alex, do you still have that necklace you made with obsidian?"

"The snowflake obsidian? Which one?"

"Both. You have an arrowhead with black onyx stone on a chain and you have another with an amulet about the size of a dime with an obsidian stone in the middle and two sterling silver feathers. I think the chain on both is sterling silver, right?"

"Those are some of my most expensive pieces."

"Which is why they haven't sold," Abby reminded him.

"You can give me the family discount."

"I'm not family," Alex reminded her.

"Well, you are practically family. You've lived with us long enough. I'll pay you. I just need them shipped today. Your post office has that do-it-yourself machine in the lobby, right?"

"I suppose you want them in boxes."

"Of course."

Dillon climbed onto Abby's lap and waved at Sam's image on the monitor. He babbled and attempted to bang on the keys. "Guess it's time to sign off." Abby grabbed Dillon's chubby hands. "He's getting antsy. We'll get those in the mail today."

"Thanks. We'll talk soon. Jake and Carl say hi. Love and kisses."

Sam clicked out of Skype and sat back. Somewhere in the house she heard a cell phone ring. Carl emerged from the kitchen, cell phone pressed to his ear. Jake was on the deck, a cell phone pressed to his ear. She tailed Carl onto the back deck.

The two men hung up at the same time. "Please tell me you two weren't talking to each other."

"Sure. Isn't that what you women do?"

"Hardly, Carl. Did you hear any results?"

"Yes. The paint flakes are a match to the color used in the 2016 Prius. Whether it was Nicole DuMorney's car, we will never know. According to Betty Murphy, once the case was determined an accident, the car was sent to be recycled then crushed at a facility near Charleston."

"What about DNA?" Sam asked.

"She swabbed the steering wheel, gear shift, and door handle for touch DNA," Jake said. "It's a long shot since it's been almost a year since anyone drove the car. And it would be a gift to any defense attorney since it could be argued that just because someone drove the car doesn't mean they were the person who was the last to drive it."

"We shed hundreds of thousands of skin cells every damn day. Think of that next time you don't feel like dusting." Carl laughed when he saw Sam's reaction. "I'm only saying."

"Thanks. I needed that image in my mind."

"The killer doesn't have to know we can't prove he was the person driving. He just has to think we can get results." Jake was a master at having a poker face. Sam had seen firsthand how Jake could make a case with very little evidence. The suspect never saw it coming.

"Why don't you call Milla, Sam, and tell her the results from Quantico. We can let her break it to the pastor. Until we get a confession from the killer, ask him not to tell the parents. Milla can do that after she has a confession."

# 50

Milla entered the church, hearing music even before crossing the threshold. The song coming from the choir loft was beautiful... *Halleluiah* by Leonard Cohen. It was her mother's favorite. Rather than an organ, whoever was singing was accompanied by a piano. She was probably walking in on a choir rehearsal.

The sun's rays struck the stained glass windows spreading a kaleidoscope of colors across the pews. Milla found the stairs to the loft in the vestibule. She climbed the stairs as quietly as possible, which was difficult since the old wood was creaking under her feet. When she reached the top she saw Jonah at the keyboard, his back to her. There wasn't anyone else in the loft.

She wasn't sure if it was the song that filled her with such immense reverence or the magnificent beauty of the church. She didn't want to move, wanted to hear every lyric. And when the music and singing finally ended, she wanted him to play it again.

Jonah pushed away from the piano and stood. Maybe it was the look on Milla's face that made him stop.

"That was absolutely beautiful."

"Thanks." He lowered himself onto the piano bench as Milla sat on a chair facing him. "You heard back, didn't you?"

"I'm sorry, yes. All they can prove is that the paint flakes are from a 2016 Prius. Without Nicole's Prius to check if paint flakes on her car match what was found on the Bel Air, we don't have concrete proof. We will, though, once we get a confession."

Jonah nodded. He leaned forward, elbows on his knees, hands prayer style tapping his chin. "It's odd. I don't feel anything. Not sorrow, pain, anger. I'm not even numb." He looked across at Milla. "I don't even care if all of my questions are answered. What was she planning? Why was she so secretive? She had more in her life than most people, why be so greedy?" He washed his hands over his face and chuckled. "Nicole must have picked the stupidest love-sick man alive."

"At least you weren't left at the altar."

Jonah raised his head and studied Milla's face. "No. You? Who would ever leave you standing at the altar?"

Milla felt her face flush. "Didn't know he and one of my bridesmaids had been seeing each other for months. He used my credit card to buy her a ring. Found out later he used our honeymoon tickets and took his girlfriend on the cruise that was meant for us." It still stung as Milla could hear the venom in her words. She sighed and shrugged. "Just as well. He might have pushed me overboard."

"He was a fool." Jonah's gaze dropped to his hands where he had been kneading them. "Is that why you have so little furniture in your house? Ready to pick up and move the next time your heart gets broken?"

Milla stared at him. Was that really why she had so few furnishings? She had always told herself it was because she was waiting for an offer from a larger police department, a city where there was more action. So why have too many belongings to move? She shook her head. "You do too good a job of reading people, Jonah."

"Oh, I don't know about that. Detectives do a pretty good job at that, too."

"Not really. If I were a hard-ass like the guy I am supposed to be partnered up with, I'd be treating you like a suspect in Nicole's murder. I would be suggesting that you found out about Nicole and her deception. You and Angela plotted her death. You may have been the one driving the Bel Air; and when Angela double-crossed you, maybe promising her ex she'd split this phantom treasure with him, you were the one to kill Angela."

The silence in the choir loft was intense. "Wow." The pastor whooshed out a long breath. "Guess the question is, why haven't you slapped the cuffs on me?"

Milla cocked her head as though sizing him up, then crater-like dimples formed as she smiled. "Gut instincts. I've met your mom and I don't think she could possibly raise a killer. You have a kind face; and that voice of yours is mesmerizing. I just have one request."

"Uh, give you an alibi for the night Angela was killed?"

"No. I want to hear that song again."

Phil paced from one end of his deck to the other, then back inside the condo to the laptop on the corner desk. His condo was near the county administration office building in an upscale complex. His ex-wife had taken him to the proverbial cleaners, claiming the house, the car, and the summer home in the Hamptons. Phil kept the trust fund from his parents which was quite sizeable. Everything that his ex kept would keep her and their son comfortable for the rest of their lives, provided she invested wisely. Since she made sure he would never have visitation rights, he made sure in the divorce decree that she would never get another dime from him.

Back to the deck. Phil stood and looked out over the construction across the street which forced him to keep his screen door closed. Nothing like a good wind to coat the deck with a film of dirt. He looked back over his shoulder to the corner desk as if willing the laptop to tell him something.

In an attempt to make a quick name for himself, he had a feeling he had jumped the gun. The two hicks from Kentucky might have been clumsy, but they weren't stupid, not by any means. Tyler, the brother who hadn't been incarcerated, had lived in Heyward Bluff long enough to know his way around. Phil doubted he would be so stupid as to let Travis take a wrong turn and drive into a lagoon. Those damn *what if* questions were nagging him. What if the lagoon had been a meeting place? What if that meeting went sideways? Tyler had killed Angela Douglas. The forensics proved it was his hands around the victim's neck. If Travis had been that pissed off at her for framing him and sending him to prison, Travis would have been the one to bestow the final blow. If Travis was so jealous of any man Angela had ever been with, why only drug John Doe? Why not kill him, too? What if the Goodwin brothers weren't responsible for the drugging?

Phil knew he wasn't well liked in the department. He was a hardass...check. He felt superior...check. He didn't care what people thought of him...check. He felt bad for what had happened in Miami. What wasn't in the report or on his record was that he had punched out the police commissioner. Not because Brice Nolan fired him or spread lies about Pam Nolan refusing to get a divorce or any other multitude of lies. It was because he had pictures of the injuries Pam had sustained at the hands of her abusive husband. Brice made sure she never went to the hospital so there wasn't a record. Yes, Pam had gone into the suspect's house first. Phil tried to pull her back because he knew Pam Nolan was on a suicide mission. She had never drawn her gun. Was Phil bitter? Hell, yes. Nolan had the mayor and the press in his hip pocket. They had skewered him on the front pages, quoting just enough to leave doubts in everyone's mind, including his own wife. And when Phil went to retrieve the photos of the injuries from a locked drawer in his home office, someone had taken them. Phil's wife had let Brice Nolan search his desk, anything to punish him. And Brice was going to let everyone think that Phil had been the one to pound all those bruises onto Pam. So yes, he was bitter. Brice Nolan had him between a rock and the proverbial hard place.

The last thing he needed was to get on the wrong side of this investigation. "Oh, hell." He slammed the door shut, then returned to the desk to re-read the autopsy and crime scene reports for the tenth time.

# 51

"You're up early." Carl pointed at the coffee pot on the warmer sitting on the bar. He was seated on the deck catching the first hint of a sunrise.

Jake poured two cups of coffee and set them both on the table before taking a seat.

"Looks like you stuck your finger in a light socket."

Sam raked fingers through the knots of curls. "Thank you for the compliment."

"What on earth bird makes all that racket at night? I could barely sleep." Jake seemed to inhale his coffee.

"That's a whip-poor-will. Known for its song which almost sounds like its name. A male will stake out its territory and call for a mate. I think the one we hear has claimed the lot next door. They are becoming rare these days."

"No wonder." Jake rubbed the sleep from his eyes. "People have probably shot them."

"Nice, Jake. Mom would have you tarred and feathered. They are a sign of death in Native American lore, you know." Sam doctored her coffee with cream and sugar.

"She's right. The singing is a death omen, according to some." Although Jake and Sam had thrown on gym shorts and tops and brushed their teeth, Carl looked as though he had already showered and was headed to the office in long pants and a dress shirt. Does this man never sleep?

"The sound is comforting in a way," Sam said. "Guess it gets to be white noise, like those wind chimes in the corner of the front porch."

"Those are as ceaseless as that damn bird," Jake grumbled.

"As I said, their numbers are dwindling." Carl brought over the coffee pot and filled everyone's cup. "They like to nest on the ground which makes them snacks for cats, alligators, coyote, you name it."

"Guess they haven't learned to make a nest in the tree. Anything that dumb deserves extinction."

"Nice, sweetheart. You are spending way too much time with Carl."

"Quiet, and watch the beauty of the sunrise," Carl ordered.

And so they did. The dark purple and blue of the horizon was turning to lavender and rose. If one doubted that the earth was spinning, one only needed to see the sun as it slowly crept into view.

"I never get tired of watching the sunrise and sunset." Carl did something they had never heard him do…he sighed.

So they sat quietly, sipping their coffee, and watching the wonders of nature as if any sound might halt the transformation. The mystery of the case could wait for another half hour.

Milla decided today would be the day. She had had a long talk with Hoodoo who had tap danced around the living room as though she understood everything Milla had said and was thrilled with her decision. Milla still felt Hoodoo was just a cat, but there wasn't any harm in letting Hoodoo think she wasn't. Course, the young detective disregarded the fact that Hoodoo had tap danced on a book on the *Burning of Heyward Bluff* the little brat had knocked off of the coffee table, a book Milla had checked out of the library on Friday.

When she entered the precinct she saw the chief returning from the breakroom, cup of coffee in hand. He arrived near Phil's desk just as Milla approached. "A minute of your time, Chief Ray, in your office." Then she turned to Phil. "You may as well join us. It's time we came clean."

Phil looked puzzled. Lucky for Milla, he closed his gaping mouth.

"Okay." The chief closed the door and then sat behind his desk. He looked from Phil to Milla. "What do you need to come clean about?"

"The statement to the press which Phil gave was a ruse." Milla held up her hand to silence Phil. "I know you wanted to tell the chief, but that's on me. We have four deaths now, Chief. I felt as long as the real killer thought the case was closed, he wouldn't leave town, and that would buy us more time." She saw Phil start to open his mouth again, but she silenced him with a stern look.

"Four?" McComb parroted.

"Travis and Tyler weren't working alone. Yes, Tyler killed Angela, but their vehicle did not fly into that lagoon on its own four wheels. Someone pushed it."

"And how could someone take two strong guys on their own?"

"They were drugged, probably with the same drug that was used on Angela," Phil said, now realizing what had been eating at him. Because it was assumed the two men took a wrong turn and ended up in the lagoon, a drug test was never completed. "There's a new guy at the M.E.'s office. I was going to tell him I wanted a tox screen done, but with everything that's been happening, it completely escaped me."

Chief Ray slid his gaze from Phil to Milla, still not convinced.

"When I went to return the photos to the Douglas house, a realtor arrived and the attorney got involved with him. I walked through the wrong door and ended up in the garage."

"The wrong door? You mean you didn't remember where the front door was?" The chief was beginning to look amused, or was it irritation?

Milla hurried on. "The garage was spotless, as though Angela couldn't wait to get rid of everything that the old man, I mean her husband, owned. Except for one item. A tarp covered a 1957 Chevy Bel-Air. It was pristine, until I lifted the tarp. The entire right side was damaged." Milla turned to Phil. "This is what I haven't had time to update you on. So my apologies." She turned back to the chief. She then filled him in on the theft call she took on Friday regarding a prized heirloom that had been stolen from Mossy Belden's house."

"Wait. You mean the same Mossy Belden who Angela Douglas had been assisting?" The chief was having a hard time keeping things straight. The two men sat dumbfounded as she mentioned Jonah Belden and his fiancée and how Milla had seen a photo of Nicole with Angela.

"Whoa, wait, Milla. Jesus, you are rambling." The chief pressed his hands to his head. "Something tells me the Chasen Heights constituents have their bloody fingerprints all over this. How did you get paint chips off the Bel Air sent for testing without me knowing it? And that would have taken ages."

"Mister Underer sent them to Quantico."

"Of course." McComb plopped his elbows onto the desk and pressed a fist to his chin. "Is there anything else I should know?"

"Well, we still have to figure out the treasure map."

"Treasure map?" The two men said in unison. McComb

turned to his star detective. "You didn't know any of this, did you?"

Phil tossed a sideways glance at Milla. Was that irritation or amazement on his face?

"Phil's been so busy," Milla started, "that I didn't want to toss my out-of-the-realm of possibilities suspicions at him. And besides, I knew you both would be upset if you knew Sam and the guys were still involved."

"God, is it too early to retire?" McComb whispered. "I need everything typed up and on my desk. Details, I want details and a timeline."

"I already sent it to both of your computers."

This time Phil actually smiled.

# 52

Jake kissed the top of Sam's head, her hair still damp from the shower. "Find anything useful?"

Sam had been searching the Internet for information on Dover Webbing. "His ancestors go all the way back to the Civil War. No wonder he was so knowledgeable about the War. He even has a Facebook page."

"Is he from Montana by any chance?" Jake asked.

"No. That was the first thing I checked. His one ancestor, Anchor Webbing, was a Lieutenant Colonel and the right hand man to Jefferson Davis, the President of the Confederate States of America during the Civil War."

"Everything keeps coming back to the Civil War."

"You noticed that, too." Sam scrolled though another site as Jake leaned over her shoulder. "Says here that Anchor Webbing accompanied Davis when he travelled to his southern Confederate Headquarters on Hilton Head Island on a plantation known as Coggins Plantation. It was owned by a William Pope who also had that carriage house across the street from the Church on the Bluff. You remember the church docent filled me in on that property." Sam continued scrolling then stopped when she saw a grainy picture of President Davis and Anchor Webbing. In the background was a plantation house with a dark-skinned man and boy standing at the foot of the stairs like foot soldiers. The caption said they were servants and gave the names of B. Hashi and L. Hashi. The images were too far in the background for Sam to make out the details, but her thoughts returned to the little boy she had seen by Mossy's house.

"I hear your gears moving, Sam."

She turned her head just as his lips found hers.

"Love the sound your gears make."

"Ummm. Love the effect it has on you."

"Hey, no time for that," Carl barked. "I heard you mention William Pope's carriage house. That's the property across the street from the Church on the Bluff."

"One day when I was at Mossy's, the little boy pointed to that property. He's telling me something. I just know it." Sam pushed away from the table and stood. "I'm going to make another trip to Mossy's house. Care to join me?"

Sam stopped at the carriage house property and stood outside the fencing. The pulsing she felt surging from the ground was strong. She turned and walked through the church grounds toward Mossy's house, feeling the thrumming increase. Carl and Jake were standing at the edge of the bluff looking at the May River stretching before them. Tourists strolled along the gravel beach below them while boats anchored at piers were preparing to cast off.

"Good morning, Mossy." Sam waved at the woman who rose from the swing and waved back.

"I hope you are coming for tea."

"Of course. And we stopped at that new bakery for goodies."

Sam didn't climb the stairs, though. She continued to the large azalea bush where the little boy seemed to always appear. *I'm here*, she said in thought only. *Do you have anything to show me?*

It was as though he climbed out of the azalea bush. The boy

beamed when he saw Sam. "Wish you knew English," Sam said. "I have so much to ask you."

The boy smiled and stretched out his hand to her. Again she saw the coin he had shown her before.

"Hey, hon, are you going to join us?"

Sam turned to see the men climbing the stairs and Jonah emerging with a tray of glasses and a pitcher. "In a minute." She turned back to see that the boy was gone.

"That nice detective called," Mossy said. "She's stopping by, too, along with her partner, although they may be awhile."

Everyone took a seat, except for Carl who kept his eyes peeled on trees, shrubs, even boats on the river, as if expecting an ambush.

"Jerry Nolan told me a little about the property across the street, the Squire Pope Carriage House."

"He also owned plantations on the island," Mossy said.

"Right. In my Internet search, I found a picture of two servants at the Coggins Plantation. It said their names were B. Hashi and L. Hashi."

"Hashi? That was my father's middle name," Mossy said. "He said it had been handed down through generations."

"I asked Alex about the name and he said the language the Yamassee used was Apalachee and the words translate to sun and moon. He thinks the B and L stand for Big Hashi and Little Hashi."

Mossy nodded. "That makes sense."

Sam pulled the treasure map from her purse. "The little boy I keep seeing pointed to that property. Do you think that the map might be of the carriage house property?" She laid it out on the coffee table. Carl finally took a seat and everyone studied the map.

"Come to think of it," Jonah said as he looked across the lawn toward the carriage house, "I've seen what I thought were flashes of light coming from that property at night. Thought someone was using a flashlight or the moon was reflecting off of something."

"You think someone was looking for buried treasure?" Mossy asked.

"If they don't have this map, they don't know where to look." Carl pointed out the obvious. "The map is certainly crudely drawn, like someone was in a hurry. Strange thing is, the paper doesn't look ancient. I would expect it to be falling apart. And you showed this to both Angela Douglas and your son's fiancée?"

"I showed it to both of them," Jonah confessed. "It just came up in the conversation and neither of them took the map with them."

"Actually," Mossy started, looking a bit flustered, "I may have shown Nicole the original map."

"Original map?" the voices echoed.

# 53

"Mom, what do you mean original map? I thought this was the original."

"My father drew that one. He never trusted that the original might get lost or stolen. Filled my husband with all kinds of stories about a hidden treasure. One thing for certain is my father wanted to make sure the original was kept in a safe place." Mossy started to knead her hands.

Jonah reached over and placed his hand on Mossy's. "It's okay. Do you remember where the original map is kept?"

Mossy looked up at her son. "I was cleaning out that old chest of drawers upstairs. I think Nicole was helping me. It was in a flat white box."

Jonah raced into the house leaving a stunned group of guests.

"Do you remember if this was before or after Jonah showed the copy to Angela?" Jake asked.

"Oh, definitely before because I didn't have a home companion until Jonah hired one."

"And how did he discover Angela?" Carl was starting to follow a timeframe in his head.

"At the church," Jonah replied as he returned. He handed what looked like cloth to Carl. He unfolded it and placed it in the center of the coffee table. There was a lot more detail on this map.

"That's deerskin," Sam said.

"How does the color not fade?" Jonah asked.

"They use natural mineral and vegetable pigments. The brown pigment could be from cottonwood buds, the red by burning clay, and the blue from the indigo plant." Sam pointed at the X. "Mossy is right. Her father didn't give his paper copy as much detail as this one."

Jonah leaned forward, then cocked his head. "That isn't an X. It's a cross. That depicts the church."

"THIS church?" Sam looked next door at the clapboard structure. "Do you think the treasure is buried here?"

"Can you read this thing, Sam?" Carl asked.

"This row of squiggles is probably the May River. These two parallel lines are quite a distance from the cross that's drawn."

"And what's this?" Jake pointed at a row of dotted lines running from the cross to the parallel lines. You did say pirates drew maps with only symbols they could understand," Jake reminded Carl.

"No pirate drew this," Sam said. "It's definitely Native American, and probably your ancestor, Mossy."

"My father claimed the deerskin one was sent to Hashi's wife after she fled south. Guess she gave it to her remaining son or daughter and it's been handed down ever since."

Carl studied the paper copy, and then the deerskin. "So, if Angela stole the paper copy, it was obvious to whoever wanted it that it was missing some pieces to the puzzle. These squiggly lines you think represent water, Sam, could be the ocean, not necessarily the May River."

"I'm not sure." Sam turned to Mossy. "We already know they worked at the Coggins Plantation on the island so maybe it does represent those waters. I still think it's here because I see the boy here."

"And since Pope owned the property across the street which Jefferson Davis is known to have used, he would have brought the servants with him. So I definitely think it's this area," Jonah said.

"I just counted these dashes." Sam pointed at the map. "There are forty. What if that means forty feet?"

Jake walked over to the railing and looked toward the street. "Can't be right, babe. If you count from the road, that puts you in the middle of the church. And who's to say where the road actually was back in the 1860's?"

"Why not paces?" Mossy suggested.

"Let's check it out." Carl left the porch trailed by everyone but Mossy who stood by the railing. Carl walked to the end of the church building, then walked forty paces.

"That's it!" Sam said as Carl stopped right in front of the azalea bush. "That's where I always see the boy. Mossy?" she called up to the woman. "Do you have shovels?"

Jake groaned. "Never fails. Whenever Sam is around, I always end up with a shovel in my hands."

Jonah walked around the back to a shed and returned with two shovels. He handed one to Jake and took the other.

"I'll take second shift." Carl turned to Mossy where she had moved to the end of the porch closest to the azalea bush. "Did this house ever have a storm shelter?"

"I think so. Matter of fact, I think it was near where you are digging." Mossy took a seat on one of the chairs and watched from above. The digging was painstaking and soon the men were stripping out of their shirts and draping them on the stair post. Sam carried all of their glasses down on a tray and set it on a wrought iron table next to a bedding of tiger lilies.

Carl relieved Jonah of his digging duties. With each digging of the shovel, Sam could here the thrumming increase. Out of the corner of her eye, she saw someone approaching. It was Luke Parsons.

"Don't stop on our account."

The men stopped digging. "Our?" Sam wondered.

Luke hooked a thumb over his shoulder toward the porch where Dover Webbing sat in the chair next to Mossy, a gun in his lap, pointed at Mossy. "Yes, do continue, please."

"My uncle is a pretty good shot, but that close, even I couldn't miss," Luke said.

"Uncle." Sam was starting to put pieces together. "I know he wasn't born in Montana. I looked him up. I bet you were, though."

"Born and bred."

"I bet you've been the guy lurking around the carriage house across the street at night. I've seen dim lights flashing off and on. Thought it might have been a reflection from boats on the water."

"What were you using, a metal detector?" Carl rammed the shovel into the ground and heaved the dirt onto the lawn.

"Top of the line. If I had known Angela had worked here, we might have figured out where she got the map. Instead, we had to rely on our ancestor's notes."

"Yep, would have saved ourselves a lot of hunting," Dover added.

"So, Anchor Webbing didn't give you specifics." Jake gripped the shovel tighter, wondering if he was close enough to hit Luke. Unfortunately, he wasn't, not with a gun pointed at Mossy. He and Carl had left their weapons in the Cadillac.

Dover held up the deerskin map. "You obviously had a better map."

"Put it down." Mossy's voice couldn't have been more stern

if she were carrying a nun's ruler. "It isn't yours."

Dover handed it to Mossy. "Well, ma'am, seems I don't need it now."

"Keep digging," Luke ordered.

"Yep, we wasted a lot of time searching at the old Coggins Plantation site. All my ancestor wrote was one-hundred-twenty paces from the house." Dover shook his head. "Damn idiot."

"Little hard to search on a private country club. Those are all gated communities now, aren't they?" Carl slammed the shovel back into the earth. They were working up a sweat while he wondered how soon until Milla and Detective Lawson showed up.

Sam didn't want to hear about how much time Luke and his metal detector spent on the island. She wanted other details. Jake climbed out of the trench and handed the shovel to Jonah.

"I take it Angela didn't trust you with the map she stole from Mossy."

"No, pretty lady, she didn't," Luke said. "Said her husband told her the treasure was gold, either pirate treasure or a lost payroll for the soldiers. Uncle Dover got close to Gordon Douglas when they were engaging in those reenactments. Then Gordon up and dies. Left us with trying to negotiate with his wife. That got us nowhere."

"And Nicole?" Jonah asked. "How did you involve her?"

"Damn, she was good." Luke laughed and that's when Jonah knew Nicole hadn't been faithful.

"Shut up, boy," Dover said. "You've been flapping your gums long enough."

"Doesn't matter," Sam said. "We already have the paint fakes off of the Bel Air matched to Nicole's Prius."

"Yeah, just waiting on the DNA from the car to see which of you two were driving it." Jake was pulling his bluff.

Luke whipped his head toward his uncle.

Jake sensed they were going to clam up so he switched gears. "So your ancestor, Anchor Webbing was it? Was he stealing the chest for himself?"

"Nah, he was loyal to President Davis. Davis and his wife were fleeing Heyward Bluff before the Union troops arrived. Didn't have time or the means to haul the chest with him so Anchor buried it."

The next strike from Jake's shovel hit something solid. He brushed dirt away only to find a piece of rotted wood. He held it up, then tossed it aside. With visions of buried treasure, Sam and Milla joined the others surrounding the coffin-size hole. Jake and Carl brushed dirt away and came up with more pieces of wood."

"If this was a storm shelter, I think this is what's left of the stairs." Carl tossed two more pieces of rotted wood onto the grass. He scraped with his shovel, but this time instead of wood, he hit a metal object. "You know, I don't recall pirates using metal chests. Theirs were made out of wood."

"So what is this?" Sam said.

# 54

"My father always said there's nothing more dangerous than a woman with a lot of time on her hands."

"I'll take that as a compliment." Milla was starting to warm up to Phil. She had anticipated a firestorm after her revelation in the chief's office. Instead, he seemed grateful that she had found a way out of the corner he had managed to box himself into. Sam was right. She had eliminated an enemy. "I have a feeling you had your doubts about how the brothers died."

"Yeah. Something kept gnawing at me about the lack of skid marks. Hell, if I was headed for a body of water, I would have thrown myself out of the vehicle. Never know if there were alligators in that lagoon. Thought maybe the brakes weren't working. However, techs didn't find any indication that the brakes had been tampered with. If anyone is still in danger, I'd bet my money on the owner of the map."

Milla studied his profile. His military style hair was graying at the temples. At least he wasn't vain like other cops who dyed their hair. While he wore long pants and a short-sleeved shirt, Milla preferred khaki shorts and a sleeveless blouse. And for some reason, Phil had stopped wearing ties.

Phil drove past a line up of cars parking along the shopping district as they headed toward the river. "Turn before the church. There's what looks like a dirt road, but it's actually a street," Mossy said.

"It's hard getting used to the streets here. No curbs, some asphalt, some dirt, some that go to one single wide trailer. This isn't Miami anymore."

"I had the same problem when I moved here." Milla pointed at the white house just past the church's rectory. Mossy's front porch was small compared to the back. Phil pulled onto a gravel patch and they got out. A wind chime by the front door hung as listless as the trees draping the roadway.

They climbed the four stairs to the screen door. Milla was just ready to knock when Phil stopped her and pointed. Through the screen they could see past the living room and into the back porch. A man was seated next to Mossy.

"That's Dover Webbing," Milla whispered. "Does he have a gun on her?"

Phil quietly pulled the handle on the door. It wasn't locked. They crept in and made their way to the front porch.


They were gathered around like scouts at a campfire. The men were covered in dirt and sweat by the time they freed the chest from its grave and heaved it up onto the grass.

"Open it," Luke said, his eyes wide in anticipation.

"If history serves me correctly, this isn't a pirate chest. It's a Confederate paymaster chest from the Civil War," Carl said. "And if you are expecting gold, you will be sorely disappointed. They used Legal Tender notes in order to save metals. I would think your uncle knew that, son."

Luke swung his gaze to his uncle. "Is that true?"

"Just open the damn chest." Dover stood, the gun still pointed at Mossy

"Looks like it needs a key," Carl pointed out.

"I've got a key." Jake raised the shovel and slammed it against the latch. The rusted pieces fell apart.

Luke fell to his knees and lifted the lid. The paper money was clumped together and covered in a fungus. "It's all, and don't know, decomposed or something."

"What do you expect? It's been subjected to the elements, even though it's been buried," Carl said. "If this were the dry sands of Egypt, the money might have survived."

"Four people are dead for a pile of rotting paper?" Jonah couldn't believe the stupidity of criminals.

"Tip the chest over. Get the paper out," Webbing yelled. "We ain't done yet."

Carl and Jake slowly turned toward the porch. Webbing may have short hair and bifocals. Matter of fact, he looked unusually distinguished, certainly not how he looked the last time the two had heard that phrase.

"Sonofabitch," Jake said. He was at first amused, but quickly switched to anger. "You're the old fart who sat next to us at the bar. I want my twenty bucks back."

Carl snapped his fingers. "Now I remember. You were sitting next to Angela at the bar dressed like an old miner. You're the one who spiked her drink."

"That old reenactment outfit always comes in handy. Now empty the damn chest."

Luke pushed the chest over and scooped the moldy clumps of paper out. Jake noticed Phil and Milla slip out of the house and onto the porch. "There's nothing else here, Uncle Dover."

Phil put his gun to Dover's head. "Drop the gun, nice and easy."

"Shit." Dover held his arm up and Phil took the gun.

"Thank goodness," Mossy said. "What on earth kept you two

so long?"

"My partner had paperwork."

"You wanted to stop for a coffee." Milla tossed her handcuffs to Carl and he did the honors.

A fleeting shadow caught Sam's attention. The boy was standing several feet from her, smiling. Then his gaze dropped to the trench where they had found the chest.

"Jake." Sam pointed at the makeshift grave where a skeletal arm had been exposed.

"What's happening?" Mossy made her way down the stairs and toward the cluster of people.

"It's a skeleton, Mom." Jonah grabbed her arm and led her across the lawn.

Phil led a cuffed Dover Webbing down the stairs to the digging.

Carl and Jake jumped back into the trench. It didn't take much scooping of dirt to find, not one, but two skeletons. "Looks like one adult and a child."

Sam looked down at the skeletons, knowing that the child was probably the boy she had been seeing. "Check the boy's right hand."

Jake was careful when touching the hand. "There's something there."

"Yes!" Webbing cried. "It was in the chest all along. The kid must have stolen it." He moved away from Phil. "Let me see. Let me see."

All heads turned to Webbing.

"Uncle, what are you talking about? I thought you said we were looking for gold."

"You're a stupid ass, Luke. You think I went through all this just for some non-existent pirate or Confederate gold? This is the Holy Grail, you idiot!"

Jake handed the coin to Sam. "It's in pristine condition. It isn't even tarnished."

Carl studied the coin in Sam's palm. "It's a Confederate half dollar. Confederate money isn't worth much, except to a collector."

Sam noticed the boy standing near the blooming azalea, smiling at her. He showed his empty palm, then disappeared.

"It's worth a fortune." By god if there weren't tears streaming down Webbing's face. "Jefferson Davis gave the first coin off the press to his wife. Before fleeing Heyward Bluff, she hid it in this chest. My ancestor didn't find that out until he met back up with Davis. By then, the town was overrun with Union soldiers, but he remembered where he had buried the chest."

Jonah stared at the skeletons in the grave. "He hadn't sold his son into slavery and stolen some treasure. He fought to protect his son."

Luke struggled against the restraints and scowled at his uncle. "You weren't planning on sharing any of this with me, were you?"

"Hey, I didn't tell you to get caught up with two women, but you couldn't leave it in your pants."

Everyone remained silent, letting the uncle and nephew go at it.

"You're the one who thought Nicole was a threat. You're the one who ran her off the road."

"Shut up, Luke."

"You're the one who told me those two screw-ups had to be eliminated."

"Shut the hell up." Webbing struggled against the strong arms holding him back. He turned to Phil. "We want a lawyer."

"Of course you do." Phil gave a nod toward Milla. "I'll call Betty Murphy and get her crew here. You call the substation and get a patrol car to cart these two away. Let's take them up to the porch until the car gets here. If they cause any trouble," he added with a chuckle, "we already have their grave dug."

# 55

The next day Mossy and her guests stood at the railing of her porch watching Betty Murphy and her crew continue their work under a canopy protecting the area where the skeletons were found. It had taken Betty several hours yesterday to gather a crew, get a tent erected, and cordon off the area. They were meticulous in cleaning and labeling each bone. Curiosity seekers were kept at bay by two uniformed officers standing by a row of wooden horses just off the street. "We haven't had this much excitement out here since a guy backed his boat and truck into the river," Mossy said.

"Is it my imagination, Mossy, or did the number of flowers on your azalea plant double overnight." Sam had researched Encore azaleas so Mossy was right. They should only bloom three times a year, not all twelve months.

Mossy walked over to a potted plant at the end of the porch. The flowers were scarlet in color, the same as the ones on the azalea bush. She carried it over and handed it to Sam. "Jonah dug up a small shoot from our plant so you can have something to remember us by."

"How sweet, but I'm afraid it won't survive our winters."

"I have a feeling nothing will kill this one."

Sam accepted the plant and set it on the coffee table. There were two narrow trunks, each with a multitude of flowering branches. She hoped Mossy was right about the plant surviving Midwest winters.

Jake and Carl crossed the lawn carrying bags of take-out food. They paused to watch Betty in action. She and her assistants looked more like beekeepers in their white scrubs. "You must be hot in those uniforms," Jake said.

"You haven't seen what I'm not wearing underneath." They walked closer as Betty held up a skull. "This was a boy about five years of age. The way the bodies were positioned, the adult male was shielding him. Didn't stop whoever killed them from putting one bullet in each of their heads. This was an execution."

"Did you find the bullets?" Carl asked.

"Hank," Betty called out to a balding man standing by a table of boxes. "What did you find out about the bullets?" Betty turned back to the two men. "Hank is a pro when it comes to ballistics, no matter what era."

Hank picked up an object and carried it over. He held it between his thumb and index finger. "Since the Union burned the town, I thought it would have been a bullet from a Union soldier. But it wasn't."

"How can you tell?" Carl cocked his head to study the conical-shaped bullet.

"Below the single groove you can just make out the CSA 1041…Confederate States of America. Jefferson Davis owned two Kerr five-shot .44 caliber revolvers. He bought them as a pair and gave one to his closest advisor."

Sam leaned over the railing, having heard what Hank had said. "Let me guess—Lieutenant Colonel Anchor Webbing."

"Correct." Hank carried the bullet back to the table and carefully placed it back in a bag.

"Were you hungry?" Jake asked. "We have enough."

"Thanks, but we've already eaten," Betty replied. "Have a lot I need to get done before dark."

They left Betty and her crew to their work. By the time they set out plates and drinks in the dining room, the rest of the guests arrived. Phil came with Chief Ray while Milla stopped at the church to rescue Jonah from a cluster of tourists.

"Burgers, chicken, salad, subs. You went all out." Milla asked.

"Didn't know what everyone liked so we tried to cover all bases." Carl grabbed a burger for himself and sat down.

The dining room table could seat ten people comfortably. Windows were wide open and the overhead fan had been set on high. Once everyone had their food and drinks, Detective Lawson filled them in on their interview with Luke Parsons and Professor Webbing. "Once we got them to the precinct, they each couldn't wait to make a deal and throw the other under the bus."

"Didn't they ask for a lawyer?" Jonah reached for a packet of salad dressing, then handed one to Mossy.

"They changed their minds pretty quick. Professor Webbing had letters and documents regarding his ancestor. It confirmed everything the professor said. Everyone was fleeing Heyward Bluff before the Union soldiers arrived. President Davis realized he didn't have the time or room to take the chest so he asked Anchor Webbing to hide it. Then they would come back later for it thinking the Confederate soldiers would push the Union back." Lawson refilled his iced tea, then grabbed another mini sub. "Anchor didn't trust the servants. He suspected they saw him placing the chest in the storm shelter. After killing them, Anchor filled the storm shelter with dirt, burying the two along with the chest. With the Union soldiers just an hour away, he took off to join Davis. When Anchor met up with him, that's when he found out that Davis' wife, Varina, had hid her Confederate half-dollar in the paymaster chest for safekeeping. She feared losing it or having it confiscated should they be caught on the road."

"Just like a woman," Carl said under his breath.

"It's a shocker you're still single, Carl." Sam said.

"It appears Anchor wrote cryptic instructions on where to find the chest, which the professor couldn't make heads or tails out of until he met Gordon Douglas. Explains why Webbing struck up a friendship with Gordon and why he got into reenactments. Since the Squire Pope Plantation on the island was the officers' quarters where Davis spent much of his time, Gordon Douglas thought that was where they should look first. Anchor may have written one-hundred-twenty paces from the home, but he never said which home. Ended up being the carriage house."

Phil took a breather to eat so Milla filled in more of the details. "Nicole DuMorney..." she looked over at Jonah.

"It's okay."

"Anyway, Nicole had met Angela and Gordon Douglas on a cruise. She and Angela struck up a friendship. She'd sometimes stay overnight at Angela's after her husband died and she overheard a little too much. Now that we know about the original map, we can only assume Nicole might have mentioned it to Angela. While Luke is off on the island fighting the mosquitos in the dark searching, Angela inserts herself into Jonah's life. By getting close to Mossy, she is attempting to see if the map Nicole eluded to actually existed."

"Did either of those ingrates explain how the Goodwin brothers got involved?" Carl asked.

Milla grabbed a chicken leg off of the platter and set it on her plate. "Remember, they were opportunists. Tyler finds out through Becky where Angela is living, picks up Travis from prison, they see her with Luke, convince Luke to cut them in. If anyone could get Angela to talk, it was Travis. But all they did was spook her and the rest is history."

Carl scooped potato salad onto his plate, then passed the container to Jake. "It was probably the first time she realized she made a deal with the devil. Professor Webbing had been waiting a long time to find that coin. He would be damned if anyone got in his way and I doubt he planned to share it with anyone, not even his nephew."

"You're exactly right, Carl." Chief Ray had raised his head from his third piece of chicken to join in. "Any publicity or suspicion of what they were searching for would have brought hoards of treasure seekers down here."

"Okay, no one is going to bring up the elephant in the room." Jake looked to Chief Ray who was busy licking his fingers.

"Saving the best for last," Chief Ray said.

"Yes, exactly where is that coin?" Sam asked.

"In our safe. I sent pictures to a numismatic expert in Columbia. He says if it is what he thinks it is, you are talking priceless. Four were minted and only three have been accounted for, two of which showed up in an auction house in 2015, the first in 2003."

"How priceless?" Phil asked.

"Millions, if not hundreds of millions of dollars. But it has to be authenticated. Originals are made of silver, copper, and some trace elements. The weight is the key. An original weighs 189 grains. There are a lot of restrikes and fakes out there, but this expert was pretty sure this one is the real deal. And since it was found on Misses Belden's property, she owns it."

"What? Oh, I couldn't. I would prefer to donate it to a museum."

"You may feel that it's only right to donate it, but like it or not, there's a finder's fee of five percent of the value."

"Five percent?" Mossy almost dropped her fork. "I don't know. I just…"

"Yes you do," Sam said. "You need eye surgery and you certainly could use central air." Sam waved a napkin at the sweat running down her neck.

"I guess Jonah could build that youth center he has always wanted."

"Let's not jump ahead of ourselves here. I prefer you not let that coin out of your sight," Jonah said.

"Don't have to. That expert is flying here tomorrow with a guy from an auction house in New York City."

# 56

A private service was held at the church for Big and Little Hashi. The remains would be cremated and urns given to Mossy. There was a small gathering at Mossy's house afterwards, with Sam, Jake, Carl, and Milla in attendance.

"What is this?" Milla took the box from Sam.

"Just a little something from us." She handed a similar box to Jonah.

Alex had also sent Sam a dreamcatcher to give to Mossy. "I love it. We used to make these when I was a child. I managed to lose every one of them." Mossy fingered the delicate feathers hanging from the circle. Alex's work was all about color and this dreamcatcher had blue beads, and blue and tan feathers.

"Sam, this is beautiful." Milla quickly put her necklace on.

"What kind of stone is this?" Jonah held up the arrowhead necklace.

"Snowflake obsidian."

"I know that name," Milla said. "It's for balance of mind and spirit."

"And shields you from negativity."

Carl let out a sigh. "Nothing but volcanic glass. But hey, whatever works."

"Carl."

"Yes, ma'am. I'll shut up. Don't want to interfere with their Chakra."

"So when do you leave?" Mossy asked.

"Tomorrow morning. Jake and I are treating Carl to dinner for his hospitality."

"Then I guess this is goodbye. And thank you so much for all your help and the necklace." Milla gave each of them a hug.

Sam gave Mossy a hug. "Soon you will have your twenty-twenty vision back."

"You can count on it." Jonah shook Carl's and Jake's hands. "Drive safely." He lifted the azalea plant and handed it to Jake.

"Mossy, have I ever told you how many plants Sam has killed?" Jake said. "She isn't exactly known for her green thumb."

"This one will always live. I can feel it." And Sam could.

As they walked to the car, Sam made a detour to the fence surrounding the property across the street. How long had the spirits been attempting to be heard? How many years had passed since that fateful day in 1863? Today, the air was still. She no longer heard the whispers, nor could she feel the ground pulsing beneath her feet. Little Hashi and his father were finally at peace.

Jake came up behind her. "About ready?"

"What a shame they plan to put a park here. Would be the perfect place to build a house."

"Hate to see what might be unearthed when they start digging. Besides, I like Carl's house. It has a better location. And he said we can come stay any time."

"I'm going to miss this place."

"We can come back."

"Promise?"

"Promise."

Sam turned and gave one last look at the bluff overlooking the May River. Yes, she would definitely return.

Find out more about the other books in this series and the author's mystery/urban fantasy series she writes as Lee Driver.

Visit **www.sdtooley.com**

Once there, be sure to sign up for her newsletter.